"I was hooked by the third chapter. . . . Devoto's strongest talent lies in her creation of living and breathing characters [who] rise from the pages of Devoto's book and become real people we know."
  —*First Draft* (Alabama Writers' Forum)

"Roy Rogers would have liked it. . . . Devoto writes with sensitivity and charm in bringing the characters to life . . . engaging and believable."
  —*Montgomery Advertiser*

"When you find that little slip of history, mirth, and the joys of a summer childhood, beautifully detailed in a new, fresh book with an even newer, fresher writer, you just have to indulge the urge to crawl up inside the tome and savor all the warm and fuzzy memories of your own childhood."
  —*Opelika-Auburn News* (AL)

"So much happens in this warm, funny debut novel that the poignant climax seems almost an afterthought . . . worth reading because of its fresh approach to a 'polio summer.'"
  —*Library Journal*

"What a joy to happen upon a novel that should appeal to preteen-age and centenarian alike, as well as everyone in between . . . splendid . . . ought to win a literary prize or two."
— *The State* (SC)

"Devoto is a talented new voice from the South with keen insight reminiscent of Eudora Welty or Harper Lee . . . a poignant and memorable debut."
— *Library Booknotes*

"Many memorable characters. . . . Tab's antics bring heartache as well as laughter and suspense."
— *Roanoke Times*

"Affectingly details the bittersweet last summer of childhood . . . deftly evokes a time of blissfully ordinary comforts."
— *Kirkus Reviews*

"Devoto captures the feel and imagery of the 1950s South through a delightfully crafted and entertaining tale."
— *Newport News Daily Press* (VA)

Pat Cunningham Devoto

My Last Days as Roy Rogers

WARNER BOOKS

A Time Warner Company

Copyright © 1999 by Pat Cunningham Devoto
Reading Group Guide copyright © 2000 by Pat Cunningham Devoto and Warner Books, Inc.
All rights reserved.

Warner Books, Inc., 1271 Avenue of the Americas, New York, NY 10020
Visit our Web site at www.twbookmark.com

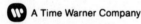 A Time Warner Company

Printed in the United States of America
First Trade Printing: February 2000
10 9 8 7 6 5 4 3 2

The Library of Congress has cataloged the hardcover edition as follows:

Devoto, Pat Cunningham.
    My last days as Roy Rogers / Pat Cunningham Devoto.
       p. cm.
  ISBN 0-446-52388-7
  1. Rogers, Roy, 1911– —Fiction. I. Title.
PS3554.E92835M9 1999
813'.54—dc21   98-22788
                                      CIP
ISBN 0-446-67564-4 (pbk.)

Book design and composition by L&G McRee
Cover design by Wendell Minor

For the sisters: Jo and Sal

Prologue

Whenever I am caught in a summer rain, the memory of that last polio summer comes back to me. Perhaps there were others. Certainly there were others. Summers in which we lived round about the great illness of our youth, reshaping and changing our lives to conform to its dark ways.

For us, me, Maudie May, and the Brothers, it was no more than some dreaded, distant voice of authority to be sidestepped and dodged at every turn.

To the adults in our world, it appeared as a giant headlight and they the deer, caught in its beam, afraid to turn in any direction else they or theirs be struck down.

To all of us, that last summer was the messenger of great changes to come.

Chapter 1

There were two seasons in life, the season of school and the season of no school.

All other happenings—Christmas, Thanksgiving, spring vacation—all were just short practice sessions leading to the real thing. I was appalled by those who cried on the last day when we were "let out" for the summer. My thinking was, some genetic disorder must be the cause. It was usually Jenny Lou Harris. Her mother was the school librarian. That explained it.

Summer brought with it the cicada's whine, death to hundreds of lightning bugs that made up my Ball-jar lantern, weather so hot and filled with humidity that my sandals would mildew if left in the closet untended. Afternoon showers as if dumped from a bucket and minutes later bright sunshine to steam everything dry or at least bring it back to its original limp, soggy condition. The showers passed almost without notice, since I was in a perpetual state of damp anyway. As long as there was no streak lightning, we were free to roam in the downpour. Water rushing past in the street gutters would be frantically dammed with mud and sticks to make small wading pools. The more formal among us changed to swim suits for the afternoon rains. The rest of us made do with whatever we began the day in.

It was May and already hot as blue blazes, but Grandmother had explained that the weather never bothered us. Our family had been so long in Alabama, our blood had just naturally thinned out to accommodate itself to the situation. People like us did not suffer from the heat.

May always dawned with the hope, however faint, that we might pass through the whole summer in this way, unfettered by the changes that we knew must come in June when polio season began.

It began for me that June as I sat on the curb in front of my house making a mud dam while steam rose from the still-wet streets. It arrived in the person of Mary Leigh McKnight, my fellow fifth grader, expertly pedaling her Schwinn to a pinpoint stop in front of me.

Mary Leigh was my age but light-years beyond me. Holder of straight *A*'s, wearer of pearly white lipstick, possessor of the ultimate status symbol, blond naturally curly hair, she was so far removed from me as to make comparison, not to mention competition, unthinkable. That's why Mary Leigh liked me.

Of course I blamed my lack of social skills on Mother. A person could not possibly get popular and sophisticated with a mother like mine. She cared too much about everything I did. On the other hand, Mary Leigh's mother let her ride all over town on her own. I knew there must be some correlation.

She poured out the latest. "Well, Tab, I guess you heard what they did."

"What who did?" I was putting the mud I had brought from the driveway in between the rocks and sticks. Water was still getting through.

"Don't tell me you don't know." Mary Leigh pulled the handlebars back and began circling as she talked.

"I said, I didn't know, Mary Leigh. I been busy making this dam, as you can see." I shaded my eyes against the sun to follow her circling. She glanced unseeing at my mud dam.

"Well, everybody in town is talking about it. I thought for sure you would know, since you love to go to the movies so much."

"I told you, Mary Leigh, I don't know! And if it's what I think you're gonna say, I don't want to hear about it."

"They closed all of them down for the summer

again, that's what. You can't even go over to Huntsville and see one, because they closed them over there, too."

The pool had closed down last week. Poor Mary Leigh had pedaled her little legs off trying to be the first to tell that news to the few blocks of bungalows that made up our neighborhood.

The Crystal Plunge was the gathering spot for my older sister, Tina, and her myriad of junior high school friends. Fed by a natural spring, the water passed through several filters right into a large concrete rectangle. All of Bainbridge was very proud of our pool. Ice-cold water on the hottest of days. It worked great except for the occasional snake that happened to find its way through the filter system. Of course they were only water snakes. I was sure no self-respecting moccasin would venture near Tina.

Poor Tina had been pitiful over the pool's closing. Swim class at the Crystal Plunge was working on its annual water ballet. This year's theme was "Hawaiian Holiday." For weeks the sounds of "Sweet Leilani," and rhythmic splashing of feet filled the air around the Crystal Plunge. Now all was silent. After the last practice, Tina came home carrying her feather headdress like a wounded bird found by the roadside. She pinned it to the bulletin board on her side of our shared room. Afterward she threw herself across the bed, arm flung over eyes, mumbling something about the Fates and Esther Williams.

Mary Leigh had stopped her bike and was standing on the ground, pretending to adjust the mirror on her handlebars. Of course both of us knew she was only checking her lipstick to see if it was pearly enough. "Oh, it's no big deal," she said. "We don't have but one movie in town anyway and it shows the same picture all week."

"So what if we only have one movie, Mary Leigh. Don't forget we also got the cartoons, and newsreels, and serials, good stuff like that. A person can get a real education at the movies, you know."

Although steeped in the social graces, Mary Leigh was not as politically concerned as I. "Remember, Mary Leigh, that part of the newsreel they showed last week where the man with one arm biked all the way across the United States with his dog?" Mary Leigh didn't remember. I changed the subject.

"You want to help me make this dam? We can build one big enough for the both of us to wade in."

"No thanks. I don't want to take off my shoes and socks. Besides, I might get my new shorts dirty. Did you notice my new shorts?"

"Yeah, real nice, Mary Leigh."

She was smiling at herself in the handlebar mirror. "Well, see you later, Gal." That's what Mary Leigh called everybody, Gal. She said it made you sound more social. She stood on her bike pedals and pumped off down the street toward town. Red, white, and blue handlebar streamers flying in the wind. I watched her naturally curly hair bounce up and down until finally she was out of sight.

I dried my hands on my shorts and headed to the kitchen. Up the back steps, I let the screen door slam behind me. Of course she was always the first vent for my frustrations.

"Okay, Mother." I stood there with hands on hips, giving her my "mean" look. "Why did they close down the movies? Just explain that to me." I was tapping my foot on the linoleum floor. Then I raised my hand before she could give me some plausible explanation. "Hold it. Just hold it. Don't tell me. I know why."

"If you know, why did you ask me?"

"It's because they think we'll catch it at the movies, which is silly to me because they haven't closed Sunday school and we might catch it there, and they never close the doctor's office and that place is full of germs."

Mother smiled. "Would you like a nice glass of iced tea to cool off?"

"I do everything they say to do, stay inside for spraying, wash my hands all the time, but they keep adding stuff on." I shook my head no to the iced tea, then plopped down in a chair at the kitchen table and started balancing the salt and pepper shakers on top of the sugar bowl.

Whenever I came inside in the summer, I always ended up in the kitchen. The chair on the left side of the table was mine. Just as you had a bed, you had a chair at the kitchen table. Mine was by the window overlooking the common driveways between our house and the McMillans' house next door. The breeze from the attic fan danced the window curtains and began to dry my wet clothes.

Mother was busying herself with some sort of cooking that involved large mounds of flour. She was not "to the stove born," so the end product of her labors was sometimes a surprise to us all. To add to her lack of skill was the fact that the stove was as old as the house and sat on an uneven floor. All her dishes cooked up lopsided. We pretended not to notice.

Custom intended that all meals consist of at least one or two meats, three or four vegetables, and hot bread washed down by gallons of iced tea. All of this was followed by an occasional—I might even say a rare—dessert. Often our father would forget himself. "What's for dessert?" We would turn our heads to her and smile in anticipation.

"What's for dessert? What's for dessert? The twins have an ear infection, Charles junior got poison ivy, Tab skinned her knee so badly it took me an hour to stop the bleeding, and Tina spilled nail polish all over the coffee table."

He would quickly pick up the sugar bowl. "Nothing like a little sweet taste to finish the meal," he said as he downed a teaspoonful of sugar and passed the bowl on to the next one of us. We would dip our teaspoon into the bowl and give extra sugar to our iced tea glass or take it straight. Sort of like Holy Communion. We were absolved of our dessert sin.

In addition to the cooking, there was Mama's maid problem. Suddenly I realized Estelle was missing. "Where's Estelle, Mama? I thought she was always here by now."

"Estelle won't be coming in today." Mother looked resigned as she cranked out more flour. Estelle was the fourth maid we had had that year. In Bainbridge if you had a maid, it didn't mean you were rich. It only meant that the maid could get a good meal in the middle of the day and take home a little, very little, money at the end of the week. Not much cash money was involved because there was not much cash money to be had. Still and all, maids and Mama just didn't seem to get along.

"Did Estelle quit on you, Mama? That's the fourth maid—"

"No! Estelle did not quit on me. We just had a mutual understanding and . . . and she left."

"Grandmama says maids quit on you 'cause you're from the North and don't know how to talk to them. She says you're gonna use up all the maids in town before long." Grandmother, my father's mother, had lived in Bainbridge since the time of the caveman, as far as I could tell. In my eyes she was Mohammed or the Mountain or both and must be deferred to in all matters. Mother, on the other hand, was not such an easy convert.

8

She gave me one of her looks. The one where her eyes were half-closed and her mouth was a perfectly straight line across her face. "Tennessee is not exactly up north, Tab. Your grandmother exaggerates, as usual. Besides, we had servants when I was growing up. Did I ever tell you about the Indian cook we had? He was a real Indian. He belonged to one of the Cherokee tribes in the Smokies."

"You told me before, Mama, a million times, but that doesn't count."

"I don't know why it doesn't count. It's all the same. I simply tried to write out a list of duties that Estelle would be responsible for each day and she got huffy and left."

"Remember the time Para Lee worked for us and you tried to teach her to make a corn soufflé and it turned out so terrible and she got huffy and left? She said the only time the Lord wanted corn to rise up was when you popped it? Remember?"

Mother didn't like to be reminded of her maid problem. She glared at me from the flour bin. "All I did was post a simple list of duties, now what's the matter with that?"

"Estelle got huffy 'cause she couldn't read the list," I said.

Mama's cheeks burned red. "How was I supposed to know that?" She looked at me suspiciously. "How did you know that, Tab?"

"Well, Grandmother says—"

"Oh, never mind what your grandmother says.

9

That's all I ever hear around here, what your grandmother says. Let's get back to the subject at hand. Who told you the movies were closing?"

"Mary Leigh. She rode by on her bike just now. Her mother lets her ride all over the place on her bike, you know."

"Like Paul Revere spreading the news."

"Like who?"

"Oh, never mind, go ahead."

"Well, that's all there is to it. They closed the movies all over this part of Alabama and nobody has any say about it. Why do they keep closing all the places that are good and none of the places I hate?"

Mother was smiling now as she poured milk into a bowl that was, I hoped, the beginnings of a cake. "Maybe if you're lucky, they'll start closing some of the places you hate. There has been some talk of closing the whole town down."

"What does that mean, close the town down? You can't close down a whole town." Not that I cared at this point. Everything of any meaning had already gone by the wayside.

"Oh, it's just talk that gets started every summer when the polio comes. If things get really bad, they'll close down all the places where more than a few people gather." She walked over and raised the window by the kitchen table higher. Another hour or so and the house would be closed against the heat of the day. This week's advice concerning

10

polio said that you must be careful not to get too hot. If you did, you might catch it. Next week another surefire safeguard would be in vogue. Mother went back to stirring her bowl. "I phoned Cora Johnson this morning. Her Jimmy came down with it last Wednesday." She stood shaking her head as she stirred. "He ate a banana the night before he got sick. Now Cora is telling everybody who'll listen that the bananas gave it to him. Something about they came from Mexico."

I gagged. "Mama! You let me eat two this morning! You told me bananas were good for—"

"I did and they are. Bananas weren't the cause, sweetheart. Cora, Mrs. Johnson, is just trying to make some sense out of it. The paper said the count is already up to one hundred and ten people and it's just barely into June."

She took salt and pepper from the cabinet above the counter and added it to her brew. Pepper did not portend a sweet after-dinner delicacy, but you never knew.

Life in Bainbridge was to Mother like dropping Tallulah Bankhead down in the middle of the Amazon rain forest. Mother had been born and raised in very comfortable circumstances in the city, educated to be a classical musician, and was on her way up north to study when love struck. Fifteen years and five children later, Mother and Bainbridge still did not live as one.

Mother could not get it through her head that

baking a good cake for the missionary circle was more important than spending an afternoon reading *The Adventures of Tom Sawyer* to us as we huddled in a circle around her rocking chair on the screened porch. Or that visiting Great-Aunt Lizzie on the tenth anniversary of her husband's passing was more important than putting her feet up and reading the editorials in the *Birmingham News.* In a town filled to overflowing with her husband's relatives, she was besieged from all sides but undaunted.

Grandmother Rutland, on the other hand, was just as determined to have her see the light of accommodation, and I, brainwashed from the time I was old enough to take Grandmother Rutland's hand and walk up the steps of the First Methodist Church of Bainbridge, I was her willing accomplice. Me and Grandmother must, would, lead Mother into the path of righteous Bainbridge culture no matter how long it took.

You take my name, for instance—Tabitha Goodloe Rutland. It was a perfect example of Mother's and Grandmother's turn of mind. The Tabitha was Mother's idea. She thought it sounded pretty off the southern tongue. The Goodloe was from Grandmother's side of the family. Grandmother said that Great-Great Uncle Preston Goodloe died the death of a wonderful military hero up at the Battle of Shiloh during the War. Mother, being less than reverent when it came to family folklore, said that more than likely he died of a large case of Jack

Daniel's at home in bed. I didn't mention her theory to Grandmother.

Now she was squishing what appeared to be dough between her fingers and talking at the same time. "I sure do hate to see the movies close. I was looking forward to seeing that new picture with Lana Turner that's coming next week." She brushed a straggle of hair off of her forehead with a floury hand. "Well, look at it this way, Tab, after what happened last week, you and your friends might not be allowed back in the movie anyway."

"That was not my fault, Mama." I bristled. "I told you that. It was all Miss Blankenship's fault. She should have known we weren't ready to serve our fellow man." That was not true in the strictest sense, but then, why burden Mother with the actual facts of the story. She wouldn't have believed it was all Maudie May's doing anyway.

"What are you talking about?" Mother said, too busy consulting the Ladies Help League Fifth Anniversary Edition of *Fascinating Foods of Bainbridge* to pay real attention to me.

"That's what Miss Blankenship called it. Serving our fellow man," I said.

"Miss Blankenship means well. You girls will just have to bear with her."

She reached down in the cupboard and got out—a frying pan?

Chapter 2

Having just graduated from Millsaps College over in Mississippi, Miss Blankenship had come back to Bainbridge to get married or teach school, whichever came first. Since Miss Blankenship was on the plump side and hadn't even been asked to be a contestant in the Maid of Cotton contest, we all were certain she would teach school in the fall.

The Maid of Cotton was the only contest worthy of consideration. No tacky bathing suit competition, and every business in town sponsored a contestant. Given the narrow age eligibility and the large number of businesses that had to find a competitor—even Tommy's Battery Shop fielded a candidate—the main requirements were that you be female, the right age, and breathing. But alas, Miss Blankenship did not make the cut. I had great empathy for Miss Blankenship, fearing I, too, would be in the same shoes a few years down the road.

The Reverend Mengert suggested that the mothers would probably like to have Miss Blankenship as our scout leader. Any suggestion that he made was usually followed as law. The Reverend was Episcopal but somehow he transcended all religious bounds. It helped that the Reverend had the only church service broadcast on the only radio station in town. In addition, Reverend Mengert had originally come from somewhere out west, so he had an accent like none I had ever heard. Given these circumstances, I knew from the time I was old enough to listen that the Reverend was, in fact, the real voice of God coming to us over WRAY, "your voice of north Alabama." Even after I was enlightened by Grandmother, I had a sneaking suspicion she didn't know what she was talking about. She was just jealous because he wasn't Methodist.

There was even proof of my God theory. Every Sunday afternoon when "The Greatest Story Ever Told" came on the radio, from up in New York, He was there. At some point in every story the voice of God would speak and tell the wayward what they were doing wrong. Before God spoke, an angel chorus would sing a few bars. Then it was God's turn. God sounded exactly like—God WAS the Reverend Mengert, and I knew everybody else in town thought so, too. It was just less than polite to bring it up in everyday conversation.

Grandmother even said he should have been a Methodist, like us. It would be more becoming to his nature. But, she said, he was descended from a long line of Episcopalians (not to mention from On High), so he was stuck where he was.

Anyway, Miss Blankenship was positively itching to try out her new Mississippi education. First off, Miss Blankenship decided that we should stop doing ordinary things like making pot holders and papier-mâché masks and do something to serve our fellow man, like taking up money for the March of Dimes.

When the March of Dimes began each year, everyone, but everyone, marched! Mothers went from door to door collecting dimes. The Lions Club solicited money down at the fire station. Mr. Neeley's hardware store was always the first to donate electric fans to the children's polio ward when it was set up each summer. Merchants all over town contributed candy, ice cream, comics. No one dared to tempt the fickle finger of fate by not doing his fair share.

Just the fact that we were asked was reason enough for our Scout troop to meet Miss Blankenship in front of the Majestic Theater on that Wednesday morning. Of course if you volunteered, you got in the movie free. I had been the first one to volunteer.

When the day finally arrived, I was so overwhelmed with this opportunity to serve my fellow man that I conveniently forgot to tell Mother that admission was free. She gave me a whole twenty-five cents to squander.

I stood in the kitchen for scrutiny. "Right over left, left over right," Mother said.

"I know, I know. I thought I did a good job."

"You did. Your scarf was just a little lopsided. Don't forget your belt. And Tab, I believe I would change those red socks if I were you. That's not in the official Scout dress code, is it?"

Nobody appreciated my flair for color. Not even Mother.

I always walked the three blocks to town. That is, it was three blocks to River Street and River Street was town. Bainbridge began as River Street eased away from the bridge over the Tennessee River and wound uphill. Streetlights followed the road to its crest and continued as it flattened out to form a corridor of lights and buildings. On summer evenings the lampposts were almost obliterated by swarming willow flies up from the river. The street ended at what was the focal point of its existence, Bainbridge House. Huge white columns on a porch two stories high. It was evident to all that J. James Bainbridge had laid out the town. Even the courthouse was shuttled to one side. Grandmother said J. James had not cared to have it in the center of things, disturbing his view.

Only a few buildings held the slightest interest for me. On one side of the street was Woolworth's, filled with the necessities of life, toys and the dreaded school supplies. Farther down was Western Auto, stocked with the required transportation, shiny new bikes decked out in battery-powered lights and plastic handlebar streamers. On the other side of the street was the Majestic Theater, my ticket to the world, and Mason's Corner Drugstore, where you could get delicious grilled chili dogs and cherry Cokes if you had the money, which I never did. There were other stores—Pendleton's Floral Fair, Cravy's Dry Cleaners and such, but they all faded when compared to the likes of Woolworth's or the movies. Of course there was the park a few blocks over and the Confederate statue down by the courthouse, but they were only pictures to look at on my way to more important things: testing out the bikes at Western Auto, studying the candy counter at Woolworth's.

In the third grade we had been introduced to Bainbridge history by Miss Locklear. She had taken on this task in order that we might be indoctrinated to her view of things long before regular Alabama history was required. Miss Burke, eighth grade Alabama history, had only been instructing for twenty years and therefore was not thoroughly grounded in the subject. Besides, Miss Locklear had a few things she wanted to get off her chest.

First off, allowed Miss Locklear, there was

Andrew Jackson, sent by the federal government to march through with his big army, disturbing our quiet town. He was on his way down to fight the Battle of New Orleans and he could have left us alone and crossed the river up around Huntsville if he had wanted to. Later on came Nathan Bedford Forrest, poor boy, running for dear life, being chased all up and down the valley by Yankee troops and them tearing up everything in sight and not paying us back for one bit of the damage. Last and certainly not least was that the federal government came in to dig up the river and build the TVA dams, which flooded all the good bottomland. Of course it was completely beside the point that Miss Locklear's daddy had some of the land that got flooded and—"I would probably be a millionaire today if I still had it."

By the end of the third grade we were thoroughly disgusted with the federal government and its bloodsucking ways, believe me.

When I arrived at the Majestic, our troop had gathered outside next to the coming attractions poster. It said Roy and Dale were scheduled to make their usual Saturday appearance.

Mary Leigh, Marilyn Travis, Betty Jo Smithson, and Sally Barber were already there. Mary Leigh, in official Scout uniform covered with merit badges, was holding court, giving long, complicated descriptions of how she had earned her latest cooking badge. No human person could win that many of those little sewed-on felt circles. I suspected that her mother sat home at night turning out fake merit badges to put on her uniform. Another instance in which my mother had failed me miserably.

"Hi, Gal," Mary Leigh called over her flock of admirers.

"Oh my gosh, oh my gosh." Marilyn Travis grabbed my arm. I looked up, to see her staring in the direction of the Majestic ticket cage. You didn't see him often, but when you did, you just had to stare. He was talking to the lady who sold tickets. We all wondered if he would go in and watch the movie, too, or would he just go behind the concession counter and grab a handful of candy bars and not pay for them, or pour himself a free Coke, two straws.

The first thing we were always told to remember about him is that we are not impressed by his money. Oh no, Grandmother said! He might be rich as Croesus, but that didn't faze us. He might be smart as blinding light, but we couldn't care less. It was just because he went to school up East and had nothing to do all day but sit around and learn.

For heaven's sake, the man had probably never even been on a farm. So where could he possibly belong? He didn't fit in with ordinary people. He wasn't colored. He wasn't even Yankee. He was J. Stanley Rosenstein, owner of all the movie picture houses all over north Alabama. The most amazing thing about J. Stanley Rosenstein was that they said he didn't even like the movies. He inherited the picture shows from his father.

He was walking toward us now, just casual as you please. No tie, short-sleeve shirt, great big head, little skinny body, big ears that he used to hook on his horn-rimmed glasses. I was appalled that someone with access to so much free candy could be that skinny.

All us girls watched him with our mouths open as he came closer.

He was thumbing through a book in his hand as he walked past. Walking away from Susan Hayward starring in *Canyon Passages*? The man could have been from another planet. I said to Marilyn Travis, "I think he is actually reading that book."

Miss Blankenship walked up and clapped her hands. "Girls, let me have your attention."

I knew she was fat on the outside, but I thought Miss Blankenship had a sweet face. Round Santa Claus cheeks that tended to glow crimson when she got excited, which was most of the time. She had purchased her own Scout uniform. Even had a hat stuck to the side of her hair with bobby pins. I was determined to help Miss Blankenship be a success in her first venture into the world of Scoutdom.

"Now, girls, as you know, polio is a deadly disease, especially here in Bainbridge. Every summer we suffer its ravages. This is our chance to serve our fellow man in the fight to rid our country and

Bainbridge of this monster that takes its toll on young and old all over the United States."

She paused, clasping her hands over her bosom and looking down at the sidewalk. I thought for certain she was going to offer up a prayer, but she took a deep breath, raised her head, and said, "Are there any questions?"

I stepped forward. "Yes, ma'am, Miss Blankenship. Is there a cartoon after the main feature?" She looked mournful. She must not like cartoons.

"I have no idea, Tab. Now, everyone line up," she said.

We marched down the aisle of the old Majestic, stepping over chewing gum wrappers, old Coke cups, and stale popcorn. J.W., one of my fellow fifth graders, said once he had run across a rat eating popcorn on the floor of the Majestic. I never believed J.W. but I had felt something hit my feet from time to time. I pretended that it was the person sitting behind me. After we were settled in the front row, Miss Blankenship returned to the back of the theater. "The faces are too big up this close— you'll ruin your eyes, girls." Mary Leigh and I sneaked back up the side aisle to the candy counter in the lobby.

"A Baby Ruth, a Long Boy, a Coke, and a box of popcorn. Make that a small box of popcorn, please." I blew the whole twenty-five cents. Mary Leigh got a Coke.

"A Coke, Mary Leigh? One Coke? That's not

worth the trouble," I said as we headed back down the aisle into the cool dark smelliness of the Majestic.

Mary Leigh was like that. My trip to the lobby was for food, while Mary Leigh's was for smiling at everybody she saw and making sure everybody saw her. When we got back to our seats, she took two sips of her Coke and started to put it on the floor.

"Don't do that. I'll drink it."

The movie was just beginning. Susan Hayward was the star and my favorite. Actually, it was a toss-up between Susan and Roy Rogers. After the main feature came the cartoon, the news, and then our part of the program began.

Now there appeared on the screen a man telling everyone that if they gave their money to the fund-raisers who would pass among them, the money would help find a cure for polio. The scene then switched to a man in a hospital room. Except for his head, he was closed up in what looked like a large steel barrel. The man spoke only as the barrel allowed him to, its motor pumping slowly up and down with a hissing noise.

"If you will help"—*sssssss*—"us find a cure"—*sssssss*—"by making your donations"—*sssss*—"I will be most grateful"—*sssss*.

Mary Leigh reached over for some of my popcorn. "What's he talking like that for? He sounds like a spaceman in a Flash Gordon serial." She had

24

been searching the seats to see who was there and hadn't been at all interested in the screen.

I, on the other hand, had hung on every word. This was far more dramatic than Susan Hayward. I turned my head to hide my watery eyes from Mary Leigh. "He's in an iron lung, stupid! That's the way you talk when you catch it. You feel terrible. You can't breathe. They put you in an iron lung and then—you die."

"Well, President Roosevelt had it and he looked all right to me the last time I saw him on the news-reels."

"That's all you know, Mary Leigh. He was president, so they kept him alive for a while, but he's dead now, isn't he?"

"Well, I guess so. I never thought of that, Gal." She smiled at me.

Over all of this, a voice from the screen was singing a divinely beautiful version of "You'll Never Walk Alone." As the song ended, I was drying my eyes with my Girl Scout scarf. Mary Leigh took out her compact to put on more pearl lipstick. As she was the cosmetic leader of our class, she must have felt duty-bound to use up one whole tube each day.

"Was that the most terrible thing you ever saw?" She checked her hair in the mirror. "That man was disgusting with all that sweat pouring off his face. Why do you suppose they let people like that be in the movies?" Mary Leigh did not care much for suf-fering of any kind.

The lights came on and Miss Blankenship walked down to us, holding round paper cartons with slits in the top. I began to feel somewhat guilty about wasting my twenty-five cents on candy. Now I had nothing to give to the paper cartons. Oh well.

She sent us to our places in the theater. My job was to collect up the center section with Mary Leigh as my partner on the opposite aisle.

Downstairs there was a center section and two small side sections. The balcony and a projection booth were upstairs. The balcony was reserved for colored people. They paid at the ticket booth outside and then went through a side door and up the stairs. I had always thought that this was unfair. They were allowed to see not only the movie but also everything else that was going on in the seats below. Besides that, there were no ushers with flashlights in the balcony. Ushers were always watching to make sure you didn't do anything stupid when reels were being changed. I had even been told that J. Stanley Rosenstein himself sometimes watched the movie from the projection booth on high.

Flushed with my newfound authority, I stood at attention by the right-hand front-row seat, March of Dimes box in hand.

Miss Blankenship gave the signal and I started my carton down the front row toward Mary Leigh. This was a summer-morning crowd, friends our age whose mothers wanted some peace and quiet for a while. Not a big money group, but good for a few tokens and pennies, maybe a dime here and there.

I waved to friends as I moved up the aisle. A few popcorn kernels landed at my feet. I looked up to see Maudie May sitting on the front row in the balcony, her hands resting on the brass railing.

I waved back and passed the carton again. More kernels of popcorn. This time she pelted me on the head, using a slingshot she had made from a thick rubber band. I smiled and looked up just in time to be hit right between the eyes with another kernel. Somehow I didn't feel Maudie May knew the importance of my duties. I would have to find a weapon of retaliation. The next time the March of Dimes carton came to me, I pretended to adjust the top and grabbed a penny before I passed it on to the next row. I put it in my pocket to wait for the right moment.

Mary Leigh was waving to all the boys she knew. J.W. was a particular favorite of hers. In fact, he was a town favorite. His father had been killed in the war. His mother had had to go to work to support the family. As a result, he had been allowed to come and go as he pleased, with very few rules and regulations. Except that every adult in town knew he was untethered and would reign him in when they felt it appropriate.

At this particular moment J.W. got the idea that he should impress Mary Leigh, so he grabbed the heads of the Martin twins, who were sitting in front of him, and bashed them together. It made an awful cracking noise. While everyone was staring at the twins to see if their noses would bleed, I saw my chance to get back at Maudie and sailed a penny up toward her in the balcony. The problem was that my aim was just a little low. The penny ricocheted off the balcony railing and hit Claudia Sands in the back of the head. I glanced up at Maudie. She was shaking with laughter and reloading her slingshot. Claudia was sitting a few rows in front of J.W., so she thought the hit was part of J.W.'s grandstanding. Claudia was not as refined as the Martin twins. She was also twice as big and about half as smart, thirteen or fourteen and still a year behind her grade in school. She looked up at me, rubbing her head. I smiled and tried to look innocent. "That J.W. just beats all I ever saw. Is your head okay, Claudia?"

One of the girls sitting next to her began to laugh. Claudia's eyes narrowed. "My head's okay, but J.W. ain't gonna be," she said.

Not being of the best background, Claudia was very disturbed by this whole thing. Claudia's people lived out on the edge of town. Her daddy was a part-time janitor at the jail when he wasn't in it sleeping off a bad night. Well anyway, Claudia stood up, turned around, and began to look for J.W. in the audience. When she spied him, she leaped up on her theater seat and began to step over to the row behind her in pursuit. "This is your unlucky day, J.W. Quinn," she shouted as she grabbed the head of Marcy Payne to steady herself.

Even though he wasn't quite sure why it was happening, J.W. stood on his seat, turned around, and began climbing over to the row behind him. He started walking from arm to arm over the theater seats to escape. All the time he was smiling and waving at Mary Leigh whenever he got a chance.

This made Claudia even madder. She began stepping on people's arms and shoulders to try to catch him. Now other members of the audience who were being trampled didn't take kindly to either one of them. In addition, Maudie was unloading her spare ammunition on anyone within range. People began to get up out of their seats and join in all the chasing around, sure they were hapless victims, never knowing that Maudie sat in the balcony like Cecil B. DeMille, directing the mob scene with her slingshot.

Now Mary Leigh let out this very loud scream. I couldn't tell whether out of fear or happiness. Then I must admit things did get a little out of hand. Ushers were running up and down the aisles trying to catch Claudia. March of Dimes canisters became footballs spiraling through the air, spraying coins as they sailed. Ice from empty Coke cups was deposited down the nearest back or dumped on an unsuspecting head. Everything was in a wonderful state of turmoil, reminiscent of an Errol Flynn movie when he ran around swinging from the curtains, fighting off whole armies.

Miss Blankenship was standing in the middle aisle wringing her hands. Any empathy I had for her was fast disappearing. She was on the verge of tears over such a trivial matter, for heaven's sake.

Things finally got back to normal when Maudie May ran out of ammunition and the ushers caught J.W. and Claudia and threw them out of the movie. I, for one, believed they certainly deserved it. So immature. Meanwhile, I was on my hands and knees trying to pick up the money that had fallen out of my canister when somebody had grabbed it out of my hand.

Still trying to look out for poor Miss Blankenship's best interest, I walked over to her with my money. "Look, Miss Blankenship, I think I collected almost fifty cents for my fellow man." She told me to line up with the rest of the girls and walk out and not to say another word. I was stunned by her lack of gratitude.

As we marched toward the lobby, I looked up in the balcony, to see Maudie May, elbows resting on the balcony's brass rail, hands holding her smiling face.

Chapter 3

It had been earlier in the summer when Maudie May and I met for the first time. I was in my side yard putting the finishing touches on what I considered to be an exquisite set of teacups I had expertly crafted out of ivy leaves. Now I was giving serious thought to matching saucers made from pieces of pine bark. All of this would be artfully displayed on a tablecloth made of a large elephant-ear leaf that I would whack off of Mother's prized plant in the front yard.

Just then Maudie and the Brothers came walking along home on the dirt road that ran beside my house. I had seen Maudie and her little brothers before, but we had never spoken. I didn't even know if they were kin to each other. They didn't look at all alike. Maudie was very light brown. The lightest brown colored person I had ever seen, and the Brothers were dark brown, very close to black. I decided to make polite conversation. Seeing it was Saturday, I knew she had just been to the Roy Rogers movie like everyone else.

"Well, I guess Roy is the best of all the cowboys," I said. Maudie stopped walking. She stuck her hand down into the popcorn bag she was carrying, trying to fish out the last of the good pieces. Then she started to talk without looking up. "Just how old you think I am?"

"How old?"

"Yeah, how many years am I?" She lifted her face from the popcorn bag and stared at me, not smiling.

"Well, uh, you're a lot bigger than me and I'm ten, so I guess, I guess you're fourteen or fifteen."

She let out a disgusted breath. "I"—she put her hand on one hip—"is thirteen and three months, which means I ain't been studyin' no kid stuff like cowboys. But if I was to, I'd say Roy ain't no good. I only goes to see Roy 'cause the Brothers likes him. Ain't that right, Brothers?"

The two little boys walking just behind her looked up at Maudie, smiled, and shook their heads. They looked to be about the same age. Maybe five or six. "Y'all twins?"

"Naw, they ain't twins. They is a year apart. Miss Mama say they the very last two she gonna have. I sure hope so, 'cause I get tired of watchin' out after childrens. They was crazy about the horse chase at the end of the movie. Ain't that right, Brothers?"

The Brothers smiled again and nodded. That day and every day that summer the Brothers always wore the same thing, knit shirts with blue and red and brown stripes stretched across their stomachs, short pants, and sometimes shoes, but more often not. I had once asked Maudie why the Brothers never changed clothes. Maudie was indignant. Of course the Brothers changed their clothes and I was just blind if I didn't see that some of their shirts had the blue stripe and then the red stripe and others had the red stripe and then the blue stripes. She said I was just not a person who was particular about colors, so I wouldn't notice that. She deigned to explain that they had lots of shirts, only it took an expert like her to notice the difference in them. Besides, she was the one who had to wash them out every night.

"I guess you think Roy Rogers has the best horse there is," I said, trying to get the Brothers to talk. "I guess you think Dale is the most beautiful one." The Brothers still didn't say a word, just looked at me.

"The Brothers ain't allowed to talk to no strangers," Maudie said, still not smiling.

"Oh, sorry, I didn't know," I said.

"Course now if I was to judge, I would say the best one is Gene Autry. Can't nobody outshoot and outfight old Gene. Besides, he got a horse miles better than Trigger." She wadded up the popcorn bag and threw it into the bushes. "Now Champion a horse don't nobody want to mess with."

"Champion isn't even a pretty color like Trigger. Champion's just a plain old brown horse." I lowered my head waiting for a verbal assault and added in a soft voice, "Well, it seems to me he is anyway."

"That's all you know. I saw in *Silver Screen* where it say Champion knows one hundred tricks. Can't no other horse know one hundred tricks. Why, he can say yes and no just by shakin' his head 'bout anything you wants to ask him."

I rolled my eyes. Even I was hard put to believe that. "That's silly. You can't teach a horse one hundred tricks."

"Are you sayin' I'm lyin'?" Maudie turned her head and cut her eyes to me.

"The Brothers don't likes to hear peoples sayin' I'm lyin'. Do you, Brothers?"

The Brothers stared at me with sullen faces.

"I . . . I, uh, didn't mean you were lying exactly. It just seems to me—"

"Never mind what it seems to you." Maudie came over to me and took one of the ivy teacups out of my hand to hold up and inspect. "If it say so in *Silver Screen,* then it's so." The Brothers closed their eyes and nodded their heads yes, like Maudie was the preacher and they were giving her the big "Amen."

Maudie looked at me like maybe she thought I didn't even read *Silver Screen* or maybe she thought since she was so large—I dared not think fat—well, maybe she thought I was scared of her. I stood up straighter to try to gain equal footing.

She handed the teacup back to me and brushed her hands together like maybe they were dirty now. Her chubby fingers pulled down the skirt of her print dress. It was riding up her waist, it being probably two sizes too small. "Come on, Brothers, we got to get a move on."

They walked down the road a way and stopped. Maudie turned back to look at me and think. After a minute she took a step back toward me. "Course it ain't ladylike to play cowboys and things, but I'm gonna head on down this here road and make a hide-out ranch for the Brothers to play in. You wanta come?"

The road? The dirt road? She was asking me to come with her down the scary, dark, forbidden dirt road? My mother, my father, all, had warned against going down the road any farther than my backyard. It followed a creek and both eventually ended up down at the river. It was rumored to be a hangout for local drunks and anything else the mind could conjure. I knew even Maudie's house was not far down in the dark reaches of the road.

I jumped at the chance.

I pitched the cups back in the yard and brushed the dirt off my knees. "Course I myself am ladylike also, but all I was doing was making those pretend teacups, so I guess I'll come."

35

"Well, come on. Me and the Brothers knows the best place," she said.

We walked down the road past the dirt trail that led to Maudie's house. The sun jumped in wherever it could through the thick trees that arched overhead. For the most part, it was deep shade and getting deeper the farther we walked. Gigantic kudzu figures towered over us, their paws hung with trailing kudzu vines swaying in the breeze. There were four or five Negro houses on its path and way off in the woods a few whites were rumored to live. The stream, White Rock Bottom, for its limestone base, was said to be perfect territory for bootleggers.

"You sure it's all right if we go down this far?" I asked, seeing my mother's face before me. Maudie pretended not to hear me. "You know my name?" she said.

"No, but I know your mama. She works for Mrs. McMillan, next door to my house."

"Yeah, Miss Mama done work up there since I can remember. Truth be known, me and Miss Mama used to live up at Mrs. McMillan's when I was a baby. That was after she had her first batch of children and before the Brothers come along. Claude and Tot and Leroy had gone on off up north by then, so for a spell it was just me and Miss Mama living up there over the garage. That was before Mr. McMillan got hisself killed in the war and Miss Mama kept right on having more babies."

We walked on, not saying anything. She took a deep breath and let it out slowly. "I remember it. Peoples don't think I remember it, but I remember it! Mr. McMillan say, 'Now, Miss Mama, the circumstances are such that as long as it's just the two of you, our garage is plenty big, but don't go having more children, because there won't be space for others.'" She was shaking her head and muttering to herself. "The circumstances! The circumstances! Now what he suppose to know about the circumstances?"

"What does that mean, 'the circumstances'?" I asked her.

She looked up at me like she had forgotten I was there. "The circumstances? Well, let's see. That's like I is here and you is there and those are the circumstances. Tomorrow I may be there and you may be here and them would be the circumstances." She gave me a pretend smile. "Do you understand that?"

"No." I shook my head.

"Well that's all right. It don't make no difference anyhow. I'm just used to the Brothers listenin' when I talk. I didn't mean nothin' by it. Miss Mama say I'm gonna fry my brain if I don't stop thinkin' all the time."

"Why do you call her that, Miss Mama?"

Maudie looked at me like I wasn't too bright. "What do you mean, why do I call her Miss Mama? 'Cause that's her name, Miss Mama. It's the name she was born with."

"Oh."

"Now my name, if you want to know it, is Maudie May. Miss Mama say she give it to me because it have a nice sound to it. She say it kind of roll off your tongue like a movie star or some such. Course I don't care about that, but that's what she say. What's yours?"

"Tab. It's short for Tabitha."

"Kinda funny name ain't it, Tab?"

"Well, kinda."

"What grade you in, Tab?"

"Going on sixth. What grade you in?"

"I ain't in no grade. I been keepin' the Brothers 'til they old enough to go to school. Then I'm gonna start back. Course I used to be in school, so I knows all about it. Ain't that right, Brothers?" She didn't even wait for a shake of their heads, just continued on.

"Come next fall I be startin' back."

"What grade will you be in then?"

"Well, I, uh, well, what grade do you think I'll be in? You're so smart, you being in school continual and all, you guess."

"Well, I guess eighth, maybe even ninth."

"Eighth?" she said, thinking about it. "Do that sound right, Brothers? Eighth?"

Then she smiled to the Brothers and shook her head up and down. "I believe you exactly right. Eighth is where I'll be. In good old eighth grade. I wonder, do they still have the Blue Horse paper with the coupons on the back you can save up for prizes? Miss Mama says she's gonna help me save up all the coupons she can find."

"Oh yeah. I'm saving up for a bicycle. Only it takes fifty thousand coupons. I got two hundred so far. I think you sure are lucky, Maudie, not to have to go to school or do any homework."

"Oh, Miss Mama makes me practice my readin' and sums every afternoon when she gets off work. I read all the old magazines she brings home. That's how come I knows so much. I reads *Silver Screen* to Miss Mama all the time."

I was beginning to have great respect for Maudie. She didn't go to school and she learned to read by using movie magazines. How brilliant. Why had the thought never occurred to me? I must ask my mother about this kind of education.

By now we had walked farther down the road than I had ever been before. Here the trees and bushes were thick on both sides. Kudzu climbed in all directions up the tall pine trees. Some of the vines even crawled a little way out in the road. Off in the distance you could hear the cry of a pileated woodpecker. She stopped at a place where a wide path led off into the woods. There was a mailbox on a wooden post beside the path.

"Well, here it is." She put her hands on her hips and rocked back on her heels, so satisfied.

"Here what is?" All I could see was a dirt road

and a path and a bunch of kudzu vines strangling the pine trees.

"That's it." She pointed. "The kudzu vines. We gonna make the hideout behind the vines underneath the pine trees."

"I don't know about that, Maudie." I squatted all the way down to the ground to see if I could see under the vines. "We can't get in there. It's too thick."

"There you go again, sayin' I'm lyin.'" She was shaking her head. "Follow me."

I followed her back up the road a few yards from where we had come. She crossed over to the opposite side of the road from the vines and walked into the thick bushes down a little slope. At the bottom of the slope was a creek. It led to a big drainpipe that ran underneath the road above. I was amazed. "How did you know about this?"

"I been livin' round here all my life. I know 'bout where everything is and where everybody lives. We can walk through to the other side. Ain't much water in the pipe except when it rains, and then we can take off our shoes and wade through. This here is the most perfect way to get in and out of our hideout. I know 'cause I been here before, lots of times."

Of course, I kept saying to myself, I wasn't afraid of snakes if she wasn't. We walked through the big pipe and came out on the other side of the road, still in the creekbed. Everything on the

40

slope and up to level ground was covered over with old blackberry bushes strangled by kudzu. Maudie turned left and walked up the slope through the bushes to level ground. There were four or five big pine trees that held thick ropes of kudzu leading from the ground all the way into the top branches of the trees. It was so dark and shady, I felt like we were in a cave, except if I looked real hard, I could see out through the leaves to the spotted sunlight on the dirt road and path just a few feet away.

"This place must have armies of chiggers just waiting to pounce on the first real person they ever saw," I said.

Maudie pretended not to hear me. "Now, ain't this a perfect hideout," she said, "just like in the movies. We got our own secret entrance and everything. We can set right here and can't nobody that passes on the road or down that path out there see us one bit. It's just like a fort, safe from everything and everybody."

"I bet I'm gonna have ticks all in my hair next time Mama washes it. I know a nice place up under the magnolia tree in my grandmother's yard."

She paid not one bit of attention to what I was saying, just kept looking around at the vines and glancing out to the road on the other side of the kudzu. I decided to try again. "It sure does have a lot of sticker bushes in it. Look at my legs. They're full of scratches."

"Course they is right now, but when we clean out all the briers and makes room, it'll be perfect for anybody that wants a 'real' place to be," Maudie said.

I knew she was right. It was a real hideout, not just a pretend place to be, like we built in our side yard on summer nights with old army blankets. It was cool and shady away from the heat. Probably Roy and old Gene had chiggers and ticks, they just never let on. There was no way in or out except through the drainpipe. We were surrounded by thick bushes and kudzu.

Maudie turned to the Brothers. "Old Gene hisself would like it. It puts me in mind of the fort in *She Wore a Yellow Ribbon*, starring John Wayne."

"Yeah! We can clear out this space," I said, entering into the spirit of it, "and over there we can make another place for the Brothers. That can be the stable. I know! The Brothers can be Trigger and Champion and you and me can be Roy and Gene."

The Brothers turned to Maudie May with wide eyes. "Don't worry, she ain't gonna ride you. You just gonna stay in the stable and do tricks like stompin' numbers with your feet when we ask you how much is two plus two. Things like that."

The Brothers breathed a sigh of relief.

The very next minute we started to work on our fort. I volunteered to run back out the drain and up the road to my house and get old garden gloves to pull out the dead brier bushes. Maudie got a big kitchen knife from her house to cut down the small trees and branches that were in the way.

Chapter 4

It had taken almost two weeks to clear our hideout. Every morning after breakfast I made straight for the woods.

"Don't you want more cereal, Tab?" Mama asked.

"No, ma'am, two bowls is plenty. I gotta go."

"You and your friends must be having a good time doing whatever it is that you're doing. Are you playing with Mary Leigh or J.W., or Miss Mama's child? What's her name?"

"Oh, sometimes I play with one or the other or just whoever."

"You aren't going down into the woods, are you? I've told you that's off-limits."

I shook my head no. An answer to her question,

but not as binding as a spoken promise. She took the cereal bowl and dunked it in the hot soapy water in the sink. "Playing around on the dirt road is all right as long as it's close to our yard, but don't think about going down any farther toward the river. Edna says there are rumors of bootleggers down there, white trash. Those people can be very dangerous."

I shook my head again, in agreement, and slipped out the back door.

Finally we finished clearing out all the briers and bushes without messing up any of our kudzu cover. Old sticks and small logs were stacked in one corner. Briers and extra vines were placed in another. All of the poor displaced chiggers had immediately taken up residence on me. Each night as I painted yet another infestation with clear nail polish, I visualized armies of chiggers in their little chigger houses suffocating to death all over my body. The thought that old Gene and old Roy had suffered untold chigger misery in their woodsy adventures had never occurred to me before. Yet another reason for great admiration.

I brought an old hammock that was stored in our garage to hang between two pine trees. The Brothers gathered rocks and put them in a circle to make a place for a campfire like old Gene did in the movies. Maudie cut down some strong branches and tied them together with short rope pieces. Then she attached short stick legs to make a table.

We rolled four big stones up from the creekbed to use as chairs. I brought an old red-and-white oil-cloth to put over the stick table and a candle in a jar top for decoration.

What if, we thought, the whole town came down with polio and half the people were dead and what if our mothers and fathers were dead, too? Why, we theorized, we might have to come here and live forever and ever.

We made a shelf between two pine tree trunks. This was the place to keep our bucket of creek water as a washbasin. The idea was that if you washed your hands all the time, it would help keep you safe from polio. Of course, we forgot the other theory, which held that creek water might give it to you.

One day Maudie had another idea. "Now we need some pine needles to go on the floor so it won't get muddy when it rains. If we go on down the road, toward the river, we'll come to a good stand of pines we can get needles from."

As she talked, a thing she did quite a lot, Maudie was looking down the dirt path that ran into the woods. "Where does that path lead to, Maudie?"

"What path you talkin' about?"

"The one you keep looking at on and off. The one right out there." I pointed out to the path in the sunlight.

She looked at me with narrowed eyes. "Who cares where that path goes? I don't know where that path goes or who goes on that path. It makes me no mind. Probably just some old white trash. Miss Mama say don't mess with them. They ain't no count. She say they is niggers and Negroes and they is whites and white trash and the baddest of the whole bunch is white trash." She walked over and started tightening the ropes on the stick table as she muttered to herself, "And that's what lives down that road, just plain and simple white trash."

"How do you know that? We haven't even seen anything moving on that road."

Maudie was still fixing the table. "I told you I been living here all my life. I know about every-thing around here. You can believe me. Old man Jake is just about as sorry as they come."

"Well, if he's all that sorry, how come we got a hideout so close to him? Maybe we ought to think about moving our hideout up—"

"We ain't lettin' no sorry no-good run us off. We been here and we gonna stay here!"

"But if your mama said—"

Maudie smiled at me like my sister Tina did when she had decided I was too young to carry on an adult conversation. "Now Tab girl, don't you worry none about that. Let's go get us some pine straw."

We left by the drainpipe and brought back big armloads of straw to spread all over the living room and the kitchen and the Brothers' room.

We had made our third trip and were on our

hands and knees spreading pine needles on the floor when all of a sudden I felt Maudie grab my arm. I looked up, to see a man staring into the kudzu from the sunny path. I knew it must be white trash. It couldn't be anybody else. My mama was gonna kill me.

He was old. I couldn't tell how old, but his hair and beard were white. He had on bib overalls but no shirt. The most impressive things about him were his huge strong arms. They hung down beside his overalls with the fingers half-clinched. Old leather shoes with the sides cut out to make more room. And eyes, eyes that I knew must be looking right at me. If the Reverend Mengert was God in disguise, then the devil himself had materialized in the form of old man Jake. I stopped breathing.

Maudie looked at the Brothers and put her finger to her lips, but they were already standing stock still, watching him.

He squinted for a few minutes more and when he didn't seem to see anything, he bent down slowly and picked up a rock, which he tossed into the kudzu. Still nobody moved. He stood there for the longest time staring out of the sunlight into the vines.

Slowly he turned and walked to the old mailbox. He kept an eye on the kudzu while he felt with his hand to see if there was anything in the box. When he found that there was nothing there, he shuffled back down the path into the woods.

49

My heart was beating so loud in my ears, I didn't hear her at first. "I told you. I told you." Maudie began shaking my arm that she still held in a tight grip. "Can't nobody see us in here no matter how close they is. And him thinkin' we was a rabbit and tryin' to flush us out with a rock. We wasn't no more than ten feet away from him." Maudie was laughing like it was all a big joke.

"Is that . . . is that white trash?" I managed. "How do we know that? It . . . well, it might be just a farmer, you know, in those overalls. That's what some farmers wear. I'll bet it was a farmer, Maudie." I looked at her. "Don't you think it was a farmer, Maudie?"

She sighed. "No, it wasn't no farmer, Tab. That was Mr. Jake Terrance. Everybody knows him. He makes all the whiskey for peoples around here."

My heart was slowly coming back to a normal beat. "Well, it just seems to me that if you wanted whiskey, you would go across the river to one of the wet counties and get it."

"Oh girl, you sure is young for ten years old. The whiskey is legal for over there, but some peoples don't like you to know they drinks even legal whiskey, so they get it from old man Jake. But he can't never see us in here, so they ain't no need to worry. We as snug as a bug in a rug." She took two handfuls of straw and threw it up in the air and started laughing.

Then we began to throw pine straw at each other and laugh like crazy. The Brothers watched us with big smiles on their faces. Then they started throwing pine straw, too.

"You're right, Maudie. I'm not worrying about it," I said, the ultimate false bravado. "I'll bet old Gene and old Roy would even like a place like this. They wouldn't worry."

"You sure right 'bout that. Can't nothin' ever get to us in here." Maudie jumped up off the pine straw. "I'm gonna go right on out to the drainpipe and get some soft rock to write our name on the inside of the pipe. Enter the mighty Fort—" She stopped. "Fort what? What's gonna be the name?"

"How about Fort Apache, like in the movie?"

She thought about it a minute. "No, Apaches is Indians. We ain't got no Indians around here. What's the worse thing we got in Bainbridge? Something like Indians that goes around killing and doin' destruction."

"Well, the only thing we got around here is polio, but everybody's got polio. That's no—"

She interrupted: "Fort Polio, that ain't so bad a name. Everybody sure is scared enough of it. I'll put 'Enter the mighty Fort Polio and never fear!'"

Chapter 5

Not every waking moment was spent in the fort. During "spray time," it was mandatory to stay inside. Flies were everywhere in the summertime and maybe, just maybe, flies were the cause. On designated afternoons, listed in the newspaper, certain parts of town would be doused with large rolling clouds of DDT dropped into every nook and cranny from the local crop-dusting plane. This was perfectly wonderful, the local paper assured. DDT never hurt anybody and it might control the flies. Just one precaution. It probably would be best to stay off the streets during this time and be sure and park your car under the nearest tree. The DDT dust did have a tendency to stain clothes and cars a light yellow color.

For me, it meant the inconvenience of being cooped up inside with my sister Tina for an hour or so. During this time I would try to divert her, because if I didn't, Tina would end up talking the whole time about Tom Lyle Brown, her latest boyfriend. Oh, how Tom Lyle was so cute. Oh, how he smiled at her when she saw him in the Woolworth's the other day. And oh, how she went over and sat next to him in Sunday school last week, only he couldn't share his catechism with her, but it was only because he was already sharing with DeDe Marsh. And wouldn't everybody just fall over dead if they knew about her and Tom Lyle being boyfriend and girlfriend. I thought to myself as I shuffled the cards, Probably the first one to fall over dead would be old Tom Lyle himself, since he probably had no idea in the world that he was Tina's boyfriend. It was not that Tina was nuts, I had decided. No, she was like everybody in her grade. They were all practicing for when it would be real, only after a while, they forgot to tell the difference.

We both sat on our beds, me playing solitaire, Tina studying the latest copy of *Seventeen*. I would steer the subject to a story she liked to tell.

"So, Tina, tell me again how come it is we don't live in the country anymore? Pop still is a farmer, and besides, I love the farm."

She yawned and stretched her arms out, tired of the *Seventeen*. "The plantation, Tab. It sounds better to say 'plantation' than 'farm.'"

"But Mama says it's all the same. She says Pop works like a slave, and when the crops fail, nobody gives a hoot what you call it."

"Our mother," she said knowingly, "is the reason we had to move off the plantation in the first place."

"Well, I remember she did say there wasn't any electricity and indoor plumbing when she lived up there. Mama isn't always wrong, you know."

"That's beside the point, Tab. It was family tradition. Our family had lived on that land for just ever."

"So what exactly did happen?" I said, to get her started. Of course I knew what happened, but it was better than Tom Lyle Brown. I dealt out my first hand of solitaire.

"Well . . ." She put down her magazine and leaned back against her bed pillow.

"When Mother met Pop in college, it was so romantic. They decided to get married and come back to live in Alabama. It was their turn to carry on the tradition, Pop being the oldest son and all. But Grandmother and Granddaddy were still living on the farm. So Grandmother said she would move into town. Only Mother said that was all right, that she would just as soon live in town with paved streets and indoor bathrooms and cars and things like Mama was used to in the city where she came from." She paused and pointed to me. "Did you know she told me Knoxville had five movies and they showed different pictures all week?

55

"Well anyway, Grandmother said no, she and Granddaddy would sacrifice living on the lovely farm so Mama and Pop could carry on the tradition of living on the beautiful old plantation. You know Pop—he's a great believer in tradition, so he said that was real nice of Grandmother to offer and we would take it. They moved in town to the house on Ridge Road and we went to live in the country. That's how we came to live out there." She looked over at me and waited for me to look at her before she raised her eyebrows and said, "For a while, that is."

Tina continued, warming to the tale. "Well, when we first moved out there, I was only a kid, but I remember it. All the workers would come to the front porch of the big house every day and stare at Mama and Mama would chat about what a lovely day it was, like they were Mrs. Vanderbilt come to call. How were their children, and would they like some iced tea?"

Tina shook her head. "Poor Mother, she just didn't know how to treat the help. She still doesn't, if you ask me.

"Why, Pop would come out of the fields from working with the field hands and say that Mama should tell all the house workers what their responsibilities were. And Mama would say she didn't even know what her responsibilities were, much less theirs. Pop said they must make a garden, churn the butter, clean the kerosene lamps, stuff like that.

"Mama would say that the only butter she ever

saw came from a store but that she would give it a try. Mama was always willing to give it a try. I'll give her that.

"Mama would say to the workers, they needed to plant a garden and make butter, but the workers would kind of lower their heads and smile, and some days they would say it was too hot to make butter or it was too early to plant peas and Mama would say that sounded reasonable to her. Then Pop would come home for lunch and Mother would be cooking and listening to the Texaco broadcast of the Metropolitan Opera and all the workers were sitting on the back porch listening to the opera, too.

"Mama even decided one time that La Wanda— she was supposed to be Mama's main helper around the house—well, La Wanda had this real lovely high voice and Mama said she bet she could teach La Wanda to sing the 'Bell Song,' just like Lily Pons on the Met broadcasts. Mama's musical training just popped out. She couldn't help it. She used to all the time walk around humming some tune from an opera nobody ever heard of." Tina put her hands behind her head, smiling, and hummed a few bars from *Carmen.*

"So anyway," she continued, "the workers said that sounded like a good idea to them. They said that La Wanda was sure the best singer in their church choir. They smiled real polite and stopped work to watch Mama commence with the lessons.

Mama started out teaching La Wanda, but Pop came home in the middle of one of the sessions and said it was a noble idea to teach La Wanda but it wouldn't fly and for Mama to be more realistic. It was not songs, but food, that everybody on the plantation needed.

"Then Pop said, how come there was no butter and why wasn't anybody working in the garden. Mama said on account of it was too hot for the butter and too early for peas. Pop said he had better get somebody to help Mama learn the farming ways.

"That's how Will came up to the main house. Did you know that?" She looked over to me to see if I was still listening. "Before he got the job of helping Mother, he helped Granddaddy."

Tina said she thought Will would rather work for Granddaddy, in that Granddaddy spent most of his time riding around in his Ford Ranchero. But Will got assigned to the main house to help out. It was a good thing Will came, too, because it was just about time to take the hams down from curing.

"Now, and this is the best part," Tina said. "One morning a few weeks after Will came, he and Mama went to the smokehouse. It was right out back of the main house. I can still see those big pieces of pig hanging from rope tied to the rafters. Will cut down the ham Mama selected and carried it back to the kitchen. 'First off, Miss Mary, you needs to cut the bad places out of the meat.'

"'What bad places, Will? If there are any bad places in pork, we should throw the whole thing away. You should never take chances with bad meat, especially pork.'

"'They is always some bad places, Miss Mary. When the smoke don't get to some places on the meat, the flies will get in the ham and lay eggs. You has to cut them places out.'

"Now, Mama looked at the ham for a long time and said she thought that was disgusting and she wasn't going to have her family eating meat like that and for Will to throw it away.

"Will said he didn't believe Mama wanted to do that. If she threw away that ham, they likely as not would find bad places in the other meats hanging up to smoke, and they couldn't throw away all the meat. 'Then what we gonna eat all winter? This here is the only pork we got and the only pork we likely to have all winter for the white folks and the colored folks. We lives in the country now. We ain't in the city no more. This here ain't just for you and your family. The smokehouse meat go to every family on the place.'

"Mama looked at the ham for a long time and then took the knife and began to cut where Will told her to. Only she didn't do it for long. She got white around the mouth, and gave the knife to Will and told him to finish cutting. She went over to a chair in the corner of the kitchen and sat silent for a long time. After that, Mama didn't listen to the

Met broadcasts much more. She didn't try to teach anybody else how to sing. She just worked all the time.

"Will would come on up to the house every morning and tell Mama what the workers were supposed to do. Then when the workers came, Mama would go out to the back porch and tell them what Will had told her.

"Grandmother came out to visit every once in a while. She and Mama would sit in rockers on the front porch. 'You are so lucky to live on the old plantation, my dear. Very few people are blessed with the traditions and heritage of a family like ours. We are the only family in the county that managed to keep the same plantation through all these years.'

"Mama rocked back and forth in her chair while she peeled peaches for supper. 'We certainly are not like most people,' Mama said."

Tina said we might still live on the lovely farm if the ceiling hadn't fallen in on Mama. She was sweeping the rug in the living room one morning and a chunk of ceiling plaster came loose and fell on Mama's head. "I don't think it hurt so much, because it wasn't a big piece of plaster, but Mama just stood there with tears running down her face.

"Will came rushing in and began to pick up the plaster pieces. He said the ceiling was put up there such a long time ago and made of molasses and horse hair and clay and such that it just naturally fell off every once in a while.

"Will said he would have some of the workers repair it that very day. Mama said not to bother, that she had decided to move into the twentieth century.

"I remember, when Pop came home for dinner that day, he and Mama went up to their room and had a long talk. When winter came, we moved to town."

Chapter 6

Although it had been ten years since we moved from the farm, Mother was only slightly more at home in town. She tried singing in the church choir. It seemed a natural, given her background. After a few weeks she had made the mistake of suggesting to the choirmaster that they sing something other than the likes of "The Old Rugged Cross." The choirmaster was offended, but, more importantly, Miss Locklear, third grade teacher/Sunday organist, was insulted. She didn't know anything other than songs like "Old Rugged" and wasn't about to learn new ones. It was a big mistake to offend Miss Locklear. She was one of only three organists in town and the Presbyterians and Episcopalians had the other two sewed up. Besides, the rest of us loved "Old Rugged." One was not truly blessed unless the strains of a familiar hymn had washed over you of a Sunday.

After a year or two of pushing for change in the choir loft, Mother would often throw over the whole Sunday school business and send us along with Pop while she stayed at home. It was the only day in the week she was free to put her feet up, pour herself a second cup of coffee, and read the Sunday edition of the *Birmingham News* without children underfoot. Every time this happened Grandmother informed us that God was taking notes.

Right after Sunday school every one of my group, Mary Leigh, J.W., Tommy, et al., would rush down to the Men's Bible Study Class to beg for any free leftover doughnuts. Even Tina was not too sophisticated to race us down the stairs. After eating as many doughnuts as we could politely stuff in our mouths within a five-minute period, we would trudge back up to the sanctuary and take our places in the proper pews. Our family was the fifth row back on the right-hand side. Grandmother had long ago staked out our row. In front of us was Mary Leigh's family. In front of them were Tommy and his family. Next came the Lane sisters, and so it went all over the church. We were stacked in like meticulously sorted fruits and vegetables at the Piggly Wiggly.

Tina had explained to me that you never, but never, sat on anybody else's row and they never sat on yours. "It would just look perfectly pitiful if you did, like you didn't know what you were doing." To make sure that I never embarrassed her by taking an improper seat, she explained that it was written somewhere in the Bible that "Jesus sitteth on the right hand of God the Father Almighty and everybody else sitteth in their right row." I knew she must be lying through her teeth, but I couldn't take the chance. I considered her a biblical scholar after she got a free Bible for five years of perfect Sunday school attendance. So I always sat in my right row even though we were a very tight fit when all the uncles, aunts, and cousins were there.

New people who came and went every ten years or so sat in the back or the balcony. Nobody worried about them.

Next on the Sunday agenda was eating at Grandmother's house. A mixture of food and, now that I was old enough to sit at the big table, fascinating adult conversation. I felt it my responsibility to act as a social buffer between Mother and the rest of the clan. This particular Sunday, it was nigh on to impossible.

The meal began as usual. Dora, Grandmother's maid, was feeding the little children in the kitchen. Laughing and crying could alternately be heard. The sounds of silverware clanking and iced-tea spoons swirling in tall wet glasses were a background noise to everyone at the table talking at once. I had spilled my first teaspoonful of sugar on the tablecloth but had managed to get the other five in the glass. Grandmother was constantly ringing her little handbell to try to get Dora to bring out more biscuits, but Dora had her hands full in the kitchen and wasn't about to bother with Grandmother's bell. I was doing my best to grab some portion of whatever serving dishes were being passed by me. I had filled my plate with two pieces of fried chicken, string beans, watermelon-rind pickle, squash casserole, and fresh fried corn. This I considered a dainty helping, in as much as I wanted to save room for dessert, rumored to be pecan pie.

Granddaddy was sitting at the head of the table, eating and not saying a word, as usual. I was devouring my first piece of fried chicken when Grandmother began to tell a story about her next-door neighbors, the Doland Myerses. Mr. Myers was famous for his heavy drinking. There had been other stories, but this one was a doozy, Grandmother assured us. Everyone at the table turned to listen to her.

It seemed that Mr. Myers had gotten drunk as a river coot last Thursday, Grandmother said. It was his reaction to Mrs. Myers pouring out all of his cabinet whiskey. Poor little thing, she had become overzealous after attending a Baptist revival meeting. Upon seeing all the empty whiskey bottles, Mr. Myers had jumped in the car and driven across the river to a wet county to drown his sorrow. After his sorrows were sufficiently drowned, he had driven back home ready to do battle with the first thing in sight.

By this time everyone at the table was having a big laugh over yet another attempt of Mrs. Myers to sober up Mr. Myers. I did notice, out of the corner of my eye, that Mother was not laughing like everyone else. I looked in her direction with a big grin on my face to give her the idea that this was something she should be amused by.

Grandmother continued. "Well, the first thing he saw was Katherine's thrift plants running all up and down the driveway. You know how she keeps that yard in pristine condition? Well, no more." She started laughing and had to stop and take a drink of iced tea. "He took that Buick Roadmaster on a run around that yard like he was plowing a field. He would run over all her flowers going up the front walk and put the car in reverse and run over all her flowers going back down the walk. You have never seen such precision for one so drunk."

"I could use old Doland Myers during spring plowing," Pop said, smiling.

"Everybody in the neighborhood was coming on out to watch," Grandmother said, "because every time he reached the end of one row, he would honk his horn to signal he had finished. Katherine even tried to go out and talk to him as he was plowing along, but he wouldn't roll down his window."

I looked over to Mother again. Despite herself, she was smiling. Good! I could enjoy my dinner and not worry about her.

"Well, finally, finally, things came to a head when he started toward her Pride of Mobiles," Grandmother said.

There was a collective gasp from the aunts seated at the table. "Oh my heavens," Aunt Helen said, "Katherine has the prettiest azaleas in town."

"Don't I know it," Grandmother said, while the men at the table smiled at each other.

"So what happened?" said Uncle George. "He plowed down her Pride of Mobiles and she came out and shot him."

"Serves him right, too," Pop said. "He should have known better than to come between a woman and her flowers. Especially a woman and her front-yard flowers."

"Don't I know it," Uncle George mimicked Grandmother. "Remember the time I accidentally mowed down Helen's tulips?"

Pop raised his eyebrows. "How could we forget. You were saved from an ugly divorce by an emergency shipment from Burpee."

"Oh, you boys stop that foolishness. That's not what happened at all." She took another sip of tea as a dramatic pause before the conclusion.

"No, Robert saved the day."

"Who?" Mother said.

"Robert, he's the colored man who works for the Myers and lives in the garage apartment behind their house," Pop told her.

"I might have known it would be Robert," Uncle

George said. "If it hadn't been for Robert all these years, they would have had to put Doland Myers away a long time ago."

"So what did he do?" Aunt Helen asked.

"He came around the side of the house, awakened by all the commotion, I guess, slipped in the front seat when Doland stopped to put the car in reverse, and turned off the key. As simple as that. Doland just sat there in a stupor, with a smile on his face."

"Old Robert holds that family together," said Pop.

"Poor old Katherine," Aunt Alice said. "Out in front of the whole neighborhood he's making a fool out of himself. She must have been mortified."

"She would have been better off staying in the house and pretending it wasn't happening," Grandmother said.

"You know, I don't know why Katherine Myers puts up with that," Mother said. "Can you imagine being married to someone who stays drunk more than he stays sober? Why . . . why, I could more easily be married to Robert than Doland Myers. At least he's sober. Doland Myers is just one step above white trash."

"Robert who?" Grandmother said.

"Robert, their helper who lives in the garage," Mother said.

The table got quiet. I had been finishing off my second piece of chicken and hadn't paid too much attention to the subject of the conversation, but I knew Mother had been the last one to speak and she must have made another social gaffe.

Mother looked around the room, surprised at the silence. "Well, that goes without saying, doesn't it?"

I looked up to see Pop poking his fork at the fried okra. He cleared his throat. "What Mary meant was that Doland Myers's drinking has gotten all out of hand. He's certainly not an example to anybody."

Mother's face turned red. "What *I* meant was . . . that I would rather be married to a colored man who was honest, hardworking, and a responsible member of the community than to a white man who was a raging alcoholic."

More silence. Dora was standing in the doorway with hot bread. She began to serve everybody biscuits, only she passed over Mama when it was her turn to get one. I compensated for her by taking two.

"I never heard of such a thing," my aunt Alice said. Then she started to giggle. Aunt Alice always giggled at everything, death, marriage, birth. All events elicited the same response. "Married to a colored man? Mary, you do beat all." She raised a shaky iced tea glass to her lips and tried to sip it.

Then Uncle George had to get into it. He glared at Mother. "You talk about poor white trash. Now that's poor white trash talk if I ever heard it," he said.

70

Pop folded his arms across his chest and gave him a long, mean look. All of the sudden nobody was eating; everybody was sitting up straight. Everyone could tell he was about to give Uncle George down the country, when Aunt Alice put down her tea glass and saved the day. "Oh my heavens, can you imagine Mary, when she interviews to become a member of the Ladies Help League, saying something like that?"

Grandmother had recently nominated Mother for membership in the local women's charity organization. One of her ongoing attempts to make Mother fit in.

Aunt Alice began giggling again. "I can just see all the ladies sitting there strangling on their cups of coffee." Everybody started to smile at the thought. "Why, can't you see Miss Delphi Jones? She would probably spew coffee halfway across the room, like somebody had hit her on the back in midswallow."

"We would have to get Doland to bring over a bottle of Black Jack to revive her," Aunt Helen put in.

People began to smile and snicker at the thought. Me loudest of all. I punched Aunt Alice on the shoulder, "You are such a card, Aunt Alice," and laughed as if it was the funniest thing I had ever heard. I didn't know what Black Jack was, but I knew it was up to us girls to make everybody happy again. A thing I could not seem to get across to Mama.

71

Then Pop started smiling too and sat back easy in his chair. "Well, one thing's for certain. My Mary will sure add a real spark to the Ladies Help League with all her Tennessee notions."

Everybody relaxed and laughed, all except for Grandmother. She muttered under her breath, "She will if they let her in." Nobody heard that comment except me and maybe Uncle George and Aunt Alice. Maybe Dora.

Chapter 7

We had pretty much settled into a routine at Fort Polio. The Brothers spent their time up in the tree house Maudie had added as a lookout for Mr. Jake. She had found some old boards at her house. I had happily lifted all my father's tools from his toolbox on the back porch and contributed them to the project. First I had taken his new hammer, then a bag of nails. After that I had decided it would be much more efficient just to take the whole box. It saved me constant trips back and forth.

We started by nailing boards between two trees that were draped with kudzu vines. After we had added steps enough to oversee the path to Mr. Jake's house, we dragged up several boards and nailed them together for a floor. It was a wonderful

lookout through the kudzu vines to all the surrounding territory. Then Maudie brought an old
barge rope she had found down by the river. We
tied it to a top pine tree branch for a quick way
down.

From dawn to dusk every day we labored in our
new fort. Making stick chairs, clearing out a path to
the drainpipe, bringing up stones from the creek
to outline our different rooms. Of course, I
explained to Maudie, I had other friends and I had
other things to do, so don't get the idea that I
thought this was the best thing that had happened
to me since peanut butter. Oh no, I was also a member of the all-boy secret club in our neighborhood
and on occasion I would have to leave this ordinary
place and attend a secret session of my other club.
My popularity was boundless.

"Is that right?" Her eyes sparkled with the coming verbal battle. "Well now, let me see here. You say
you a member of a secret all-boy club?"

"Yes I am." Knowing I had impressed her.

"What's the name of this here club?"

"Well, the name of the club is, uh, The Secret
Club. We just call it, The Club for short." I had not
one clue what the official name of the club was,
having never been let in on that secret.

"And you say The Club don't have no girl members?"

"All except for me."

"Well, how come in all this time we been build-

74

ing this here fort you ain't had no meetings? Least ways, I ain't seen you go to no meetings."

"That's because we don't have many meetings," I said, patronizing.

"Them boys ain't about to let you be a regular member of they club. You dreamin'."

"Listen, Maudie, J.W. and Tommy and Bean said if I brought refreshments to the club meetings, then I could be a member. So I'm a member. You're just jealous 'cause you aren't a member."

"And what do you do at these here meetin's?" She egged me on.

"I don't know, but it's only because I'm a new member. There's only been one meeting since I joined. I spent all my time getting refreshments. I had to make three trips back to my house for lemonade and peanut butter and jelly sandwiches. By the time I finished all that, the meeting was over. But next time I'm going to fix everything before-hand."

"That bunch don't want no girl members."

Just then, two pinecones dropped to the ground. This was our signal to freeze. The Brothers had spotted Mr. Jake Terrance coming along his path or they had seen a whiskey car coming down the road. What usually happened was that we stood still until he walked to his mailbox to put a paper bag in or take an envelope out. The bags were to cover a jar of whiskey he brought from his still down in the woods. After he put the bag in, he would amble back on down to his house. Then a car would come along in a few minutes. The driver would take out the paper bag and leave an envelope in its place. We were used to this by now. My initial fear of Mr. Jake had turned to curiosity, then to just plain boredom with him and his whiskey business.

This day, Mr. Jake put the paper bag in the mailbox and walked back down the path. I waited, drumming my fingers on my crossed arms, wanting to finish what I had been saying about The Club. We kept still until the car drove up and got the whiskey. This time it was Mr. Newfield, the mayor. Then he drove off.

"What's the matter with you, Maudie? Didn't you hear right about The Club? I told you, it's me, J.W., Bean, and Tommy. We even have a hole in the tree down by Tommy's side yard where we leave messages."

"Messages?" She walked to the creek edge to hunt for a large stone.

"Yes."

"What messages?"

"Well, just messages. You know."

"No, I don't know."

"Just stuff. Stuff that only club members are supposed to know."

"Like?" She strained under the weight of a large rock she was bringing up from the creek.

"Kind of like, I might leave a message for J.W. or he might leave one for me."

76

"Have J.W. ever left you a message?"

"No, but he could." The truth was, I had seen the other boys use the message tree, but I had never dared use it myself. It was the ultimate secret of The Club.

"Has you ever left him a message?"

"No, but I could if I wanted to, and he would read it and leave a message in return. That's how we do it in The Club."

She dumped the rock she had brought up from the creek, stood up, and smilingly pulled the trigger. "Okay, let's see you do that."

"Do what?" My heart stopped.

"Do what you say. You leave a message in the message place and have somebody answer it."

"Uh, I would, but I don't have anything to say right now." Faint hope that she might not pursue it.

"You ain't gonna leave no message 'cause won't nobody answer it if you do."

"You think you're so smart, Maudie May. If I had a message to leave, I would, just to show you."

Maudie had taken a position sitting cross-legged on the pine-needle floor. She began making clover necklaces for the Brothers from a big stack of white clover we had picked on the roadside earlier in the day. One of the Brothers came down the rope to where we were sitting and she held up the necklace to measure it. Then she looked over at me and—"You just think you a member of The Club."

That did it. I knew, somewhere in the back of my

mind, I was Wile E. Coyote racing off the nearest cliff, Acme jet pack strapped to my back, but I charged ahead with reckless abandon. "Okay, all right, if you're gonna be so smart. I guess I'll just have to show you how we do it in The Club."

She smiled. "Okay, how?"

"Well, it's just simple. Say if you want to do something like have a football game, you would just write a message asking who wants to play and you leave it in the message tree."

"Then?"

"Then whoever wants to play just leaves a message telling you that they'll play."

Maudie got up from in front of the clover pile and went over to the tin can where we kept pencils. She tore the back off of an empty box of saltines that had been left from lunch. "Okay, here's some paper and a pencil. You write the message and I'll watch you put it in the message tree."

"Okay, okay." I turned over the piece of cardboard to the back side and wrote, "Whoever wants to play football, sign here." Underneath I signed my name and under that I drew four straight lines. After all, I was a member of The Club. They had said so at the first meeting as I lugged large sloshing pitchers of lemonade back and forth from my house. I folded the cardboard two times. "Now all I have to do is put this in the message tree and wait. You'll see," I said, hoping she might let me put it in my pocket and forget about it.

Maudie followed me to Tommy's side yard and waited while I went to the message tree. I walked back out to the sidewalk where she was standing. "See?"

Maudie May was impressed. I could tell. She would probably never mention it again. In a week or two I would tell her all about how I had played football with the boys and been the star of the game. I could see myself catching the winning pass. That was it—I caught the winning pass and the score had been tied seven to seven.

But a few days later . . .

"You been to the tree to see who signed your paper?"

"No."

"Why not?"

"'Cause, I haven't had time."

"You ain't had time 'cause you know don't nobody want to play."

"That's not it at all. I just haven't thought about it." Of course Maudie kept after me until finally we made a trip back to the tree. My message was in there just where I had left it. I took the piece of cardboard out and opened it up slowly, Maudie standing over me. All the lines that I had drawn were still empty.

"See, nobody has had time to read it and sign their name." I breathed a sigh of relief and was folding the paper to put it back in the tree when I noticed somebody had written on the back, "We challenge your team to a game on Saturday afternoon." It was signed by J.W.

I stared at the paper in disbelief. "Oh great, this is just great, Maudie. See what you got me into? J.W. and the rest want to play my team."

"You ain't got no team."

"I know that. Do you think I'm stupid? I meant we would all play together. Now they want to play against me."

"I thought you was a member of The Club and all the members played together." Maudie smiled.

"We do, except I guess they just got the message wrong. They think I want to play against them. This is all your fault, Maudie."

"They didn't get no message wrong. They ain't studyin' playin' no football with you. They wants to play against you and beat you. I told you you wasn't no member of no—"

"Oh, just shut up, Maudie. You're mad because you aren't a member and I am. You just don't know how The Club works, that's all."

"I know how The Club works. They is gonna gang up on you and beat you at football and then they gonna say you ain't good enough to be in The Club. That's how it works. I know all about peoples."

"You don't know anything. This is all your fault, Maudie. You got me in this mess. Now who in the world am I gonna get to be on my team? I have to have at least three people to play J.W. and Tommy and Bean. Maybe I can get Mary Leigh."

"Mary Leigh? Prissy Mary Leigh? The one that was in the movie with you? She ain't gonna play football."

"She might, maybe. I could get John, but John can't come out of the cellar. At least not when anybody will see. Besides, John's so little, they'll run all over him. I need somebody big and strong to throw the ball to me while I run down the field. John could center, but he can't do anything else."

I looked at Maudie. My eyes narrowed as I saw her transformed into a menacing tackle. "You could do it, Maudie! You're stronger than any of them. You could do it." I jumped up. "This'll be great. If we can get John out of the basement for a little while on Saturday, and you and me, we would have a team."

"Don't look at me. I ain't playin' no football. I don't even know how it works. Besides, I ain't a member of"—she put her hands on her hips and raised her eyebrows—"The Club."

I ignored her. "You don't have to be to play this one time. Just this one time. Come on. Please, just this once."

"You crazy. I ain't even studyin' 'bout playin'." She turned and walked back up the path to the sidewalk. "Come on, let's go back to the fort. Bein' in The Club don't make no difference no way. I was just funnin' with you 'bout them boys."

Chapter 8

That night at supper, Tina eyed me suspiciously as she passed the tomatoes. "J.W. told me he was going to play you in football on Saturday after the movies. Is that true?" Not waiting for a reply: "What is the matter with you, Tab? Girls are cheer-leaders, not football players. Mother, tell her she can't play."

Mother looked surprised. "Is that right, Tab? Do you have a football team?"

"Well, sort of." I busied myself with putting a slice of tomato in my biscuit.

"What do you mean, 'sort of'?" Tina glared at me. "Do you or don't you?"

"I did say I wanted to play, so I guess I'll have to have a team."

Mama looked over to my father. "I don't know if you should be playing such a rough sport, Tab."

Pop was buttering his biscuits while they were hot. He looked up at me and winked. "I don't see how it could hurt. At this age they're all the same size anyway. In fact, most of the girls are bigger than the boys. Who's on your team, Tab?"

"I'm not exactly sure yet. I was going to get John, but he can't get out of the cellar."

"John who?—can't get out of the cellar?" Pop stopped buttering and looked over to Mother. "Has Edna put John down in the coal cellar again this summer?"

"Yes, sir," I said. "He's been down there since school let out. But he's loving it. She brings him new toys every day."

Pop shook his head.

"They only use it for coal in the winter," I said, embarrassed that John seemed so weird to everyone except me. "His mama swept out all the coal and made it real nice." Still there was silence from my father. "The other day he got a whole new train set. Now he has it running all over the floor. Sometimes I watch him through the window when he runs it. And you know what? Last week, Mrs. McMillan brought him two sets of Tinkertoys. That's nice, isn't it?"

"What in the world is Edna thinking about?" Pop looked at Mama like she could do something about it.

She was pouring everybody more iced tea. "You know Edna. She told me that the coal cellar was the coolest place in the house. She says she can't stand the thought of having him exposed to polio when he plays with the other children. I think since her friend Janice had a child come down with it last summer, she's sort of gone crazy about keeping him out of harm's way. You have to take into account he's the only child and all she has left, not to mention the fact that she thinks he is a budding genius." She looked an apology to Pop. "I should have remembered to tell you, Charles, but with all that goes on around here in the summer, somehow it almost seems normal." She put the iced tea pitcher back on the table and sat down. "She says as long as he's happy, she'll keep him in the cellar through the hottest part of the summer."

"That beats all I ever heard," Pop said. "I'll bet Big John Mac is turning over in his grave. How does she know being around the other children will help or hurt? Why, if we thought it would do any good, we would keep ours in the house all summer."

"I know, I know. It's just that Edna . . . Well, people have to cope with it in their own way, I guess. Remember, Charles, I packed up all the children and spent a good part of the summer in Knoxville last year, just to escape."

"That was different. Your parents live in Knoxville. It was a natural thing to do, visit your parents. It's not like we panicked."

"I don't wanna leave here again this summer."
Tina was starting to whine, as usual. Such a big cry-
baby. But I was just as glad. Now everybody started
talking about polio and if we might leave town.
They forgot about my football team. I sat back to listen and have one more helping of creamed corn
and another hot buttered biscuit with a slice of
tomato in the middle.

The next morning I walked over to the McMillans' house, plopped down on my stomach in front
of the window to John's cellar room, and gave it a
tap. John pushed a chair over to the wall and stood
on it to reach the latch. He was two years younger
than I and little for his age. In my eyes, he always
looked like he was on his way to a party because his
mother dressed him in a freshly starched outfit
every day. He wore a white shirt with a Peter Pan
collar, short pants, and matching blue socks. His
straight black hair was always parted and every hair
in place. Because he never ventured out in the sun,
his face was white and delicate-looking, like a china
doll wearing glasses.

The window swung back on its hinges and John
hooked it to a latch on the ceiling. If I was ever ban-
ished to a cellar, this would be the one for me. The
whole area had been cleared out except for the furnace, a big easy chair, and a few garden tools in the

corner. Other than that, it was wall-to-wall toys and books. The ceiling was hung with squadrons of airplanes, models of World War II British and American fighters. The shelves that had once held garden tools were now lined with every imaginable toy. One wall had a set of encyclopedias and every Big Little Book ever printed. Other shelves and tables were stacked with comics in neat piles, intermittent with jars of marbles, rows of tops and yo-yos. A train set spread its tracks around the furnace and back again. He had saved every toy he ever got and somehow also managed to keep them all in good condition.

"Look down here at my new set of Lincoln Logs." He hopped off the chair and walked over to his train set. "Mother was going to give them to me tonight, but when I jumped in bed with her this morning for our talk, she said she just couldn't resist giving them to me right then. See, I built this train tunnel three feet long."

"Yeah, real nice, John, but I guess you get tired of staying down there," I said, eager to get on to my reason for this visit. "You probably would like to come out and play some."

John looked up at me and pushed his glasses back on his nose. "Why would I want to do that? I like it down here. Tomorrow Mother's going to bring me a—"

"Yeah, well, that's fine, but it just seems to me, John, if you stay down there all summer, you won't be able to get out and walk in the woods or play football."

"I don't like the woods. You get chiggers, and I don't know how to play football. Last year in Miss McReynolds' class, when we went outside for supervised play, well, one day we had a game of kickball. I didn't enjoy it in the least. I never could kick the ball past first base. They always put me out."

He stopped looking at me and began to look around the room. "Did you see my new Roy Rogers gun and holster set?"

This temporarily diverted me from my mission, Roy being my hero and all. "Where did you get that?" It was the most beautiful thing I had ever seen. It was made completely of white leather, with red glass, set in diamond-shaped designs, on the holster and belt. There were genuine cowhide strings hanging from the ends of the two holsters.

"That's the best thing you got. Where did your mother get it?"

"Mother didn't. My mother's friend, down in Lower Peach Tree, sent it to me. It came in the mail yesterday. I can't wear it, though, because it's so heavy it pulls my pants down. I'm going to hang them on the wall until I get bigger."

I saw my opening. "I guess that'll be a long time, then, because you're never going to get bigger down in that basement."

He gave me a curious look through his big glasses. "What do you mean? Mother said the other day that I looked like I had grown an inch."

"I guess you know it's a scientific fact that you can't grow unless the sun shines on you at least once a week. It's vitamin D and all. I read it in the paper the other day. Why, when you get out at the end of the summer, you'll probably be a foot shorter than everybody else your age, and you're already pretty short, John. That's why you need to come out and play a little football this Saturday. So what do you say?" I gave him my best Roy Rogers smile. That was where you smiled real wide with your mouth and squinted your eyes up so much that you couldn't see out of them. Roy did it all the time.

John sat down on the floor to continue building more bridges, but out of Tinkertoys this time. The Lincoln Logs were used up. "What article? What paper? I read the paper every day and I didn't see anything."

"You read the whole newspaper?" I had forgotten that his mother had started him reading the paper when he was just a little thing. Now in addition to all the regular books he read, he was a walking encyclopedia of newspaper knowledge. One of the things I liked about John was that he was so smart, but it was also one of the things that I found most disgusting.

"Of course I read the whole newspaper. Miss

Mama brings it down to me every morning. I sit right there in my chair and read it and have my morning coffee."

"Your mother lets you have coffee?"

"With lots of milk in it. She says I'm the man of the house now that my father died. Before she leaves for work every morning she tells Miss Mama, 'Take him his paper and his coffee.' So what day was that article in the paper?"

"Well . . . well, it wasn't the *Bainbridge Times*. It was in the *Birmingham News*. Yeah, the Sunday *Birmingham News*. Do you read that?"

"No, we don't get that."

"Good—I mean, that's too bad, because that's where I saw it. My pop said, 'Look at this article, Tab. I wonder if Mrs. McMillan knows about this?' So you see, it's a genuine fact. So I guess you almost have to come out and play football this Saturday. Me and Maudie May will come over around one o'clock when your mother is taking a nap. We can pull you up out of the window. You can play a little football in the sunshine and then we'll put you back in the basement before your mother even wakes up."

"But if I need sun to help me grow, I'm sure Mother wouldn't mind."

"No, we don't want to tell your mama, John, because she probably didn't read the article. She won't know about the sun and all. You can surprise her and tell her later. Probably at the end of the summer would be a good time."

John was beginning to make a large windmill to go on top of his Tinkertoy bridge. "All right, if you say so." He didn't even look up. He wasn't interested in me anymore.

I lay there in the grass with my chin on my hands, trying to decide what I could do to get Maudie to play.

In the end, she had to play. It wasn't a question of her wanting to or not wanting to. She had to. I didn't plan it. It just seemed to come to me naturally, like I was born to be devious and underhanded. I used the only thing that I knew she couldn't resist, the Brothers.

"The thing about it is this," I said to Maudie. "Poor old John is stuck down in this dark old cellar all day long by himself. His mother won't let him come out except to go to Sunday school every Sunday. He was saying to me the other day how he would love to play a genuine game of football and I said we could play except we don't have enough players. So then he started to cry. You know he's two years younger than me, so he's still just a kid and all. It's so sad."

"Don't you 'so sad' me," Maudie said. "Miss Mama work up there for Mrs. McMillan every day. She say John got more toys down in that cellar than the whole toy department at the Woolworth's. She say when she take dinner down to him every day, she can't step around for them toys down on the floor. She say they is planes hangin' from the ceiling, trains runnin' every which away. She say that boy done saved every toy he ever had and—"

"Yeah, yeah, he does have a lot of stuff, but he never gets to come out and play."

"That don't make me no never mind."

"Okay, I tell you what, Maudie. Now here's an idea. What if the Brothers could go down and play with all his toys one day? What about that?" I said it loud so the Brothers would hear. They stopped playing marbles to listen. "Why, you should see all the stuff down there. There's a glass pickle jar—must have a million marbles in it."

"Don't you start goin' on 'bout that cellar. The Brothers can't go to no cellar. Why, if Miss Mama ever found out, she would have my hide. Beside, she works up there all the time. She's right there in the house."

"You know what else he's got?" I turned and started talking directly to the Brothers. "He's got a genuine Roy Rogers gun and holster set."

The Brothers put marbles in their pockets and came closer.

She turned to the Brothers. "Ain't no use you studyin' 'bout no toy cellar. We ain't goin'." She hardened the look on her face. "Miss Mama would catch us sure."

"Not if we let them play down there on Saturday

afternoon. Your mama just works 'til noon on Saturdays. We could leave them in there while we play football."

"No, no. Just plain no. I ain't gonna."

I shrugged my shoulders to the Brothers. "I'm sorry, Brothers, I was gonna fix up a good time for y'all."

The Brothers looked pitiful. I started talking only to them. "You know, there's a stack of Captain Marvel comics in the corner. Must be three feet high. On one shelf, there's probably ten yo-yos and tops lined up side by side."

Their eyes were all glazed over. I even heard them talk to Maudie for the first time in front of me. They turned to her so pathetic, and in a tiny voice one of them said, "Please, Sister, can't we go?"

Maudie gave me a dirty look. "Okay, okay, okay, you can go play in the toy cellar, but only as long as we at the football game. Then we'll be right back to get you."

Success! I grabbed the Brothers' hands and we started dancing around in a circle. "Oh, the joys of the toys! Oh, the joys of the toys!" Faster and faster until we all fell down laughing, on the pine-straw floor. Even Maudie smiled at us a little.

Chapter 9

I was used to all of John's toys, but somebody seeing them for the first time would be surprised. "The Lord! Will you look at them toys," Maudie said. "Look like Santa Claus done throwed his whole bag down there."

Maudie and I were lying on our stomachs, peering down through the coal chute window. The Brothers squatted beside us, ready to dive into heaven on earth. John smiled up at the window. "Why, thank you very much. I do have quite a collection. My mother even suggested that I should catalog the various items in alphabetical order."

Maudie looked at me. "What's he talkin' about, 'various items'?"

"Not so loud," I said. "We don't want to wake up

Mrs. McMillan," I whispered to Maudie. "Now, John, here's what we're going to do. Me and Maudie will pull you out the window to go play football with us. While we're gone, the Brothers can watch over your toys for you."

"I don't need anybody to watch over my toys for me. I have them arranged just like I want them."

"How do you know you don't need anybody to watch over your toys? Have you ever left them before on a Saturday?"

"Well, no, but . . ."

"So you see, somebody needs to be here while we're gone to make sure they stay safe and neat. So give us your hands."

We pulled John up out of the window and lowered the Brothers down into the toys. When we left, they were standing stock still on the basement floor, breathing in the aroma of new toys.

J.W. was sitting on the football underneath the oak tree in the corner of the football field. Actually, it wasn't a football field; it was Tommy's side yard. He lived on Oak Road also, just two blocks away from my house. One goalpost was the holly bush at the far end of the yard. The other goal was the oak tree by the sidewalk that ran up Oak Road. Tommy was leaning with his back on the tree and trying to make his yo-yo "walk the dog." A lost cause.

I walked up, triumphant with my team. "I guess you thought I wouldn't come. I guess you thought I couldn't get up a team."

J.W. looked up. "That's not your team, is it? You can't play with them. They ain't in The Club. Everybody knows you have to be in The Club to play on this field."

"You didn't tell me that," I shot back, determined not to let the tears come. "You . . . you have all The Club members on your team anyway. You just said for us to play, so here we are. Are you gonna chicken out? Afraid we'll beat you?"

"With a colored girl and a baby? You must be crazy."

"Yeah," Tommy said, "we ain't playin' no colored girl and a baby."

"Is he talking about me?" John stared up at me through his glasses.

"No, he's not talking about you, exactly."

"Yeah, I am talking about you. You're just as baby as they come. Besides, you're not even supposed to be out of the coal cellar," J.W. said.

"That's just like you, J.W. Tattletaling on somebody. That's worse than being a baby."

He stood up. I knew I had insulted him, and that was hard to do.

"I am not tattling. I just meant he wasn't supposed to be out here."

"Well, he is and he's part of my team, so let's get started. Unless, of course, you won't play us, which means we'll automatically be declared the winner."

"Come on, Tab, let's go." Maudie was standing

on the sidewalk. "I guess they is afraid to play us, afraid we'll beat 'em. I told you they would be."

Tommy rolled his yo-yo up and put it in his pocket. "You did say you would play her team, J.W., and they did show up."

"Okay, okay." J.W. rolled his eyes. "One touchdown and whoever makes the first score wins. Y'all can even go first."

"Well, we have to wait on Bean," I said. "He's not here yet." I looked up the sidewalk like I was watching for Bean. My last hope was that he wouldn't show up and we could call it a draw.

"His mama made him stay at home and mow the grass. Besides, we don't need him anyway. We can beat y'all without him. You're just stalling. Now who's afraid?" J.W. snickered.

"Okay," Maudie said, "let's get this over with. Now, how do you play this here game?"

"Oh brother," J.W. roared, "this is your team? They don't even know how to play."

"Oh yes they do. Yes they do. They just forgot," I said, motioning them over to me. "Y'all come over here in a huddle."

"What's that?" John asked.

"A huddle. A huddle. Come over here and we'll have a meeting."

Maudie and John followed me over to our side of the ball that J.W. had put in the middle of the field.

"Now here's what we do," I whispered. "John,

you stoop down and pass Maudie the ball between your legs, and then, Maudie, you throw the ball to me. I'll run up the field and try to make a touchdown. While I'm running, y'all try to keep J.W. and Tommy from catching me."

"I can't stop J.W. or Tommy. I'm too little," John whined. "Besides, I might break my glasses."

"Yes you can. Yes you can. You just grab them by the shirt and hold on and, Maudie, you try and stop them, too. You're bigger than they are anyway."

They didn't like it, but we finally got ready to go. John walked up to the ball and put his hand on it. J.W. and Tommy got down on all fours and started to growl. John took his hand off the ball and walked back to me.

"I don't think I want to play this game. Those boys seem very mad." He took off his glasses and began to clean them to get a better view of the situation.

"Sure you do." I put my hand on his shoulder. "Remember the sunshine. Remember you need to be outside."

"Yes but . . ."

"Never mind, never mind, just give the ball to Maudie. She'll do the rest."

"Yeah," Maudie said, "you just give the ball to me and I'll give it to Tab. Let's get goin'." John edged back to the ball. J.W. and Tommy were making snorting noises again.

"When I say go, you give it to me," Maudie said. She took a deep breath. "Go!"

John pushed the ball between his legs and Maudie took it. She stepped back a few feet. J.W. and Tommy dove for her. She stepped to the side, just as they fell forward. Maudie looked at them piled on top of each other and promptly sat down on them. Then she handed the ball to me. "Well, go on. I'll sit on 'em while you run to the tree."

I took the ball and stared at J.W. and Tommy. They were gasping for breath under Maudie's weight and lying on their stomachs, so they couldn't get their hands up to get at her.

"Get off us, you big fat ape," J.W. wheezed.

I smiled and started to run like crazy to the tree. I ran with my hand out just like Jim Thorpe, all-American. Twisting and turning, prancing and weaving.

"I made it! I made it! We win! We win!" I jumped up and down and ran circles around the tree three or four times, holding the ball high up in the air. When I finally stopped and looked back down the field, John was wiping his glasses with his linen handkerchief. Maudie was still sitting on Tommy and J.W., using her hands to hold their shoulders down, and watching me. I walked back toward her. "You can let 'em up now, Maudie. It's all over."

"It's all over? That's it? Ain't nothin' left to do?"

"No, we won."

"Well, this is the dumbest game I ever did know about. Ain't nothin' to it." She got up off the boys and began to brush off her dress.

J.W. screamed as he rolled on the ground, trying

to catch his breath. "Cheat! Cheat!" He gasped. "You can't play like that." He took more deep breaths and got up on all fours. "That touchdown didn't count. You'll never be in The Club if you're gonna play like that. Never!"

"What are you talking about, J.W.? You said I was already a member of The Club. What do you mean I can't be a member?"

"You cheated and you can't be a member and that's that," J.W. said. He was trying to stand up.

Tommy was wiping dirt off his face. "Well, J.W., you did say if she got a team up we would play her, and you did say—"

"Never mind that. Cheats can't be a member."

"But I did what you said."

"No you didn't."

Maudie grabbed me by the shoulder. "Come on, I told you you wasn't no member. Let's go see about the Brothers."

"Yes," John said. "I don't want them messing up my toys."

"But he said—"

"Never mind." Maudie pushed me toward the sidewalk. "What peoples say and what they means ain't always the same."

I looked back over my shoulder and yelled, "We won. We still won." We got to the sidewalk and started toward John's house. Then Maudie had to go and get mushy on me. She looked at me and smiled. She almost never smiled in a kind way.

"Remember, you always got our club." She put an arm around my shoulder.

"What club are you talking about?" I pushed her arm away, still furious with the boys.

She put her head down and muttered, "Well, they is you and me and the Brothers in the fort."

"Oh, don't be dumb, Maudie. That's not a club. That's just a place to play. Nobody would ever think of that as a club."

She jerked her head up and looked straight at me. The smile had vanished. "I know that. You think I don't know that? You think I'm stupid?"

John was staring up into the sun. "Do you think I got enough vitamin D? That was quite fun. It's hard to believe we won with so little effort. I've read about football in the newspaper, but I always thought it was a real hard sport. Do you think I have a talent for football?"

"Yeah, sure, John," I said.

"Good! Maybe I'll come out again sometime and we'll play those boys in another game."

Maudie rolled her eyes. "If a frog have wings," she said.

We had walked back up the sidewalk to my house when we began to hear this loud booming noise. The closer we came to John's house, the louder it got.

"What in the name of sweet Jesus is that?" Maudie said. "Sound like somebody tryin' to knock down a wall."

All at once we all realized it was coming from John's basement. We started running toward the window at the same time.

"I forgot about the bass drum Mother gave me last week," John said as we ran.

"This is a fine time for you to think of it. Don't you know the Brothers loves loud noises?" Maudie said.

I slid into the ground by the window like I was sliding home in a baseball game. I pushed up the window and gave one big "Shhhh!" to the Brothers just as the door to the basement opened. Mrs. McMillan's voice called down to John, "John, dear, if you will remember, when I brought you that drum, we agreed you would play it on a limited basis. I think that's enough for this time."

John had crawled up beside me and now he stuck his head in the window. "Yes, ma'am," he said.

There was a moment of absolute silence while we waited to see if she was going to come down the stairs and discover everything. Then she said, "I will say that I do believe you are improving, sweetheart."

"Thank you, Mother."

The door began to close. The Brothers were standing next to the big drum in the corner, hands still raised in the air, holding one big drumstick each and grinning.

Maudie stuck her head in between John and me. "You makes one more sound with them sticks and you good as dead."

Slowly they let their arms drop to their sides and the smiles fade from their faces.

I turned over on my back and started to breathe again. John was lowering himself into the chair under the window, talking as he hopped down. "Look at this. Everything I have down here is in a mess. What were you boys thinking about, getting everything out of order? How could you be so inconsiderate?" He was picking up marbles and little tin cars off the floor. "This will take me a week to straighten out."

The Brothers watched as he counted each marble he put back into the glass jar. "Come on up here, Brothers." Maudie was reaching her hand through the window. "Some peoples just don't appreciate havin' friends."

Chapter 10

I was standing on the sidewalk across the street from my front yard. It had been several days since I was kicked out of The Club, but the memory still burned. Five or ten times a day it burned. I had found a good piece of soft rock and was getting ready to draw a hopscotch for myself. Out of the corner of my eye, I saw Tommy walking up Oak Road toward me. I was down on my hands and knees, lining out squares, and didn't even look up when I saw his Keds standing there.

"Wanta play some baseball, Tab? My aunt gave me a new ball for my birthday."

"I know, you showed it to me already." I kept drawing out squares.

"Well, you wanta play? I'll let you borrow my

glove in the outfield. We're getting ready to play down in my yard."

"No. I'm gonna play hopscotch, if you'll move your big feet so I can put the numbers in." I started drawing in the numbers.

"Come on. We only got three people. Besides, playing hopscotch by yourself isn't any fun."

"Yes it is."

"No it isn't. Are you still sore because of that football game the other day? I told J.W. he should let you back in The Club. Come on. We have to have at least four people to play."

"I'm not interested." I finished numbering. "Why don't you go get old Mary Leigh to play with you?" Then I started looking around for a good throwing rock.

"What if I told J.W. to let you back in The Club before we even start the game? What about that?"

"No, I don't want to be in The Club ever again. It's only for boys, and I'm a girl. Besides"— I decided to improvise as I went along—"I'm in another club now. Lots better than yours anyway."

"Sure you are." He rolled his eyes, then crossed them and smiled at me.

"Very funny, Tommy." As long as I was making up a club, this one was going to be irresistible. "This club"—I paused for effect—"this club is so secret, you can't even find out where we have our meetings." I picked up a throwing rock. "Of course, you're not allowed down there anyway."

"I'm allowed anyplace you're allowed and more. Boys are allowed more places than girls."

I pretended not to hear him. I had learned that from Maudie. "The other thing about this club is that we have dues, real money dues. We collect them every week." I pitched the rock I had found to the first square. "This is not just a top secret club, this is a rich top secret club. That's what it's called, the Rich Top Secret Club." I started to hop.

"Sure, you probably collect five cents a month. That's real rich. At that rate, you may save up enough to buy a baseball bat in a year maybe. Now speaking of baseball, what if I let you pitch instead of be outfielder?"

I knew that old ploy. "You never let me pitch. I'm always the outfielder and I have to run all over the place hunting for the ball when it gets lost in the holly bushes."

"Well, I might let you pitch this time if you'll come play right now."

"You'll let me pitch the whole time?" I started to reconsider.

"No, one half of one inning, and I get to choose the inning."

"One half of one inning? Big deal. I'm going to finish my game of hopscotch and then head on down to the Rich Top Secret Club to see how much dues we collected today."

"Come on, Tab, you don't have a club. Stop making things up and come play baseball with us."

I finished my hop back over number one and turned to look at the hopscotch board. "You don't know about it 'cause it's in a place you aren't allowed to go, and of course you would be too chicken to go down there even if you were allowed." I looked up at him and let my eyes shift toward the road.

"Are you talking about down at White Rock Bottom Creek? I'm not— You aren't allowed and I know it."

"Suit yourself."

"Oh come on, Tab, I'll let you pitch one whole inning. What do you think of that? A deal?" He smiled this dumb hopeful smile at me.

"No!" I said. "I told you, when I finish here, I got to go look in the Rich Top Secret Club mailbox for the club dues."

"What mailbox?"

I pitched the rock down to number-three square and started to hop again.

"Never mind, I just have to check. I'm the treasurer, so I have to check the envelope." I never looked up, just hopped on down to home and back again. Then I threw to number four. "No, I don't have time for that."

He gave up and started walking away, mumbling, "You're just a spoilsport, Tab. See if I ever let you be pitcher again." He walked on down the sidewalk toward his house.

I knew what he would do. They didn't have enough to play a regular game of baseball, just

J.W., Tommy, and Bean, so they would sit out under the oak tree and talk and complain about me not playing. Then Tommy would tell them about the Rich Top Secret Club. It would be just like me and Tina and the Bible. I knew everyone did not sitteth in their right row, but I couldn't take a chance. They would know that I didn't have a Rich Top Secret Club, but they couldn't take a chance. They would have to find out.

Soon as I finished my game, I walked slowly down to my front yard, pretending to hunt for four-leaf clovers. I was really just sitting around in the corner of the front yard by the dirt road, waiting for a whiskey car to come. Down by the street, I could see the boys sitting under the oak tree in Tommy's yard. Finally a whiskey car came. I knew it was a whiskey car because Mr. Cravy, who owned the dry cleaners, was in it, and he was a regular.

I waited one minute more, then got up and started walking real slow down the dirt road so the boys might notice me. If I timed it just right, the boys would get there just as Mr. Jake was coming to pick up his money.

After I got out of sight, I ran on down to the drainpipe and walked through to our fort to wait. Maudie and the Brothers were there, as usual. I told Maudie what I had said to Tommy. "What you wanta go tellin' them boys where Mr. Jake's whiskey money is? They liable to try and take it just to make us mad. Then they really be in bad trouble."

"I know." I smiled.

I sat down on the pine straw, facing out to the road to watch. "Serves them right. Not letting me be a member of The Club and saying we don't have a club and messing up our football victory."

"Well, I thought you said we didn't have no club. You said we was just a group."

I picked up a piece of pine straw, and started chewing on it. "Well, I changed my mind. I, well, I been thinking, Maudie. I know if Miss Mama had caught you the other day when you played football with me, well, you would have been in a lot of trouble. I know that."

Maudie didn't say anything. She came over and sat down beside me to watch the road. Sure enough, in about five minutes, here comes J.W. and Tommy walking real slow. I knew Bean wouldn't come—too scared. The minute they saw the mailbox, you could tell. They just kept right on walking but staring at it. They looked at each other and then all around to see if anybody was coming. "Well, if this is it, where's the meeting place?" Tommy said.

"Probably down that old dirt path."

"You can forget it if you think I'm going down there. It's probably some old deserted house where hoboes stay."

"Don't wet your pants, Tommy. All we're gonna do is look in the mailbox."

They had stopped right in front of the fort.

"Let's just step over there and look. We'll never know unless we look."

A pinecone dropped by my side. I had crossed my fingers and was repeating over and over to myself, Look in the mailbox. Look in the mailbox.

"You look, J.W. This place gives me the creeps." Tommy said this as he stood looking up at the kudzu.

"Oh don't be such a . . ." J.W. walked over and pulled the door of the mailbox open. "There it is, a white envelope, just like she said. It hasn't got a stamp on it or anything. It couldn't be a letter. I wonder how much they have in there and why they keep it out in the open like this."

Just then there was a rustling sound. Before J.W. had time to close the mailbox door, he was there, standing in the middle of the path, bigger than I ever remembered seeing him. His eyes just seemed to hook into J.W.'s like they were in some kind of stare-off.

I thought to myself that if J.W. would just run on off, that would be the end of it, but poor J.W. couldn't even move. Tommy began backing up as soon as he saw it was Mr. Jake. He took four or five steps and then turned tail and ran on up the road.

But not J.W. He was like a possum caught in a garbage can, frozen, as Mr. Jake walked closer and closer. J.W. held on to the mailbox as though he might collapse if he let go.

Old Mr. Jake took one or two more steps, at the

same time fishing for something in his pocket. When he reached J.W., he pulled out what was the largest pocketknife I had ever seen. He switched out the blade in one quick motion. All men carried pocketknives, but this one was different. The blade must have been six inches long.

J.W.'s eyes shifted from Mr. Jake's face to his knife, but he still didn't move.

I had thought the least he could do was run. This was not working out like I planned.

Old Mr. Jake raised his knife hand. I closed my eyes. When I opened one eye, he had brought the blade down hard, not two inches from J.W.'s arms, locked around the mailbox. We heard the blade dig down into the wood. I felt Maudie jump beside me when the blade hit.

This was just too much for old J.W. His arms let go and he fell back on the ground.

"You got business here, Boy?"

J.W. was sitting on the ground, looking up at Mr. Jake and frantically shaking his head no. "Uh . . . no sir, no sir, I . . . I got lost. I wasn't meaning to be here. I . . ."

One big strong arm went down and picked up J.W. by the collar and pulled him to a standing position, then all the way up into Mr. Jake's face. His feet dangled off the ground. With the other hand he held his knife against J.W.'s throat.

"I don't like nobody messin' round with my things. You understand that, Boy?" He waited for

J.W. to answer, but nothing came out of his open mouth. He shook him. "If your daddy wasn't kilt defendin' his country, I might have to take me a arm off here." He ran the knife along J.W.'s arm and a thin line of blood appeared. J.W. was so scared, he didn't even cry out.

"You get outta here and stay outta here, understand? Don't never come back, or next time I'll use this knife to cut you up in little pieces. You understand me, Boy?"

With that, he dropped J.W. to the ground. Still J.W. sat there like a limp puppet, staring up at Mr. Jake.

"Git!" he yelled at J.W.

That did it. J.W. took off running up the road with the wettest pair of pants I ever saw on a person over three years of age.

I turned to look at Mr. Jake. He had his hands on his hips, looking out after J.W. A half smile came on his face as he turned to get his envelope and shuffle back on down the path. We had gotten so accustomed to Mr. Jake, he had become a fixture like the kudzu vines. Now his menacing presence loomed larger than life once again. I waited for him to be well gone before I would breathe. "That . . . that didn't work out exactly like I planned it." I looked down to see my hand shaking. Trying to shift some of the blame, I said, "J.W. is just a disappointment to me. He didn't even have the nerve to run." I looked at Maudie. She was staring down the path Mr. Jake had walked.

"Did you see that? Did you see that? I knowed for sure he was gonna kill him."

"J.W. is such a baby. I'll bet he's still running." I tried to laugh.

Maudie would have none of it. "What you want to go and do something like that for? That club don't make that much difference to you. We coulda ended up with a dead J.W. on our hands."

I was afraid of what I had done, but still, somewhere inside I was furious.

"It serves him right," I said, even madder that she had seemed to take his side. Tears were welling up in my eyes. "I did it because, well, I did it because you . . . you came out to play the football game. You did it for me, and, and," I yelled out my fury, "he called you a big fat ape." I banged my fist on the ground. "I hated that!"

There was complete silence as I stared at Maudie and she stared back at me. After a moment she started shaking her head. "Well," she said, looking down at the ground, "he did do that." She thought for a moment, then raised her eyes to look straight at me and smile. "And I squashed him, too, didn't I?"

I stared back at her and then started smiling myself. "You rubbed his face in the dirt," I said, wiping the tears off of my face, remembering it.

She laughed out loud. "The Lord, I'll never forget it as long as I live. They was both right there on the ground in a pile and I says to myself, Maudie

114

girl, why don't you just take a seat." She was beginning to laugh so hard, there werc tears. "I didn't even know if it was in the rules, but I didn't care." She fell back on to the pine straw and laughed more.

"I looked down the field and there you were," I said, "sitting on the whole bunch of them." I lay back on the pine straw to kick my feet in the air and laugh. "And did you see him just now, running off with those wet pants?" I roared.

We couldn't stop laughing.

Chapter 11

The day finally came for Mother to try to pass muster. The Ladies Help League was coming to call. Grandmother had been at work for weeks contacting first one and then the other. Now the anointed hour had arrived. Mrs. Poovey, founder and president for life of the Bainbridge Ladies Help League, was to come calling for afternoon tea. If she liked Mother, she was a shoo-in. If not, well, that was not even to be contemplated. The house was abuzz. The phone had been ringing off the hook all morning. Usually it was Grandmother with some helpful hint. After the third or fourth call, Mother went in the kitchen to make refreshments and assigned me to phone duty. I immediately became Grandmother's aide-de-camp and frantically carried out her every whim.

"Be sure the children are out of the way." Tina was assigned to look after the twins and Charles junior. She had built them a playhouse in the backyard and was hovering.

"Be sure everything is thoroughly dusted. Grace Poovey has allergies." I had dashed all over the house, dusting my little heart out, but not so Mother could see me, else she think Grandmother or I—it was all the same thing—was interfering.

"Be sure the room is cool." I had clandestinely unplugged the floor fan in the dining room and repositioned it in the living room, blowing on the armchair I knew Mother would assign to Mrs. Poovey.

"Does your mother have any fresh flowers?" I had hopped on my bike and dashed to Grandmother's, five blocks away. Grandmother had cut a lovely bouquet of fresh flowers out of her garden. Promising to treat them with kid gloves, I had run out of her house, taking the front steps two at a time, slung the flowers in my bike basket, and bounced them all the way home. Arriving only minutes before the appointed hour, I had found the nearest iced-tea glass, filled it with water and stuffed the flowers in before plopping them down on the living room coffee table. Beautiful.

I looked around, fingers drumming my tummy. All was in readiness. If that Mrs. Poovey didn't like our house and my mama, she was crazy. I sat down to keep watch out of the living room window.

Mother was openly excited about joining the Ladies Help League. Only last night, at the supper table, she had said the Ladies Help League did wonderful work. Did we know, she enthused, that they obtained free braces for the children in the county who had polio? Did we know that they had raised thousands of dollars every year? She had met Mrs. Poovey but didn't know her and was looking forward to getting that chance. She was a woman who had such a wonderful influence for good. This was something Mama could sink her teeth into.

Grandmother and I were overjoyed.

"I want her," Grandmother had said, "to get to know some of the really nice people in the League. Not that she doesn't know nice people now; it's just that this will broaden her horizons."

I knew this was a veiled reference to John's mother, who lived next door and worked for a living. Working was not bad, Grandmother explained. In Mrs. McMillan's case, it was noble, even patriotic. It just meant—well, it meant you had to work and you couldn't spend all of your time doing for your husband and your children and your community.

Mrs. McMillan had already lived in the house next door for several years when we moved into town from the farm. She was one of the first people Mother met and was an outsider, like Mother, so they hit it off from the beginning. Their husbands had been teammates on the Bainbridge High football team. He had gone to the University of Alabama and met Mrs. McMillan while she was working her way through school, waiting on tables in the cafeteria. Mr. McMillan sent his bride and baby back up to Bainbridge to live with his mother while he, and so many others, went off to war, never to return. Then a year after the war ended, Grandmother McMillan died, leaving her son's widow the house and very little else. With an accent that said she had spent her early days on a tenant farm, Edna McMillan was determined that her only child never know that kind of life. She took a job at the Farmers' Co-op to provide for herself and the last of the McMillan clan in Bainbridge.

Sometimes in the evening, Mother and Mrs. McMillan would sit out on the front porch and talk. Mother liked hearing about what was going on in the working world. When I was out playing hide-'n'-seek at night, I would hide under the holly bush by the front porch to listen in.

It seemed there was this one farmer who had a mad crush on Mrs. McMillan. Eugene Waverly from up around the east end of the county. Every other day he would just happen by the Farmers' Co-op and bring her extra sweet potatoes from his garden. Now her back porch was full of sweet potatoes and she was constantly trying to give them away to Mother and anybody else who would take them.

"And how is Eugene, Eugene the Potato Machine?" Mama teased as they rocked, cooled by the overhead fan, smoke from their Lucky Strikes drifting out into the night air.

"I am so sick of sweet old Eugene, Eugene, I could scream. He means well, but he's driving me crazy. I don't want to talk about him anymore." She pointed her cigarette at Mother. "From now on, for every question you make me answer about Eugene, you have to take six potatoes off my back porch."

"I am not taking one more sweet potato. My skin is beginning to take on an orange hue. Besides, it would be an insult to Eugene, Eugene. He meant every one of those thousand or so sweet potatoes just for you."

"And did I tell you, every time you even mention his name, you have to take three more potatoes?"

"Oh no, I'm already up to nine."

"And the night is still young."

"Seriously, Edna, why don't you think about going out with Eugene or somebody?"

"You're up to twelve, and I've told you a hundred times, John is my first priority now. It might upset him."

"That's all fine and good, but what happens when you're old and gray?" Mother asked.

"When I'm old and gray, John will be governor. I'll have to help him run the state. Did I tell you the school wants to skip him another grade next fall?"

Mother sighed, defeated. "I guess eating sweet potatoes with Eugene for the rest of your life can't compare with running the state."

"You're—"

"Fifteen, I know. I wonder if they have a recipe for sweet potato pickles?"

I noticed movement outside of the living room window. A black Packard was pulling up. I peered through lace curtains and saw two women in the backseat. The driver was getting out to open the door for them. Two. Two? Grandmother hadn't mentioned two. Did we have enough refreshments, enough chairs, enough flowers? I rushed back to Mother in the kitchen.

"There are two of them and they're coming now. Two of them, Mother. Did you know that? Two?"

"Yes, Tab, I knew that. Mother Rutland phoned this morning. Her next-door neighbor, Mrs. Doland Myers, is coming along. I already know her, and she is Mrs. Poovey's best friend. She volunteered. I thought that was very nice of her."

"The one that drinks like a fish?"

"It's her husband who drinks like a fish, Tab. Katherine Myers is a sweet, kind woman with not a lot of backbone—" She looked at me and smiled. "I have to finish these sandwiches. Why don't you go keep a look out and open the door for them when they ring."

I stared at her. She smiled and then laughed at

me. "Yes, I have everything under control, 'Mother.' There's plenty to eat. Don't worry."

I dashed back to the front window. Mrs. Doland Myers was still in the car, waiting to be let out. Mrs. Poovey was standing in the street talking to her driver.

Everyone in town knew of Mrs. Poovey. The first thing they knew was that she wasn't a Poovey at all. Of course the minute you laid eyes on her, you could tell that. Rutherford Westmoreland, now that was Mrs. Poovey. It was her maiden name before she married Jesse Poovey. Grace Rutherford Westmoreland. Her mother was a Rutherford and her father was a Westmoreland, and in Bainbridge—need I say more?

Grandmother had explained the town social structure to me early on. The Rutherfords and the Westmorelands were two of the original five families that settled Bainbridge. The others being the Goodloes, the Locklears, and, naturally, the Bainbridges. Grandmother would fairly swoon when she started talking about the original five. That was because her family—she was a Goodloe—was one of the originals.

Afternoons on her porch, I was instructed in the lore. Oh, how they came here on their flatboats down the river! Oh, how they fought the Indians and settled the land! How they endured the War and famine and so on and so on. Oh, how they and their descendants were the very heart and soul of Bainbridge.

Naturally, Mother did not see it that way. Mother said, you would have thought the Holy Trinity founded Bainbridge the way Grandmother carried on. She said, if you called sitting around on the same piece of property for 150 years divine, then they certainly did qualify. I was grateful the subject never came up for group discussion.

The Rutherfords used to own some town property, two or three stores along River Street, not as good as owning county land, Grandmother said, but it did show that they were not fly-by-night people.

Now the Westmorelands were another thing altogether. They had the Westmoreland Plantation out west of town. Grandmother's eyes glazed over. "Three solid miles along the river." They used to have a big house out there and they used to have lots of horses and they used to give big parties, but that was years and years ago. Nothing was left now and nothing had been left for years, but Grandmother explained that it didn't make one particle of difference. It still showed Grace Poovey came from good lines. The fact that they were poor as church mice had nothing to do with anything. I would squint my eyes, trying to follow the logic of it all.

The story went that Mrs. Poovey was all set to marry Custus Carter III, a fellow who grew up in Bainbridge whose daddy owned and was president of First Bainbridge Bank. Grandmother explained that this was just as good as owning your own land, because you had the mortgage on everybody else's.

When he graduated from high school, Custus went on up to the University of the South at Sewanee to get his education. Only trouble was, he went home with his roommate one weekend and met an Atlanta girl. By that Christmas, Grandmother said, they were thick as thieves and poor old Mrs. Poovey was left high and dry. Her family didn't even have enough money to send her off to school so she could look for another man.

Then along came Jesse Poovey. He was from up in the hill country, north of the river. No big farms up there, just forty-acres-and-a-mule land. Jesse was not much to look at, short and stocky, with thinning hair by the time he was twenty. His best quality was that he worked harder than anybody you ever did see. Hard work alone did not weigh very much on Grandmother's scale, but she did give Jesse his due. Worked his way through trade school over in Huntsville and then started into the plumbing-supply business in Bainbridge. Since everybody needed plumbing supplies, Jesse started making good money, lots of good money. Enough so he could buy some land and people would start taking notice, which Mrs. Poovey did.

Of course everyone would have been happier had she married someone in keeping with the fact that she was descended from not one but two of the original five, although things had a way of balancing out. Jesse thought Grace Rutherford Westmoreland was the end all be all of culture and refinement, and Mrs. Poovey thought she needed to get married to somebody with money. Bainbridgians felt that this was not the ideal match, but they certainly understood the situation and tried to live with it.

They married and right off the bat had twin boys. Of course Jesse was a little rough around the edges and he did have a tendency to cat around some. It was the hill country in him coming out, Grandmother said.

Then one night a few years after the twins were born, Jesse went out and got himself killed in a car wreck down by the river bridge. He was coming home from a night out across the river in wild Colbert County, full of Presbyterians and wet. All of this was very ironic given the fact that he couldn't join the army and die a hero because of his flat feet, so he ended up getting killed drunk driving. "Quality, or the lack thereof, will out, even in the dying," Grandmother would say, with a shake of her head.

This left Mrs. Poovey to raise the twins on her own, so all's well that ends well. That's what everybody thought 'til the little boys started to grow. Seems they had more Poovey in them than Rutherford Westmoreland.

From the time they were big enough to walk around, they were trouble looking to happen. Once when they were about twelve, Mrs. Poovey caught them trying to stick Dolly, her toy poodle, on the rotisserie of her new outdoor barbecue grill. They said she was just the size of a big chicken, and besides, she barked all the time and disturbed the neighbors.

Another time, when J.W. was four or five, they tied him to a tree and were going to burn him at the stake like the Indians did in a movie they had seen. They would have, except that J.W. screamed so loud and the neighbors took pity.

After several years of this kind of turmoil, Mrs. Poovey decided to pack them off to boarding school at McCallie over in Chattanooga. Later she sent them to college at W and L and they promptly flunked out or were thrown out—no one ever knew which.

The point of the whole story, Grandmother explained, was that once she got rid of her boys, Mrs. Poovey could settle down to more dignified things.

That's when she started the Ladies Help League. It was one summer when Bainbridge had a particularly bad time with polio. So many children were getting out of the hospital without the braces they needed. The March of Dimes was trying to help, but they were just getting started, too. Mrs. Poovey saw a need and jumped right into the gap. She organized teas and bazaars and big charity balls at the VFW to help raise money.

She found out where to get the braces and what kind the children and adults required. She even sent her driver down to Birmingham with the children and their parents to be fitted with special braces when needed. She was so enthusiastic about it, it caught on with the rest of the women in town.

She was admired and looked up to by everyone. Bainbridge was especially impressed because she was a widow and had done all these good things without a man around to guide her.

I was hooked as I watched her out the window. I thought she could have stepped right off the screen at the Majestic with her hat, gloves, and dress all matching. She was tall and thin, with eyes that said she would take care of me if I ever had polio. She was Bette Davis in *Dark Victory*, Melanie in *GWTW*, compassion itself. How, I wondered, could those twins have been so tacky as to try to cook her doggy like a chicken?

The two ladies walked slowly toward the front porch. Mrs. Myers, short and chubby, wearing red, red lipstick with lots of rouge, chattering away. When they got on the porch, she rushed around and rang the doorbell so Mrs. Poovey wouldn't have to. The sound made me jump. "Mother, they're here. They're here."

From the kitchen, "I thought you were going to answer it."

"I changed my mind."

"Why don't you go sit out in the hall and if I need you to help me, you'll be there," Mother said, walking into the living room.

"Good plan." I scurried like quail to cover.

Mother went to the door in her pretty green dress with the big shoulder pads. She even had her hair curled from the Toni Mrs. McMillan had given her the night before.

The ladies came in to exchange the usual pleasantries and take a seat.

"What lovely flowers."

"Aren't they." Mother stared at the flowers as she moved the fan to a corner of the room. "I seem to have all sorts of decorating help here today. Will you ladies excuse me while I bring in tea?" She passed back and forth through the hall to bring things from the kitchen. "I didn't know you were such a flower lover," she said to me as she passed by.

When they were all settled down, I sneaked to the door to peek. Mother had moved my flowers off the coffee table to make room for the tea tray. Mrs. Myers was doing her best, twittering away about how good the tea was and how tasty the chicken-salad sandwiches were. Mother was happy. I could hear it in her voice.

"You must have used a touch of curry in these sandwiches, Mary," Mrs. Myers was saying, "that's what gives them their wonderful flavor."

"Actually, I did. I'm glad you like them. I'm not noted for my culinary ability around here."

I could see most of what was going on from the image reflected in the hall mirror opposite the door. Mrs. Poovey was the one I couldn't stop watching. She sat quietly most of the time, smiling kindly at Mother, asking a question now and again. She seemed to be content to let Mrs. Doland Myers do all the talking. At one point even Mother sat back, unable to get in a word. She looked across to Mrs. Poovey and they smiled at each other, waiting for Mrs. Myers to take a breath.

"Well, Mary, I understand that you might be interested in helping us out with some of our fall projects," she finally managed to say.

"Oh, yes indeed," Mrs. Myers said. "Mary would very much be interested in—"

Mother put her hand on Mrs. Myers's chubby little hand with the bright red nail polish. "Katherine, I couldn't have a better person in my corner than you." Then to Mrs. Poovey: "I have heard nothing but glowing reports about the Ladies Help League, Mrs. Poovey. I would love to think I could contribute something to helping the children."

"Call me Grace, Mary, and I know we will be able to use one of your many talents. We're a small group, but we try not only to help out with the polio children but to present to the community at large a face of caring and concern. We feel we have a social responsibility, as well."

"We feel we are the crème de la crème," Mrs. Myers chirped.

"Well," Mother said, "I'm sure you know what's best. I just meant that I think your fund-raising for the after-care equipment is by far your most worth-while function."

I felt a small tingle go down my spine. Mother was getting her back up over that remark about crème de la crème. She hated pretentious people, but they didn't know Mama like I did, so maybe they wouldn't notice.

"That's true," Mrs. Poovey said. "I don't mean to sound condescending, but the Ladies Help League helps in a very special way. We feel we have a responsibility to be an example to the rest of the town. We feel our example is just as important as our help." She took another sandwich off the tray and smiled at Mother.

"You do?" Mother's features hardened. I had seen this look before. It was not a good sign. I heard her teacup rattle as she tried to keep a hand steady. She stared into her cup and then lifted her head to look straight at Mrs. Poovey. "Is that right? Well, I don't quite understand. Maybe you could give me an example."

Mrs. Myers jumped in. "Well, Mary, let me see if I can explain. You see what Mrs. Poovey—I mean, Grace—means is that when we gave our lovely Spring Ball this year to raise money for the crippled children, after all was said and done—that is, we paid off all the bills: printing, invitations, decorat-ing, et cetera—we ended up making only a few hundred dollars for the crippled children's fund. Grace explained to us that the impression of responsibility and caring that we left on the community was so important that it was worth hundreds and hundreds of dollars in goodwill. We want everyone to know Bainbridge is a town where people care."

"You mean you made only a few hundred dollars from the Spring Ball? Why, Charles and I went to that, and from the looks of things, I would have imagined that you raised—" Mother stopped right in the middle of the sentence. Even I realized she shouldn't have been saying that. She swallowed hard and started talking fast. "Oh well, I certainly don't know what goes into the Spring Ball. I'm sure lots of time and effort."

There was complete silence now except for the floor fan. When Mrs. Poovey spoke, it was with a measured coldness. "Well, Mary, I hope you do realize that you certainly do not know what goes on in our organization."

"Now Grace." Mrs. Myers was trying to smooth things over. "I'm sure Mary didn't mean that we were in any way remiss."

"Oh, no," Mother said, "heavens no! Please forgive me if I gave the wrong impression. I just spoke without thinking. I . . . I took a business accounting course in college. I know how difficult it is to make a profit sometimes." Mother tried to settle down and pour herself more tea. "As a matter of fact, I thought that might be one of the ways I might be able to help out. With the books, I mean, if you wanted me to. It would be something I could do at home and not leave the children." Mother's voice trailed off, "Or perhaps you might need some other . . ."

"Now that, that sounds like a wonderful idea. Don't you think so, Grace?" Mrs. Myers pleaded. "You know how you always complain about doing the book work. This way, you . . ."

Mrs. Poovey's face had turned beet red. "I don't mind that one bit, Katherine." Then she turned on Mother. "Young lady, you certainly do have a lot to learn. Why, we have provided hundreds of children with braces through our fund-raising efforts. I have worked my fingers to the bone to make sure not one child goes without." Mrs. Poovey looked like she might be fumbling for a handkerchief in her purse, but I could never imagine her with actual tears in her eyes in public. "You may think it doesn't meet your 'magnanimous standards,' but it gets the job done. That"—she poked a finger in the air at Mother—"that is what counts. It's getting the end results."

Mrs. Myers was still trying to settle things down. "Well now, Grace, remember she is from up north and they do have a tendency to talk straight up there, even when they don't mean any harm."

Now Mother was getting mad. "I don't mean to be impolite, but why does everyone in this town think that being from Tennessee makes me a northerner? That seems so narrow-minded to me. I would have thought that . . ."

I paled. Oh, no, here she goes. Should I get another plate of brownies or, or sandwiches, or what? I was standing in the hall first on one foot and then the other, biting my fingernails.

Mrs. Poovey stood up. "I should have known better than to come here, especially after that remark you made about Doland."

"What?" Mother looked uncomprehendingly at Mrs. Poovey. "What remark I made?"

Now Mrs. Myers was upset. The whole thing was fast unraveling. "What were you saying about my husband, Mary?" She looked from Mother to Mrs. Poovey like a scared puppy.

Mother looked bewildered. "What remark am I supposed to have made? I'm sorry. I don't know what you're talking about."

"Oh, you don't?" Mrs. Poovey shot back. She had changed into a different person. Transformed from compassion to intimidation right before my very eyes. "You would rather be married to a colored man than a drunk like Doland Myers?"

There was dead silence. Mother's face went white. Mrs. Myers had a look of horror frozen on hers. She turned to stare at Mother with her big made-up eyes. "You . . . you didn't say that, did you, Mary?"

Mother looked at Mrs. Myers, not knowing what to say. "Oh, oh Katherine, Mrs. Poovey is taking that all out of context. I would never say a thing in the world to hurt you."

I rushed to get more sandwiches out in the kitchen.

When I got back to the hall, Mrs. Poovey was beinning to pull on her gloves, pushing down the fingers with hard jerks.

"Well, mother-in-law or no, I just don't think you're the kind of person who would really enjoy the Ladies Help League, Mary. Thank you for the tea. I'm ready to go when you are, Katherine."

Mrs. Myers was already headed for the door. She had her lace handkerchief out, dabbing her face, which was wet with perspiration and tears.

"Please, wait a minute," Mother was saying as they reached the door. "Won't you both come back and let's talk? I . . . I'll get fresh tea or, or make coffee."

I looked down at the paper plate overflowing with sandwiches. "Would somebody like—"

It was too late. The Ladies Help League was out the front door before you could count three. Mother was still standing there looking after them. We watched as they walked down the front lawn and the driver scurried to open doors. They drove off. We were left there, staring after them.

I took Mother's hand and led her to the sofa and to the sandwiches on the coffee table. My thought was that she needed food to help her through this crisis.

"I just feel awful. Sweet little Katherine Myers. She'll never forgive me. She made this special trip just for me and I . . . I had to go and open my big mouth and"—her voice caught—"and ruin the whole thing."

"You want a sandwich, Mama?" I took one and began to chew. "I think"—narrowing my eyes and calling upon my most sophisticated analytical skills—"I think, it was that part about you marrying the colored man instead of her drunk husband that she didn't like."

"No kidding." Mother rolled her eyes and reached for a brownie. She stared into the empty fireplace. "I should never have said anything about the Spring Ball. It just came out before I thought about it. I didn't mean to sound like a snob, but maybe I did." She took a hard bite. "Well, what was I supposed to think when she started that crème de la crème nonsense? And why do you suppose Grace Poovey brought up that Sunday dinner business? That was just plain mean. And how did she know about it anyway?"

I couldn't have answered her even if she had wanted me to. My mouth was full of chicken salad. But I knew it was probably Grandmother's maid who told Mrs. Poovey's maid and then she went on to tell Mrs. Poovey or something like that. Mother never realized that maids talked to each other so everybody knew everybody else's business.

I swallowed hard on my chicken salad. "So what if you made a big mess of it, Mama. At least you tried. It's like me and The Club and the football game."

"What?"

"Oh, never mind. See the problem here is, Mama, you have to learn to act more like Grandmother but not be like Grandmother."

She sighed. "You may be asking too much, Tab."

Chapter 12

It was with heavy heart that I pedaled to Grandmother's. I had failed her, but then again, I usually failed her. Oh, well.

She was sitting on the porch shelling butter beans for supper, waiting for me. She waved when she saw me coming down the sidewalk. I pedaled up to the front steps and pushed the kickstand down to her questions.

"Did you use the flowers?"

"Yes, ma'am." I balanced the bike and walked up the steps.

"Was the room cool enough?"

"Yes, ma'am." I took my place in the wicker swing, giving a good push off.

"Then why the long face? Sounds like things started off well enough."

"They did start off well. It was later on that things got mixed up. And it wasn't that me and Mama didn't give it a good try."

"Well, tell me what happened." She sighed.

I looked at Grandmother's anxious face and began warming to my role as narrator. I hopped off the swing determined to give it my best effort, if not in the doing, then in the telling.

"Well, now here's what happened." I began pulling three of the other chairs on the porch into position to represent Mrs. Poovey, Mrs. Doland Myers, and Mother.

Grandmother was resigned to the show.

"I said to Mother, right before they came, 'Now Mother, you go get the refreshments ready and I'll finish dusting the living room and all the other stuff that needs to be done in here.'"

"Is that right?" Grandmother said.

I held my hands together for dramatic effect. "Now"—pointing to the imaginary front door— "the doorbell rings and I say, 'I'll get it, Mother.' I run to the door and swing it open wide. 'Ladies, welcome to our home.'"

"Very nice of you."

"Of course, I didn't plan to stay long. Just enough to help everybody get settled in.

"'Sit right over here next to the beautiful flowers out of my grandmother's garden that you are welcome to smell if you are of a mind.'"

140

"So far so good." Smiling, she popped more butter beans into the colander.

"Oh, yes, ma'am. I—we were doing just fine. We brought in the chicken-salad sandwiches with the crusts cut off—tasty, tasty. We brought in the tea and the side order of brownies."

I took a seat in Mother's chair. "Mama had on her most beautiful green dress with the big shoulder pads."

I jumped to Mrs. Doland Myers eating her sandwich. "'Mary, these are delicious. Is that a taste of salt I get?'"

Then back to Mrs. Poovey's chair. I held a pretend teacup, with my little finger out. "'We know we could use you in our fall projects.'"

"Of course, all this time I am standing in the hall ready to bring them anything they want."

"Of course. And then?" Grandmother said.

"And then . . ." I stood up. "And then Mama said something that made everybody mad and they all got huffy and went home."

"What was it, for heaven's sake?"

"I'm not sure"—my eyes narrowed—"but I think it was about Mama saying she would marry the colored man over the drunk white man."

"Oh, Lord in heaven"—she stopped her shelling—"how did that come up?"

"Well . . ." I took a seat as Mrs. Doland Myers. "Mrs. Doland Myers was sitting there all choked up.

'What remark are you supposed to have made about my husband, Mary?'" I said, pretending to wipe away tears. "This made Mama turn pale as a sheet and then—" I got up and went to the Poovey chair. "'Thank you for the tea, Mary, but I don't think you would fit into The Club.' And then—"

"Never mind the 'and thens.' That cooked her goose. Everything else is beside the point." Grandmother was looking down at the butter beans in the colander. "Why would Grace Poovey bring that up in the first place?"

"That's what Mama said. She said Mrs. Doland Myers would never forgive her."

Grandmother was taking the stray pieces of shells out of the butter beans. "Oh, Katherine will forgive her. She forgives everybody. She lives to forgive. I'll talk to her, explain your mother, and remind her it's . . . let's see, that it's all part of the Lord's plan." She looked up at me. "I still don't understand it, though. If Grace Poovey wanted to tell Katherine about your mother's indiscretion, why did she choose then? They're best friends. She could have told her that anytime. Did anything else happen?"

"No, ma'am." I was beginning to feel guilty I hadn't done more. I walked back over to the swing and slumped down. "I did the best I could."

"That you did. That you did. Don't worry about it. It's over and done with," Grandmother said as she gathered up her things. "It's been a long day for you and you look hot as a firecracker. Come on, let's go in the living room and get cool. The mosquitoes are beginning to bite."

I held the front door open for her. "There's something I been meaning to ask you, Grandmama."

"Ask away, child."

"Could a white person marry a colored person?"

"Of course not. Your mother was just making a point."

I stretched out on the threadbare Oriental rug and reached my hand over to turn on the floor fan. She took a seat in her usual chair under the portrait of her mother. She pulled the ottoman closer so she could lift up her bad leg and rest it. She loosened the laces of her shoe. Her leg had been kicked by a cow once, on the beautiful plantation. Now it would swell up in the afternoons. "Well"— she sighed—"we did the best we could with that one. Maybe I should have stayed out of it, but I thought she would enjoy it."

There was silence as I lay there with my chin in my hands watching the fan turn back and forth in the big room that had hosted all the family gatherings since my memory began. The corner next to the front windows where the Christmas tree stood every year. The mantel where Uncle Tommy's vase always held fresh flowers. The portrait of Mama Jean, looking down over us all. Like the furniture in a doll's house, placed just so. It was always meant to

143

be here. We were always meant to come here. We rested there for some time in the airtight, rock-hard security of family and place.

"It's hard to know. It's hard to know," she mumbled as she let her eyes close and her head rest on the lace antimacassar pinned to the back of the chair.

After a while she roused herself. "Well now, we can't worry all day about water over the dam." Straightening in her chair, she said, "Now is the time for the stereoscope," as she lifted it off the marbletop table beside her. Grandmother was not interested in the movies, too much violence. "I don't know why your mother lets you go see that John Wayne." She selected one of the stack of stereoscope pictures from off the table. "Now, this is educational. Wonderful pictures from all over the world."

"Lemme see, lemme see." I had moved from the floor to sitting on the ottoman beside her sore foot. I massaged her ankle as she read the back of the card to us.

Then she put the eyepiece up to her face and inserted the card, picture side forward. "Ah, 'Pounding Poi with the Natives in Hawaii.'"

"Lemme see, lemme see."

"You can almost reach out and touch that palm tree." She sighed. She handed me "Pounding Poi" but kept the stereoscope and selected another picture. "We used to spend many hours looking at the stereoscope when I was a girl. This is a good one, 'Sarajevo, Austria-Hungary—Scene of the Murder of the Crown Prince.'"

"Murder? Lemme see, lemme see."

"Looks peaceful enough to me," she said. "Look at the water going under that bridge. This was before the war started, you know."

"World War Two?"

"No child, World War One. You know the crown prince got shot and that started it all."

"Oh yeah."

She handed me the stereoscope and leaned back in the chair, putting the other black laced-up shoe on the ottoman beside me. I put the stereoscope up to my eyes to look at the murder town of the crown prince. I didn't take my eyes away from it because I knew what she was doing now, looking at Uncle Tommy's silver vase on the mantel. Whenever we sat in the living room for very long, her eye would naturally turn to the silver vase and she would have to explain again.

"He was the baby, you know."

"Yes, ma'am."

"It's so nice of the other children. They never forget."

"Yes'um. Every week since he died, they send you a rose to go in it," I said, and put down "Sarajevo" and picked up "Pounding Poi."

"I would have given him the money for college if I had had it," she said.

"But it was still in the Depression here and you hardly had enough to feed the family," I said.

"You know your grandfather gave me all he had, but it was precious little. I used to take your father and go to the woods to hunt for pecans. I was that penny-wise," she said.

"You used to take all the money you had and put it in a little change purse and pin it to your bra."

"My undies," she said. She took a deep breath, leaned her head back in the chair, still looking at the vase. "I just couldn't squander that money from Aunt Rose. It was such a heaven-sent."

I looked up from the stereoscope, to see her take off her glasses and wipe her wet eyes with her handkerchief, like always. "It would have taken almost all of it to pay for his college tuition. I couldn't—"

"You couldn't take the chance," I said.

"How in blessed Jesus' name—"

"How in blessed Jesus' name were you suppose to know that he would go and get hisself killed in the war?" I got another picture out of the stack, "Picking Oranges in Valencia, Spain," and put it up to my eyes quickly.

"He was so pleased when he told me. 'Mother, you don't have to worry about the tuition; I've signed up for the air force. I can save my money and have plenty for college by the time I get out.'

"He wasn't drafted you know," she said.

"He volunteered," I said, "just before Pearl Harbor."

"Yes"—her fingers rubbed her forehead—"to serve his country."

The worst was over now. It was always over when she got to the part where he served his country. She blew her nose and put the hankie back in her dress pocket.

"Want to see 'Picking Oranges in Valencia, Spain'?" I held the stereoscope up to her.

"No, I have a better idea. Why don't we make some oatmeal cookies?"

"His favorite," I said.

Chapter 13

It had been five days since Mother had made such a mess of the Ladies Help League, and we were all the worse for wear. Pop tried to compensate by being overly cheerful at the supper table. A painful thing to witness, since he was not the joking kind. "So why did the little moron throw the clock out the window?"

"To make time fly," we answered in grumpy unison, eyes searching the ceiling. Only the twins seemed to enjoy it as they banged their spoons on high-chair trays.

For Mother's part, her attitude had manifested itself in some of her most bizarre cooking yet. To take her mind off things, she had decided to concentrate on foreign dishes. Needless to say, the ingredients were hard to come by in Bainbridge and substitutes abounded. The highlight of the week had been chicken chow mein made with hominy grits. Charles junior and I, being less than culinary experts, had thought it delicious. Unfortunately, Tina had, at some point in time, visited a Chinese restaurant on a trip to Memphis and let it be known to all of us assembled at the table that this was, in fact, fake chicken chow mein. Upon hearing the news, Charles junior thought this meant that he had been poisoned and began to gag. In ordinary circumstances none of this would have fazed Mother, but given her sensitive state, she left the room in tears.

My father decided it was time to give her a day's rest. He arranged for Grandmother to take the twins and Charles junior for the day. Tina was to visit a friend, and I, joy of joys, got to spend the day at the farm with him.

We got up early the next morning. Mother had packed our lunches and a big Ball jar of iced tea. Off we went along the big river road that led east out of town toward Huntsville. He always dressed the same way, khaki pants and shirt, big heavy boots. In his shirt pocket, his Camels. The smell from one of the big kitchen matches that he kept stuck over the truck visor danced past me in the breeze and out the window as he lighted up his first of the day. I sat in the cab of the pickup with him, pretending we were equals, off to do a day's work.

The red clay fields spread out before us as we came onto the farm. The property extended from the river road down to the river itself. When the place was first settled, the river had been its main contact with the outside world. Now the road served as its artery, bringing in fertilizer and equipment, then taking out all the farm had struggled to produce: wagons of cotton in good years, truckloads of wheat, and cattle auctioned off at the annual farm sale. It was in a world all its own, grinding out product, oblivious to the outside world and market forces that sealed its fate long before the first seed was covered with moist red clay.

The price of cotton, or wheat, or cattle was only one factor in farm survival. I had stood with him many times in the middle of a large red field, neatly curved and swirled in the planting. He would pull his pocketknife out slowly, knowing that what he found just beneath the surface could alter our lives for the coming year. We would both stoop down as he flicked the knife along a row of planted seeds. If they were cracking open with the first faint green of life, he could breathe easy for a time. If not, if we only found seeds as they had been deposited weeks before and too much time had elapsed without rain or sun, or the right combination of both, there was nothing to be done.

In the early morning when the sun was just up, you could see for miles the trails winding over the red dirt where the big John Deeres had plowed up the land. By this time in the summer, most of the fields were high with corn, wheat, cotton. Cattle grazed through the green. He had changed everything since he took over. Fields that had been washed into gullies had been revived. The cotton mind-set of Granddaddy had been shoved aside in favor of modern methods. Gone were the fifty or so families who had depended on the farm for their livelihood. Up north to seek their fortunes, and in their place tractors and combines worked the fields. Replaced by the younger generation, my grandfather had taken to riding all over the farm searching for things to complain about.

We drove up to the old house that we lived in before Mother got mad and moved to town. The foreman lived there now. Pop parked his truck and got out. Mr. Stutts was sitting in a straight-back chair on the porch, leaning up against the wall, having a chew of early-morning tobacco. If we had been in town, morning greetings would have been exchanged. On the land, quite the opposite was true. The men nodded to each other and started walking down toward the big barn.

All the workers were waiting to get assigned to the day's jobs. There were other barns and sheds, but this was the main one. Heavy equipment was parked in the bottom. Up over that was a big loft stacked high with bales of hay.

"James, you and Sam go on down to the schoolhouse field and mend the fence." Sam and James were the only two Negroes, besides Will, who were left on the place and they liked working together. "Mr. Stutts, you take Claude and Jake and the other boys on to the Houston field and finish plowing there. Joe, you and Will come with me and we'll go to the river field and start clearing brush."

Everyone started off to do his work and I was left to my assigned job, which was to look for chicken eggs in the hayloft. I found all the eggs and took them to Mr. Stutts's wife up at the big house. That finished, I came back and started to build a house in the hay bales. When I was up among all the bales and the big loft doors were open, I could see out over the fields for miles. With the cool morning breeze blowing through and the birds flying around so near I could almost touch them, it was like being on a cloud.

I finished moving the hay bales around to make my living room. I was starting to make a little kitchen before I even noticed the smoke rising way off in the distance. At first it wasn't much of a fire. Just a thin trail of smoke in the sky, like somebody was burning old dead tree brush. This would happen sometimes when the workers were clearing the fields. They would put all the scrap bushes onto a pile, then throw in an old bald tire or two for extra burning power, and set the whole thing ablaze. If the fire was hot enough, it would burn everything into a big pile of ashes. Then later, a tractor would spread all the ashes out in the field and nothing would be left except a new field ready for plowing.

This day there was a stiff breeze blowing off the river. The next time I looked up, the smoke had spread out all along the farthest hill and was rising in big dark clouds. I watched as the wind began to send it my way. Then after a while, off in the distance, the truck that Pop and his workers had used to go to the field came racing back along the river road toward the barn. It was going too fast for the ruts in the road. The wheels kept bouncing up off the ground. Finally it made the barnyard and slammed to a stop, red dust swirling around its tires. Pop jumped out and ran up to the barn to swing wide open the big wood doors. I had never seen him run as long as I could remember. I went over to the ladder that led down from the loft.

"Why are you hurrying so, Pop? What's wrong?" He didn't hear me. "I said, what's wrong?" He still didn't answer. He was trying to start the big John Deere that was sitting nearest the door. He was in the seat, trying, trying to crank it, but it wouldn't crank.

"What's wrong, Pop?" I was afraid. I had never seen him like this. "Is it the fire? Is it one of the workers?"

"Not now, Tab. I'm in a big hurry."

He had jumped down off the tractor now and was jiggling some wires in the engine. Then he hopped back up in the seat to try again. Nothing. Just the sound of the motor trying to catch. I watched as he banged the steering wheel with his hand and then looked up out the door to the smoke. So did I. By now, it was rising up along a line that kept getting wider and wider on the horizon. He jumped back off to fiddle with the wires some more. Then back into the seat. This time he put his head down on his hands, which were gripping the steering wheel.

"Start dammit." He pushed the starter one more time. It caught.

"Go back to the house and stay with Mrs. Stutts, Tab," he yelled as the tractor lurched out of the barn.

A tractor is the clumsiest piece of machinery in the world when it is not in a field plowing. This is especially true if you have a tractor with a big plow attached to the back of it, and this one did.

I sat down on the bales to watch. I could see him moving slowly along the dirt road that led to the river. Smoke rose as a thick wall off in the distance. It was plain that he was not going to be able to reach the river field in time to stop the fire from spreading to the wheat field that was next in its path. The wheat field was one of the biggest fields on the farm, maybe 150 acres. It started where the river field stopped and came all the way back to where I sat in the big barn. There was a plowed field on the left and the road to the river on the right, but nothing to stop the fire from spreading to the wheat field, and the breeze from the river was blowing right into my face. I could see the little flickers of fire now crawling over the far hill in a line from the plowed field to the river road. He could see it, too. I saw the tractor stop, then make a wide turn back toward the barn. There was one place the tractor could get into the wheat field to cut a firebreak, but it was back toward the middle of the field. He stopped in front of the gate and got off the tractor to swing it open. Back in the seat, he turned the tractor into the field and let the plow down. It began cutting into the shimmering green and gold stalks, dumping them like so much garbage back into the land, just as the fire crept into the wheat at the top of the rise.

The tractor slowly moved forward, maybe too slow for the fire. Before, it had been feeding on stubble left on the river field. Now as it caught on the wheat it started to flare up and move faster. Big flames shot up in the air and raced forward. Pieces of wheat that were on fire floated up in the air and landed ahead of the fire line. Joe and Will, the workers who had been with Pop in the first place, were following the fire line along as it burned. They were using their shovels to try to stamp out the flames, but it wasn't working. As soon as they put out one place, the fire would move forward in another place and spread out again. When they saw the tractor turn into the field, they stopped and leaned on their shovels to watch.

He was about halfway across now and the flames were racing with him to the end of the field. The smoke was blowing right into his face, so that half the time I couldn't even see him or the tractor. Finally the big round plowing disks cut into the earth all the way to the end of the field. The John Deere turned around and started to plow up another row to ensure that at least half of the wheat field would be saved.

After that, I couldn't see a thing. The wind had blown the smoke all the way to me. I went to the other end of the loft and stuck my head out of one of the windows to breathe fresh air.

From this side I could see Granddaddy's truck come roaring out of its parking place over at the big house. He pulled up in the barnyard and sat there chewing on his pipe.

After a time, the wind died down and the smoke with it. Will and Joe came back with their shovels. They put them in the barn but didn't say anything to Granddaddy, just lowered their heads when they passed him on their way home for noon dinner. Granddaddy acted as if he didn't see them.

Finally the tractor rumbled and jerked its way back into the yard. Pop was sitting there with sweat and soot all over his face and arms. His khaki pants and shirt were a mess, too, wrinkled and dirty.

He pulled the tractor into the barn, cut the motor off, and sat there. I walked over to the ladder hole in the floor and started to say something, but just then I heard the door of Granddaddy's pickup slam.

From the way he came walking into the barn, I knew he had been taking a few drinks of his glove-compartment whiskey. He spewed out his anger. "What damn fool thing have you gone and done this time? I told you to leave that scrub brush down in the river field alone, but no, you have to go and set the whole place on fire."

"Dad, you know as well as I do that when we clear that field completely, we'll have ten extra acres and square off the field. Plowing efficiency alone—"

"Never mind the damn plowing efficiency. What the hell good is ten extra acres when you burn down half the new wheat crop in the process?"

My father squeezed his hands around the tractor's steering wheel and looked straight ahead. His lips were pressed together. "Look, Dad, if it was up to you, we wouldn't have anything in that field in the first place. You would have let it go fallow for the rest of the summer. Half a wheat field is better than none. The men just got carried away with what they were doing and let the brush fire get out of hand. The wind was so strong off the river, there was no way they could stop it. I was down checking the springhouse. It was just an accident. Nothing we can do about it."

Granddaddy had been waiting to talk again, standing there chewing on his pipe. "The hell you can't! I say fire their asses, by God. Fire their asses. That'll teach 'em."

Pop began to relax in the tractor seat. He cleared his throat and started to talk to Granddaddy as to a child. "Dad, I know you're upset. I imagine it was very frustrating sitting there on the porch watching the whole thing, but I'm in charge now. You and I and Mother agreed to that. It was my decision, right or wrong."

"Well, you sure shot the hell out of any extra money you might have made on that wheat crop." He turned to go and then shouted back over his shoulder, "You keep managing like this and you'll never save enough to buy a bigger house for your city wife, much less feed and clothe the rest of us." Then he walked back out to get in his truck and slammed the door.

My father sat there for a long time with his head down. His hands were still holding the steering wheel tight. Then slowly he let loose, climbed off the tractor, and walked over to the faucet that stuck up on the side of the watering trough at the barn door. He turned on a big stream and washed his face, hands, and arms. While he was drying off with the big handkerchief he kept in his pants pocket, he looked back out into the smoldering field. There was a big black area now with a few puffs of smoke rising in the air. He turned around and kicked the water trough so hard, water from the top splashed out onto his boots.

I called down to him. "Listen, Pop, I know what. I'll go get our lunch over at the big house and bring it back here. We'll have a nice picnic up here in my hay-bale house."

He looked up, puzzled that I was there. "Tab, I thought I told you to go back to the house and stay there. Why didn't you go?"

"Oh, I forgot. I . . . I just got busy watching the fire and then watching you plow the field." I looked down at my feet. "I was gonna go, but then Granddaddy came and I didn't want to bother you while you were, uh, having a conversation."

He put his hands on his hips while he looked up at me. His face changed. "That was not a conversation, Tab; that was an argument I had with your grandfather."

He turned off the water that was still running in the trough and wiped the back of his neck with the wet handkerchief. "Go get the sandwiches and tea. We'll have a picnic. It'll sure be the highlight of my day."

I climbed down the ladder from the loft and ran across the barnyard, then the dirt road that separated the fields from the main house. I grabbed our lunch out of the pickup and was back to the barn before he might change his mind. While he cleaned up the tractor and plow, I took everything up to the loft. I made a table out of two hay bales and spread our napkins for a tablecloth. Then I put out our tuna sandwiches wrapped in wax paper and five or six saltine crackers with peanut butter in the middle. For dessert we had two big pieces of Mother's lopsided chocolate cake left over from supper. I climbed down the ladder, ran to the edge of the barnyard, and grabbed a few black-eyed Susans to put in a Coke bottle I found down around the tractors.

He climbed slowly up the ladder and sat down on the hay bale that was his chair. His legs were so long, it was hard for him to get them in between his hay-bale chair and table, but he didn't seem to notice. He put his elbows on his knees and reached down to unwrap his tuna sandwich. He didn't see my flowers in the middle of the table. He was looking down at the sandwich as he unwrapped it, not saying a word.

I, too, sat on my hay bale across from him and put my elbows on my knees in imitation. Then I started to unwrap my sandwich. The next time I looked up he was staring out at the half-burned wheat field.

Chapter 14

I lay in the fort hammock, looking up at the sun through the kudzu tangled in the pine trees. When I moved the hammock, the sun sparkled down through the trees like a kaleidoscope. I squinted my eyes watching the picture change, trying to get the uneasy feeling about Mother out of my mind. I knew there must be something I could do to make her happy, but what?

Maudie May was sitting at the stick table, getting ready to make us play school again. I was sick of playing school, but lately it was all Maudie wanted to do. She always got to be the teacher so she could do all the bossing. What's more, Maudie hadn't been to school in so long, she got everything wrong and didn't even live up to my lowly standards.

She was putting a movie magazine at each place on the table where we were supposed to sit. "Now, childrens, time for class to begin. We gonna have a fine time today. Miss Maudie May is gonna read y'all a story called"—she picked up her magazine—"'Romance Returns to Hollywood.'" I looked up at the sun through the trees. "Now this here is a good story all about the Hollywood stars returnin' home after the war got over."

I swung my feet down to the ground and sat up in the hammock. "First off, Maudie—"

"That's Miss Maudie to all you children." She waved her finger out into the air to include me and the Brothers.

"Well, first off, 'Miss Maudie,' 'us childrens' already heard that story about one million times, and second of all, that's not the way you play school anyway. First you got to call the roll, then you got to Pledge the Allegiance, then you got to do the Bible reading, then you got to collect the lunch money, then—"

"Never mind all them things, children." Maudie was looking condescendingly at me. "In my school, we does it my way. We gonna have only what's good." She glared at me from over the magazine, then held it up to start reading again.

"Sometimes I get so put out with you, Maudie May. You just think you know it all, and you haven't been to school in years. School is not fun. School is just school. You don't say, 'Gather round, childrens.' You say, 'Sit down, children, or Miss Maudie May will give you a demerit.'"

"A what?"

"A demerit, a demerit! You know, the slip of paper you get when you do bad. Didn't you ever do bad? I got three in one day last year. I was caught twice for running and once for chewing gum."

"What did you get a demerit for runnin' for? Ain't nothin' wrong with runnin'."

"I don't know why it's bad to run; it's just bad 'cause the teacher says it's bad, just like she says it's bad to chew gum."

Maudie was pretending to look through her magazine, embarrassed she didn't know how bad running and chewing were. "Ain't nothin' wrong with chewin' gum when it taste good." She said this almost to herself, eyes still on *Photoplay*.

"It's wrong, Maudie. That's how come you get demerits, because it's wrong. It doesn't matter why." I stood up out of the hammock, knowing I was going to have to be the one to teach. Maudie was obviously not schooled in the finer points of right and wrong.

"Okay Maudie, I'll show you how to do it. Now, everybody come to the table and sit down." I picked up a stick off the ground and tapped it on the table just like Miss Locklear at N.B. Forrest Elementary. "Come on, Brothers, hurry, hurry, hurry!"

The Brothers were not coming fast enough. They were taking their time sliding down the rope from their lookout. They didn't understand learning, either. I could tell that. "Now, sit up straight, both feet on the floor. All right, Maudie, open your mouth. Have you got gum?"

Maudie looked at me like I was crazy. I didn't care. She needed to learn the subtleties of higher education. I looked back at her with a pasted smile on my face.

"You know I ain't got no gum. How come you askin' me that? You're a dumb teacher. Miss Mama—uh, I mean, my teacher, she never said if I got gum, and if I did have it, then she say, 'Look childrens, Maudie May got herself some gum. Now ain't she lucky. What flavor you got there, Miss Maudie May? We would sure like to know, 'cause then we can be thinkin' 'bout how good it taste.'"

Maudie was standing up again, like she was going to try to take the class back over. I looked her straight in the eye, not believing a word she had said. "I don't think your teacher ever said that. I think you're making the whole thing up, Maudie May. Just tell me one thing. Did you ever, I mean ever, even go to school?"

Maudie looked down, at a loss for words. I stared at her, wishing I hadn't even asked the question. The Brothers were looking at Maudie, waiting for her to tell about her years of educational excellence.

She raised her head slowly and looked at the Brothers like I wasn't even there. "Now, Brothers," she said, "of everybody in this here Fort Polio, who is the best reader?" The Brothers, hands still on the table, pointed index fingers to Maudie and began to smile, shaking their heads up and down. They started squirming in their seats because they loved it when Maudie acted out. She stood up straighter and her voice got stronger. "And of everybody in this here fort, who, I say *who*, can do they sums the best?" The Brothers jumped up and down in their seats and slapped hands on the table, then pointed to Maudie, laughing all the while.

Then she turned her beady eyes on me. "Now, how you 'spect a person could get so smart if they didn't never go to no school? Why, when I get grown, I'm gonna be a world-famous teacher!"

I looked down at the ground and said in a soft voice, "Yeah, but Maudie, how come you don't know about Pledging the Allegiance and the demerit system?"

"I know all about them things. I just forgot, that's all. Besides, that's not the good stuff. The good stuff is readin' all about what's in these here magazines. So give me that stick. I'm gonna be the teacher." She took the stick and threw it over her shoulder and sat down with a smile on her face. "Now, childrens, I'm gonna read you all about romance returnin' to Hollywood." She cleared her throat. "'Dashing adventurer, outlaw, and swordsman, the fabulous Cornel Wilde returns to the screen in the daring new movie . . .'" The Brothers settled down in their chairs, faces cupped in the palms of their hands, listening to Maudie, like they had never heard the story before.

I sat there drumming my fingers on the table, watching Maudie's mouth read the words but not hearing one thing she said. My mind had switched back to Mother. What was I going to do if she decided she couldn't stand Bainbridge anymore and wanted to go back to Knoxville permanently?

Maudie had finished her first story. She picked up another old movie magazine and began again. I raised my hand, then waved it in the air when she didn't stop reading. She was so caught up in the story, she didn't want to see me. Finally she stopped. "What you wavin' your hand for, Tab? You're disturbin' the teacher!"

I rolled my eyes. "That's what you're supposed to do in school when you want to ask a question in class." Maudie dropped her magazine and folded her arms across her chubby waist. "Course I know that, but the teacher don't like to be disturbed. Now what you want?"

"Well, I wanted to ask a question."

Immediately Maudie's expression changed to that of benign dictator. "That's fine, my child. The teacher can answer any question for you. Is it somethin' 'bout the story you don't understand?"

"What happens when a mother doesn't like a place anymore and she decides to leave the father and go somewhere else?"

Maudie looked perturbed. "That don't have nothin' to do with the story at hand. You ain't been listenin', my child." She glared.

"Well, the teacher is supposed to answer any question, any question in the world that her children have. I guess you know that from going to school so much, so just answer me that. What would happen if the mother just up and left and didn't take the pop—I mean, the father—and all the children along?"

Maudie sat for a moment with me and the Brothers staring at her. Then all of a sudden she hopped up and went over to the big stack of magazines she had brought from home. "I have the answer right here, my child." She dug through the pile. "Here it is." She picked out one and came back over to the table and sat down to open it up. She looked up and smiled at me, full of confidence. She cleared her throat just like she always did when she had important things to say. "'Divorce Comes to Sonja Henie!'" She paused and looked up to make sure we were all paying attention.

I jumped up. "Divorce! Divorce! Are you crazy? Just because the mother doesn't like a place? That's no reason to get a divorce. I told you you didn't know how to be a teacher, Maudie May." Tears were coming.

Maudie wouldn't be deterred. "They does it all the time in Hollywood. If you likes somebody else, you gets a divorce. If you don't make enough money, you get a divorce. If you a famous star and your husband ain't, then you get a divorce. This here story I'm gonna read you childrens is all about Sonja Henie gettin' a divorce 'cause she want to stay on in Hollywood and not move back to Norway."

"You're not reading me any dumb story! You are just about the dumbest teacher I ever did see. I'm leaving, Maudie! Did you hear me? I'm leaving!"

But she didn't hear. She and the Brothers were too interested in divorce coming to Sonja Henie.

Chapter 15

Listen," she said the next morning as I came into the fort. I thought she was going to be mad at me for getting angry the day before, but no. "It come to me while we was havin' school yesterday. I'll be goin' to the eighth grade and the Brothers'll be goin' to first grade."

"That's what you told me—you in the eighth, them in the first."

"Well now, I forgot, it's been so long. What do the Brothers need when they goes to the first grade? I mean, do they needs pencils and paper and such?"

"School supplies?" I said, taking a seat at the stick table and trying to recall ancient history. "They need . . . let's see, they need pencils and a box of crayons, the real big kind."

"Just hold it right there," she said, jumping up from her seat to get a pencil and paper off the stick shelf. "I needs to write all this down."

"Why? The teacher will tell you on the first day of their class what they need, and then all you have to do is go out and buy it. Besides, they don't need much. The first grade is a snap," I said, remembering it fondly. It was the only grade I had enjoyed. After first grade, it was all downhill. They started giving homework and making me sit still in class for hours.

"'Cause I want to add up the cost. I done saved enough for papers and pencils for me, but I forgot the Brothers was gonna have to have somethin'. Not so much as me probably, but somethin', don't you think?" She looked at me, almost anxious.

"Well, yeah, some stuff anyway. Besides the crayons and pencils, they need lunch money every day, unless they take their lunches, and then they need a lunch box. Oh, let's get them a Roy Rogers lunch box. It has its own thermos." I was beginning to enter into the spirit of it, much like dressing dolls for a party.

"If we gets them a lunch box, it's gonna be a Gene Autry box. How much you 'spect them boxes cost?"

"Oh, I don't know exactly." I got up and went to her side. "How much you got so far?" I looked at the paper: "Pencils, 5 cents. Crayons, 10 cents each."

"Oh, and construction paper. You have to have

a pack of construction paper to make things with and to draw pictures on."

She slowly wrote down, "Construction paper, 5 cents each."

"Oh, then—I forgot—blunt-edge scissors. You have to have those to cut with, so you won't hurt yourself. I think they run about ten cents each." She hesitated and then wrote, "Scissors." Then she picked up the paper with both hands and studied it.

"This here is more money than I got saved up for my school supplies, and I don't even have the Gene Autry lunch boxes wrote down."

"They have to have lunch boxes if they take their lunch. Everybody, just everybody, will have them. We can't let them go without lunch boxes." I realized I was beginning to sound like Tina.

Maudie looked up at the Brothers, who were watching with great interest this discussion of their higher education. Then she sighed. "Okay, okay, how much you think they gonna cost?"

"I don't know. We'll have to walk down to Woolworth's and see how much. Come on, Brothers," I said. "Mr. Clovis was putting some lunch boxes in the window the other day." The Brothers were down the rope before I finished the sentence. We headed for town.

Sure enough, right there in the window, stacked in a big pyramid, were fifty or so bright, shiny lunch boxes smiling out at us. Mr. Clovis was anticipating the fall school rush. Noses to the glass, we studied each one in detail, connoisseurs of our art. They were all there, Roy, Rin Tin Tin, Superman, Hopalong Cassidy, Captain Marvel; and, down in the corner, on the bottom of the stack—the Brothers spotted it first—was old Gene himself. The Brothers were smiling and pointing.

I squatted down to get a better look. A beauty! Old Gene's smiling face looked out at us. I was sick that I had to take lunch money and didn't have an excuse to get one. "It's almost as good as Roy, don't you think, Maudie?" I looked up, to see her backing away from the window.

"Now listen here. I don't want nobody gettin' they hearts set on somethin' they liable not to get." She started walking back up the block. "I didn't see no price, but they look to me like they mighty expensive."

I jumped up to follow her. "Wait a minute, wait a minute. That's what we came for, to see the cost. Let's at least go ask Mr. Clovis how much." We were halfway down the block before she would stop and listen to me. She only stopped then because the Brothers were still at the window.

"It's gonna be more than fifty cents. I can tell that, and I ain't got more than fifty cents."

"Your mother." I shrugged. "Miss Mama can buy it for them if you tell her how much." We both looked back to watch the Brothers still poring over the tin boxes.

Maudie had her hands on her hips, studying

them. "You know, they is smart boys. I done told you that, ain't I? I know they don't say much round you, but I already done taught'm they letters and I'm workin' on numbers. They gonna be good at school 'cause I been teachin'm."

"See there. My mama always gets me a treat if I do well in something. Miss Mama will sure buy them the lunch boxes." It was settled and simple in my mind.

She looked down at the sidewalk and said in almost a whisper, "Miss Mama done got herself a new boyfriend."

"So?" I said.

"So," she said, "this one love to have hisself a beer."

"So, what does that have to do with lunch boxes?"

She shook her head. "Sometimes you just plain ignorant, Tab. He love to have hisself a beer and he takes all the money he can find to get hisself a beer and anything else he want. Miss Mama so '*in love*' with that man, she just let him take anything. I already took to hidin' my money so he can't find it."

She walked back toward the Brothers. "I know they ain't gonna be no money for school. I already know that." She called to the Brothers. "Come on, we got to get on home."

"Let's just at least go inside and see how much it is. Let's just at least see."

The Brothers ran over and pushed open the swinging doors before she could stop them.

Just going into Woolworth's was worth the walk. Me and the Brothers knew that, even if Maudie didn't. Mr. Clovis sat on a raised platform behind the cashier's counter with his usual greeting. "Don't y'all go messing up the toys."

"Yes, sir," as we passed. Overhead fans turned slowly, stirring the musty air. Oil-soaked wooden floors formed a maze of temptation. Past the candy counter and the smell of stale popcorn, turn right at the lipsticks, Tina's hangout. Back to linger over the toys that were placed in neat cubicles partitioned by little glass walls. Tops in one, yo-yos in another, marbles in another. I lingered over the marbles. The Brothers made a beeline for the lunch boxes. Maudie stopped off at school supplies, opening up one of the fancy pencil boxes.

The Brothers found old Gene and took him to Maudie. She searched the box for a price. Not finding one, she came over to me. "Take this up to Mr. Clovis and see how much he'll take for it." I did as I was told and came back with the unhappy news. One dollar and fifty cents each.

"What?" She almost moaned. "I ain't got one dollar, much less three dollars." She took the lunch box and turned it over and over, examining it. "I . . . I was thinkin' they might be fifty cents or some such."

We left to walk back to the fort. Every time the Brothers looked at her, she got mad. "Don't you go lookin' at me." She smacked one of them on the behind when he kept watching her. "I told you to stop lookin'." Then the other one. "Walk on out there in front of me or I'm gonna get a switch." I had never seen her be so mean to them. I was sorry the whole subject of school had come up. I felt it tended to bring out the worst in everybody.

We walked in silence the rest of the way back to the fort. When I left in the late afternoon, the Brothers were completely dejected, sitting up in their lookout. Maudie was swinging and thinking in the hammock.

The next morning as I walked through the drainpipe, I came upon a completely different scene. Maudie and the Brothers were bustling. She greeted me, hardly looking up. "I got a plan. I got a plan." She was smiling and working as she talked. "I"—she twisted her shoulders in rhythm—"am the man with the plan." The Brothers were tying fishing line to cane poles. Maudie was adding floats and sinkers. "I remembered all this fishin' stuff was under the house and I remembered Miss Maydean pays good money for catfish."

"Who in the world is Miss Maydean and why would she pay for catfish? Anybody can get catfish."

Miss Maydean, Maudie explained, ran the fish

camp down by the river. She bought catfish for the restaurants in town that offered it on their menus, and, of course, what restaurant didn't offer fried catfish? "Yessir, Miss Maydean, we gonna get you a fine mess of catfish and make us plenty of money for whatever we need it for. Lunch boxes, pencil boxes"— she whooped—"all sorts of stuff." She finished with the floats and sinkers and jumped to her feet.

She began to walk in circles, her mind spinning so fast, she had to move to catch up with it. "We'll put'm on a stringer to keep nice and fresh till the end of the day. Miss Maydean won't take no dead ones. We'll fish off the shore near the fish camp. No, maybe we'll take old man Jake's boat." She turned to me. "I knows where he hides it in the brush, and we'll go out on the river and fish in the deep, where the big ones are."

Of course I knew how to swim and fish, as did everyone in our river town, but the river at the fish camp was off-limits.

"Wait a minute, wait a minute. Did you say 'we'? You meant you and the Brothers, didn't you, Maudie?" I looked down at my hands. "You know I can't go down to the river. My mama won't let me. She would—"

Maudie hadn't paid me the slightest attention. She was still pacing and thinking. "And"—she reached down into her dress pocket and pulled out a nickel to raise it up over her head like a prize—"I got five cents to buy hooks. We can buy fifty hooks and put out a mess of poles."

"I . . . I bet y'all have a good time doing that," I said.

She turned to look at me for the first time. "What's this 'y'all' stuff? You comin' with us. I needs you to hold poles. The more poles the better. Besides, the Brothers is too small to catch the big ones."

"Well now, Maudie, the problem is, you see, Grandmother said the worst place in the world is the fish camp down by the river. It's full of—"

"It's full of peoples like you and me. They won't pay you no 'tention if you mind your business. The Brothers loves to go down there. Somethin' always goin' on."

"And there's the fact that it's so far away. Why, we'll have to walk way to town and then down to the bridge and—"

"We don't do nothin' of the sort. We follow the dirt road out there and it goes on down to the river. You take a shortcut through the bottom and you end up at the fish camp. Simple as that."

By this time the Brothers were squirming with excitement. By this time I was beginning to reason my way to the river. She would never know I had gone. I needed to help Maudie. The Brothers were too little to hold the poles.

She picked up the five poles she had outfitted. "Come on, let's go on down there right now. We'll look around, see what's been bitin', and buy us some more hooks. We'll need lots of hooks for when they snag on underwater reeds and rocks. See"—she pointed to a bucket in the corner—"the Brothers done dug worms early this mornin'."

Some few vestiges of conscience remained. "Well now, Maudie, I would like to do it, I really would, but like I told you—"

She stopped me cold, looking straight at me. "Who was it who helped you get John out of the basement, even though I knowed it was a ignorant idea? Who was it helped you with the football game? Besides"—she smiled—"you gonna love the fish camp."

We left the fort and walked maybe a mile on down the dirt road. As the trees began to turn from heavy pines covered with kudzu to willows that let the sun through, I felt better. We were only doing it to further the Brothers' education. This would make up for my attitude about school in general. It was not only not wrong; it was completely right, noble even. Grandmother—no, no, Mother would be proud. I began to whistle.

As the road turned to go toward town and connect with the river bridge road, we came out on a big hill that overlooked the whole river valley. As far as I could see was bottomland stretching before me, leading up to the river's edge. Off in the distance a big barge pushed its load through the channel on the south side of the Tennessee, headed toward Mississippi. The bridge, crossing into Bainbridge, was bright silver in the morning sun. Up the river the gigantic concrete spillways of the TVA dam let pass torrents of water that churned up foam and spray. In a small cove, just down from the bridge, was the fish camp. Standing there, I felt like I was getting ready to walk into a movie scene, right into whatever was going on, out of one place into another.

"Over there is the fish camp." Maudie pointed. "It's shorter to cut through the bottom than to take the road all the way round." She and the Brothers began running down the hill and across the flats to the fish camp about half a mile away.

I looked one moment longer, at the land stretched out before me, at the sun sparkling on the water, then I tipped forward and ran into the picture, following Maudie and the Brothers down into the bottoms.

I had to run to catch up with her. She carried the fishing poles over her shoulder. The Brothers were trailing along a good way behind, dragging the bucket filled with dirt and worms. We came to the river's edge, lined with trees and shrubs grown tall by sucking up the water. "First off, let's see if old Mr. Jake still keepin' his boat hid out here in the bushes so he won't have to pay no dock fee."

She walked up and down looking. "Yonder it is." She pointed to a tree half-falling in the water. I didn't see anything until we walked closer. Sure enough, there among the branches in the water was a flat-bottom boat, like all the fishermen used, complete with two oars and a minnow bucket. "Someday it's gonna come loose in a storm and the current will carry it all the way to Iuka." She looked at the Brothers, who were just walking up, and raised her eyebrows. "But for now, we may need to borrow it to get all the fish we want."

"What do you mean, 'we may need to borrow it,' Maudie? Have you done this before?"

"It just depend on if they be bitin' off the shore or only in the deep. I 'spect with all this hot weather we gonna have to go deep." She surveyed the river with a showy confidence, sticking a finger in her mouth and holding it to the air to test the wind.

"Put down them worms, Brothers. We gonna come back here to start out."

"What do you mean, 'to start out'?"

"To start out fishin'." She leaned her poles against a tree, turned, not waiting on us, and headed toward the fish camp. "We needs to see what it is they bitin' on."

"Wait a minute, wait a minute." I was running along behind her. "If we have to go deep, we take the fishing poles and—"

"And paddle up the river."

"Well, what if we run into the bridge or, or the

dam? That thing is huge and the current around the dam—well, they say it can suck you up and well—I been fishing plenty at the farm, but that's above the dam."

"The current's runnin' the other way. We float away from the dam. Then, when we get all the fish we want, we just keep floatin' back to where we was before and leave Mr. Jake's boat and take our string to Miss Maydean. I seen it done a million times."

"You've 'seen' it done a million times, but you have not actually 'done' it a million times? Is that what you're saying?"

"Seen it, done it. What's the difference? I knows what I wants to do and how to do it. That's the most important thing, ain't it?"

She was still walking fast. I was still jogging alongside, trying to keep up. "Well now, Maudie, I don't know. I'll have to think about that. It just seems to me—" We were approaching the fishing camp and she held up her hand.

"No more talkin.' We got to act like we know what we doin' so Miss Maydean will buy our fish like everybody else."

We crossed the road. Dusty cars were parked on either side of the entrance. Cars that looked as if they had taken root there. Missing hubcaps, broken windshields. And a thin layer of red dust that had settled over everything.

The camp consisted of two old graying wood buildings connected by a series of older wood walkways, some of which jutted out into the water and passed for piers. To the right of a fading Coke sign was a half-open screen door with COLONIAL BREAD stenciled across its metal brace. The smell of frying catfish mixed in with the morning air. In the window a darkened neon sign announced EATS. The other building was the bait shop, recognized by the hand-lettered sign in the window, LIVE BAIT, and underneath that but smaller, *Crickets, minnows, night crawlers.* Maudie squeaked open the door to the bait shop. "I do the talkin' in here," she said. We came into a room made even darker by the sunlight outside. Country music from a radio floated in and out of static. There was a door on the opposite side of the room, leading out to the river and the piers. As my eyes adjusted to the dark, I saw shelves full of dusty fishing equipment lining the walls. Minnow buckets hung from the ceiling. Spare wall space was covered with cigarette posters of Lucky Strike girls.

I didn't see her at first, just heard the voice. "Is that you, Maudie? Where you been keeping your lazy self, girl?" She was in the corner next to the cash register. She was at one with the easy chair she sat in. Both were overstuffed and the worse for wear. She was so large that I might have mistaken her for a part of the chair had my eyes not been adjusted to the light. The white fat of her arms and legs spilled over onto its threadbare covering.

Maudie walked over like they were old friends.

"Me and the Brothers been round, Miss Maydean. We been stayin' busy." I kept to the shadows.

"Who you got there?" she said, squinting her eyes to see me. Maudie motioned for me to come over, but I hesitated, still trying to decide who or what Miss Maydean might be.

Her voice cracked through the air. "Get on over here, girl. I ain't gonna bite you." I edged over to stand beside Maudie. The Brothers were wandering the store, uninterested in our business.

"What's your name, girl?"

"It's Tab, ma'am."

"Tab? That's a funny name, ain't it?" I could feel Maudie smiling at my side.

"Who you belong to, Tab?"

"I'm a Rutland. I'm Charles's child."

"Oh yeah, you the one got the Yankee mother."

"She's from Tennessee."

"That's what I said. And your grandmother . . . With a grandmother like you got, I know you ain't gonna cause no trouble around here. That grandmother of yours put the fear of God in a lamppost." She cackled at her joke. Now that she had put a label on me, I relaxed and moved closer.

"Heared tell your daddy went and burned up half his wheat crop t'other day. That so?"

"Yes, ma'am."

She had an old cash box in her lap and was breaking wrapped change into it. "I knew it was so. Keep track of everythin' that goes on in the county, right here in this chair. It's the river. Like bein' on a party line."

Leaning next to the chair, very close to her right hand, was a double-barrel shotgun, the kind we used for dove hunting on the farm. She saw me staring at it. "Now this here"—she tapped the barrel with a wrapper of pennies—"is for them boys that don't like the price I might wanta give'm for fish"—she winked at me—"or for anything else they don't like." She had finished breaking change into the cash box and began struggling to get out of the chair. After several attempts and one last mighty heave, she made it to a standing position. She straightened her wraparound housedress and waddled to the cash register to open it and deposit the money.

"Well now, Tab, you standin' in the finest fish camp on the river. I guess Maudie done told you that. Matter of fact, it's the only fish camp between here and Iuka." Then Miss Maydean added as an afterthought, "That little one down by the Trace crossin' don't count." She took a rag out from under the counter and chattered on. "Did you see them cars outside when you come in?" She ran the dirty rag along the counter, moving the dust around. "Everyone last one of them's mine. Done took'm in on trade. Makes the place look more businesslike to have cars out front. Most of these old boys ain't got nothin' but broke-down trucks or they come on foot. Seems like to me—"

"Miss Maydean"—Maudie cleared her throat—"speakin' of the price of fish, I was just wonderin' what the price is right now?" Miss Maydean looked up from her dusting, her train of thought interrupted.

Maudie hesitated. "That is, if I was to bring you some good live catfish, what would you give for'm?"

"You decided to go into the fishin' business? They ain't any women fishin' I know about."

"That don't mean they couldn't be." Maudie saw her opening. "Women could do it just like men. Remember Old Black Sally? You used to pay her for fish."

"That's cause Old Sally was on her last leg and needed what she could get, to live on." She cocked her head and looked at Maudie in a curious way. "Besides, she brung me some good eatin' fish." She busied herself with her dusting for a minute without saying anything. Then, "Tell you what I'll do for you gals. You bring me some good fish—don't want no carp or the like—I'll give you . . ." She hesitated and scratched her head. "I'll give you eight cents a pound prime, five cents a pound commercial. How does that sound to you?"

Maudie jumped at it. "That sounds fine to me."

"Now if you wanta see a real catch, go on out to the minnow boxes and look in that one on the left." She raised her rag to shoo us out. "Go'n out there." She pointed to the dock side of the shop.

"You know where, Maudie. But don't let them Brothers get too close. One flick of that tail'll cut you bad. Some old boys from up at Cross Roads brung him in this morning. Been out jug fishin'. That'll bring'um a pretty penny payin' commercial. Course it ain't no good for eatin'."

We turned to the sound of the screen door slamming. The Brothers had heard every word and were curious. "Now hold on there." Maudie ran after them. "You done heard what Miss Maydean said."

The minnow boxes were out next to the docks. They were made of cinder blocks and measured about six feet by three feet. Three of them lined up to hold live bait. Two men looked down at whatever was in the third one. The Brothers ran up, looked, then dashed back to Maudie. The four of us slowly stepped closer. Just as we neared the edge, its giant tail slapped and sent a splash of water up into the air.

"That old mama don't like you lookin' at her," one of the men said, laughing. When the water settled down again, we strained to find its outline. At first I couldn't see it, it was that big. I expected to see a fish swimming around in circles in the bait box. This one was so large that it took up almost the entire length and width of the box. It couldn't move except to swish its tail. Its catfish whiskers draped out over the top and each time its gills opened, they sent a ripple over the surface of the water.

"That's as big as one of the Brothers." I stared.

"Biggest one I ever got, and I been fishin' round here nigh on to twenty year." The man who caught the fish rocked back on his heels with thumbs in his belt, pleased with his day's work. Without prompting, he began the story. "Me 'n' Grady put in up by Two Mile Creek 'bout five this mornin'. We waited till we was in the middle to throw out 'cause we was aimin' to go fifteen feet down. Had the worse-smellin' day-old chicken innards you ever did get a whiff of."

"They say it's them chicken innards that's the best," the man standing next to him said, still looking down at the monster fish.

"How many jugs did you throw out?" Maudie said, watching the fish gills go in and out.

"Throwed out 'bout ten. That's all we could keep up with in the current. Course the minute this one went under, we knowed it was a big'un and we just let t'other go. They probably halfway to the Trace by now."

"How long 'fore you got a strike?" Maudie asked, eyes still glued to the fish.

"Weren't long. We floated down almost to the bridge. Then when she struck and we finally got holt of the jug, she done pulled us round for half hour 'fore she was tuckered out enough for us to get her in. After that, weren't no trouble t'all just to float her back on down here to Miss Maydean's."

"What size hook you use to catch such a fish?" Maudie smiled up at the man.

"One of them five-for-a-nickel packs. Hooks long as my finger." He elbowed the man standing next to him. "We was goin' for all or nothin'."

"And you sure got all," his friend said. "That there is a one in a million."

Maudie walked around the box, holding the Brothers' hands. "How much you 'spect that fish is gonna weigh?"

Suddenly it dawned on me why she was so interested. "Maudie," I almost yelled, "we can't bother this man with questions all day. We need to be getting on with our fishing." I took one of the Brothers' hands to try and lead us away from what I knew would be certain death at the bottom of the river.

"Oh, that's all right, little lady." The man smiled at me. "I got all the time in the world till the man gets here what buys commercial. I 'spect it'll weigh out around eighty, ninety-five pound. If Miss Maydean is still payin' good, we gonna have fine eatin' at my house tonight." He punched his friend's shoulder.

"That sure is nice for you," I said. "Thanks so much for telling us all about it. Now come on, Maudie. We got to go." I got behind them and tried to push the Brothers and Maudie back up toward the bait shop.

Maudie let herself be pushed along. Not

because I wanted it. She had other things to think about. "I got five cents. We could get one pack, but we ain't got no jugs." She was walking back toward the bait shop.

I ran around in front of her and put my hands on her waist, trying to push her back. "Now, just hold on here, Maudie." My pushing was having little effect. She kept walking. "We are not, I repeat *not,* going jug fishing. We'll all be killed. Think of the Brothers. Think of the dam. Most of the spillways are open now. Think of the barge traffic. Remember last year, that fisherman that got run down by a barge coming out of the locks?" My best efforts to hold her back weren't working. We were nearing the door of the bait shop.

Suddenly she stopped, insulted. "What you mean, 'Think of the Brothers'? You think I'm crazy? I ain't gonna let the Brothers go. They too young." She put her hand on my shoulder and smiled calmly. "It's gonna be just you and me."

I tried to make an impression by saying it very loud and pounding my fist in my hand. "No, no, no! We are not going to do that." I looked around in desperation for some distraction. "Look out there at all those fishermen." I pointed out to the docks. Other fishermen had returned with morning catches. "They caught plenty of fish and they didn't have to go jug fishing." As always, I turned to the Brothers when I was in desperate straits. "Don't ya'll want to go see what they caught?"

They immediately turned to run toward the piers to have a look-see.

"Now hold on there." Maudie had to follow them. I breathed a sigh of relief and watched after them as they picked their way along the rickety pier, stepping over missing boards and around rusty nails pulled up by years of sun and rain.

I had been past the fish camp many times, riding in the family car up River Street as it rose to catch the bridge that spanned the Tennessee. Like so many things that summer, I had seen it, but I had never really seen it. Spread out before me were four very old piers used by the fishermen to tie up their boats. Miss Maydean had not felt the need to make any repairs for years on end. There were planks missing along the walkways, cleats hanging loose or missing at the tie-up points. Old lights at the end of each pier had been shot out or never replaced. Waves from a long-gone barge slapped what little energy they had left against the wooden pilings that formed a river wall. Floating sticks and leaves lazed in the backwater, taking the waves in stride. Tied to the pilings were boats in various sizes and faded colors, all wood, wide, and flat. The fisherman's workplace. Men, black and white, mostly old, sat in their boats gutting the morning's catch and throwing the remains overboard. The heat of the sun overlaid the whole picture, leathering old fishing hands, throwing sparkles on the water, quickly turning fish remains into the scent of the river. Already I loved this place.

Now if I could only get Maudie to do right. I walked down to where Maudie and the Brothers were watching one of the fishermen sitting in his boat.

"That's a nice mess of fish you got there, Mr. Nelms," she was saying.

He untied the stringer from the side of the boat so we could get a better look. There were maybe fifteen fish, some bream but mostly catfish. "Caught the bream, on worms. I done run my trot-lines this mornin'. That's how come all them cat-fish. Got maybe two smallmouth, too." He pointed to the fish at the bottom of the string. "Them'll make some good eatin'."

"Now that's a great idea," I almost shouted. "A trotline. Why a person could get all the fish she wanted with a trotline."

Maudie walked away from Mr. Nelms, following the Brothers to the next boat down the way. "We ain't got no money for trotlines. If we had that much money, we could buy all the lunch boxes we need.

"That's a nice catch you got there," she said to the next man, who was happy to raise his catch. His stringer had twenty to twenty-five fish on it. "They sure must be bitin' good."

"Always bites good when the spillways is open. Stirs up them bottom fish."

"See there," I said, too enthusiastic. "Why, with a few catches like that, we'll have all we need."

"With a few catches like that? With a few catches like that? You know how long it's gonna take us to catch that many? Then we barely have enough money. But if we get us one big catch, we can buy everything we need and some left over for a pencil box."

"You heard the man. It's a one-in-a-million chance," I said.

She took the Brothers' hands and started walking to the bait shop. "I tell you what we gonna do. We gonna compromise. 'Compromise,' now that means you get what you wants and I gets what I want. I done read that word in *Silver Screen* the other day. Frank Sinatra done compromised with MGM and he got what he want and they got what they want. We gonna take this here nickel I got in my pocket and buy us a pack of regular hooks. We gonna fish out the whole pack and see what we got. If we anywhere near what we need, then we'll keep on with the little hooks. If we ain't, we'll go for the big ones." She opened the screen door and told the Brothers to go inside. Then she put her arm around my shoulder as we walked into the bait shop. Smiling, she said, "Now don't that make it even?"

I squinted my eyes in concentration, but for the life of me, I couldn't think of a reason why it didn't.

194

There were fifty shiny hooks in the cardboard box Miss Maydean sold us. Just looking at them gave me confidence. I knew that would be more than enough to catch thousands of fish. The monster catfish was just a distant memory as we walked away from the camp back to our supplies on the riverbank. Willow trees gave way to a mud bank four or five feet high. Below that, there was a level stretch that had been carved out when the river ran full. A red mud beach of ten or twelve feet sloped into the water. The sun was at ten o'clock as we held on to willow branches to lower ourselves down to the river's edge.

On the opposite side of the river, in the deepwater channel, at a distance of maybe half a mile, the captain of a tow, bound upriver, gave a blast on his air horn to announce his coming to the lockmaster of the dam. He pushed a cargo of fifteen barges loaded to overflowing with coal toward the massive lock doors. It would take the better part of the morning to lock all the barges through to higher ground. So heavy was the load that waves it generated on the opposite side of the river would still be three feet high once they reached us.

Maudie and I left our shoes up by the willows to better wade in and out while we were setting our poles. Of course the Brothers had no shoes in the first place and had scrambled down to wade in the water while we worked.

At the end of the first day we had made only five

cents and lost ten hooks, but I wasn't worried. I knew we could never use up a whole box of hooks.

It was late in the day when we dashed back across the bottom and home. I was just in time to take my place at the supper table. "What is that fishy smell?" Mother said, sniffing the air. I had been in such a hurry, I had forgotten to wash my smelly hands, so I shoved them between my legs, sitting perfectly still.

"Oh yuck! I can smell that, too, and it's coming from you, Tab," Tina said. "What have you been up to now?" All eyes turned to me.

I began to talk fast. "It, uh, uh, it's probably just some squirrel guts I got on the bottom of my shoe. That smells a lot like fish sometimes, don't you think? See, me and J.W. were poking a stick at this squirrel that got run over on the road today and—"

"Never mind, never mind." Mother held her hand up and kept her eyes closed. "Just excuse yourself from the table, Tab, and take your shoes off—outside—and wash your hands, and anything else that needs washing."

I jumped up and backed out of the dining room, walking on my heels, pretending great gobs of squirrel guts must be stuck on the bottoms of my shoes.

Chapter 16

"How many hooks you 'spect we got left?" Maudie said as we struck out from the fort the next morning.

"Oh, plenty, plenty," I answered, my thoughts elsewhere. Maybe I would become a commercial fisherman when I grew up. This was easy and fun and you could make big money doing it. I visualized myself at the head of a gigantic flat-bottom-boat fishing fleet. Everyone in the family would have to work for me. I would put Tina in charge of cleaning fish.

That afternoon when we stopped to eat lunch, Maudie wandered over to look at Mr. Jake's boat hidden in the underbrush. "Why don't we take this here boat and fish up and down, right out there"—she pointed offshore—"where they ain't much current. See what we can catch in water a little bit deeper."

"I don't know, Maudie. What if Mr. Jake—"

"He ain't comin'. I done saw smoke risin' out of the trees down by his place this mornin'. He busy with his business. He can't leave when he bringin' in a batch." She began to untie the rope that secured it.

To my surprise, it turned out to be very easy. Maudie and I paddled up almost to the fish camp and then we floated back down holding our poles, waiting for nibbles. That day we earned ten cents, and Maudie, without my realizing it, had eased me out into the river.

The third day, ten more cents. We had become old hands at handling Mr. Jake's boat. There was nothing to it and we were twenty-five cents to the good.

But on the morning of the fourth day . . . "We down to seven hooks," she said, counting what was left in the box.

"Let me see that." I rushed over and took the box from Maudie, the hair on the back of my neck tingling. I counted three times. Just enough for one round of hooks, with two left over. "Well, you said if we were doing good, we could buy more hooks and keep going." I pushed back panic.

"We ain't doin' that good. We got twenty-five cents and we'll have to spend five of that to get more hooks. At ten cents a day, we be here till Christmastime before we get enough for the Brothers' schoolin'."

"Well now, Maudie, don't think about that now. We still got seven hooks left. Let's see how we do today." I spent the day watching our last hooks dwindle. Each time a pole looked like its line would snag, I jerked it out of the water to recast it, but I couldn't keep up with five poles, and at midafternoon we ran out of hooks. We had four catfish, which brought us fifteen cents, but it wasn't enough. I could see it in Maudie's eyes as we walked home. "I got three old cider jugs I found under the house," she said. "You see what you can find at your house. We could use three or four more. Miss Mama wrung out a chicken yesterday and I saved the neck and the innards. They be just right by tomorrow. Only thing is the line. I got some good leader wire, but nothin' strong enough to hold a really big fish. I guess we'll have to use clothesline rope."

That night I found two old apple-cider jugs in the pantry and was trying to decide if I should take them when Mother came in and surprised me. "What in the world are you doing in the pantry at this time of night? Are you hungry? We just ate."

"No, ma'am. I was thinking I might need something to put water in. Would you mind if I used these cider jugs for our picnic tomorrow?"

"That's a lot of water. What are you and your friends doing that you need that much water?"

"I'm just trying to do everything I'm suppose to, so I won't get it." I gave her my most angelic look. "J.W.'s mother said drinking a lot of water is one of the things that will help you not to get it," I lied.

"She did?" Mother looked at me, surprised. "That's a new one on me, but I certainly wouldn't want you to do without, especially if it helps. Of course you're welcome to take the jugs. Why don't we make you a big pitcher of iced tea to go in one and water in the other. We'll even make you tuna sandwiches for your picnic. I used to love having picnics with my friends when I was little." She had taken a jug from me and was rinsing it out in the sink.

I hopped up on the counter and sat watching her. "You know, Mama, you could have a club of your own friends if you wanted to. You don't need that dumb Ladies Help League."

She drained the water from the cider jug and began drying it with a dish towel. "And whom do you suggest I get to be in this club?"

"Well, just the other day I met this real nice lady. She's kinda fat but real nice and she knows everything that goes on in town."

"Oh, really. Whose mother is that?"

"Well, I don't know whose mother she is, but she's got lots of cars all sitting around and she even has her very own shot—" Suddenly I remembered that Miss Maydean was off-limits even if, in my mind, she would have made a dandy friend for

Mother. I jumped down off the counter. "Never mind. It was probably just somebody I saw in a movie. I'll get the other jug out of the pantry."

I sat in Mr. Jake's boat the next morning, laughing to myself as I watched Maudie rig the jugs for fishing. Why had I ever been worried about us catching a monster fish? No fish in his right fish mind would ever think about biting these contraptions Maudie was making. We had four jugs. I couldn't bring myself to throw out the tea. We were saving it to drink as we paddled up the river. First she made sure the tops were screwed on good to make them airtight. To each of the jug finger-holds she tied a piece of clothesline about seven or eight feet long. Toward the end of the line she attached three lug nuts as weights. The next time we passed the cars out in front of Miss Maydean's, I was going to take a close look at the wheels to see if the lug nuts were missing. Right after the weights, she had fastened a piece of wire about five inches long, with a giant hook on the end. To finish the whole thing off, Maudie had put two-day-old chicken guts on the hooks. It smelled so awful, I had to sit downwind or get sick to my stomach. I almost laughed out loud as I watched her, but I dared not. This would be fun. We would paddle up the river toward the dam. Then we would angle over to the middle of the river to catch the current, throw the jugs overboard, and float downstream with them until we ended up where we started. On the way we could drink tea, eat sandwiches, wave to the tow captains off in the distance. When we finished, we would gather the jugs in or let them float on down the river—I didn't care. Then tomorrow, we could go back to regular fishing, once she could see jug fishing was a waste of time.

"Now I," she said as she stood in the water, trying to wash the stink off her hands, "I'm gonna be the captain, like Charles Laughton in *Mutiny on the Bounty,* and you, you gonna be the first mate, like Clark Gable. Course I don't want no mutiny."

"Yes, sir." I stood to give her a fake salute, trying to suppress a grin. "I'll do everything you say, Maudie. You tried it my way, now we'll try it your way."

She turned to the Brothers. "I could use a rope and tie you to a tree till I come back or I could let you run free, but only if you stay right here and don't go wandering off and don't get in the water no matter what. Which would you rather?" They stood grinning at her. "All right," she said, "your lunch is tied to the branch of that willow over there, but don't eat it till the sun is straight up. We be back in the early afternoon"—she smiled— "with the biggest fish you ever saw and money for a new lunch box, if we lucky."

I thought to myself, The only way we're going to catch anything is if we hit some poor fish over the head and kill it when we throw one of those jug things in the water.

"Time to cast off," she said as she pushed Mr. Jake's boat out into the water and climbed on board. We decided to sit both on the forward seat and paddle side by side. That way, the smell wouldn't be so bad.

Everyone on the river used a flat-bottom boat. They were wide, with a squared-off front and back. Four wooden cross-braces made the seats. It was easy to move about without being in danger of capsizing, but it was not easy to move the boat through the water without an outboard motor. We paddled along in silence past Miss Maydean's fish camp, staying close to shore and out of the river current. At this point, the channel crossed from the far side of the river to our side. All the barges and other river travelers must cross to enter the channel that led up to the lock in the dam.

We crossed the mouth of the channel and kept going upstream, staying close to the shoreline of the island that lay between the channel and the rest of the river. Progress was very slow. Unless we paddled constantly, we would begin to float back downstream. After the first thirty minutes, my arms were aching and my clothes were drenched with sweat. "Now here's an idea, Maudie," I said, between jabbing the paddle in the water and pulling it past me. "Why don't we throw the jugs in right here and start floating downstream right now? I bet we'll catch plenty. And we can have a drink of tea while we float."

"Nothin' doin'. We ain't even halfway to where we needs to be." She kept paddling, eyes straight ahead, looking at the dam that, I noticed, seemed bigger now. "We got to do it right to catch . . . the *big* one." She smiled.

I smiled back through gritted teeth. The big one, I thought, will probably laugh himself into a heart attack once he gets a load of those lug nuts we're using for weights.

Ten more minutes and I couldn't go on. My arms were spaghetti. Maudie took pity. She had to take pity because the boat began to travel in a circle, since I wasn't keeping up my side of the paddle. "We gonna pull into shore and rest and then go on."

"Good plan." I fell back in the bottom of the boat and lay there panting, fingers locked around the paddle that I held to my chest. Maudie steered to shore and jumped out to beach us. I lay there baking in the sun, my head not two feet away from the chicken bait that every fly onshore had immediately smelled. I was beginning to have second thoughts about fishing for a living. "How much farther?" I asked, without even opening my eyes.

"If I was to judge, I would guess another hour and we be smack up against them spillways."

"Smack up against what?" I opened one eye and turned my head in the direction of her voice.

"I was just funnin' you." She laughed as she reached in the boat and pulled out the jug of tea. "Come on, let's go set on the shore and rest. I don't know how you stand to have your head so close to them vile-smellin' chicken parts."

I sat up and began prying my fingers loose from the paddle. Now we were close enough to the dam to see it from shore to shore. In among the water and the trees and the sky was this thing that didn't belong. A massive concrete wall holding back millions of tons of water. I got out and sat onshore with Maudie, sharing the tea jug. I couldn't take my eyes off the dam. It loomed like some gigantic prehistoric troll lying across the waterway, blocking passage. Steam rose from its tail as generators ground out electricity for the valley. Its backbone was a succession of massive spillways side by side. A few were open to torrents of water that rushed over its body. Others were closed tight to all but small leaks trickling down its concrete side, which had aged to dark greens and browns in a pitiful attempt by the creature to camouflage itself.

I took another drink of tea and squinted my eyes to look again. The most forbidding part of all was its mouth, a gigantic steel door that rose up the height of a ten-story building, ready to open and swallow up boats and barges.

When Maudie said we had rested long enough,

I didn't protest. We pushed off again and continued up the shoreline of the island that ran alongside the channel. On the other side of the island, big barges pushed their cargo up to the lock door. On our side, the rest of the river spread out before us. I rowed, glancing at the dam, watching it grow larger. In the distance, the sound of the lockmaster's horn signaled barges that he was ready to open his door to them.

My arms began to ache again as I repeated my rowing motion over and over, trying desperately to keep my side of the boat up with Maudie's. As we inched up the river, signs that were posted near the dam were coming close enough to read. I glanced up through the perspiration running down into my eyes. CAUTION! DO NOT COME WITHIN 800 FEET—looked down to dig the paddle into the water again and then looked up—OF THE WATER-RELEASE AREA WHEN HORN SOUNDS! I stopped paddling and shook Maudie's arm. "You see that sign?" I said in a loud voice. By this time the roar of the spillway water was a constant noise in the background.

"We ain't within no eight hundred feet. We got a ways to go. Besides"—she kept paddling—"I ain't heard no horn."

"By the time you hear a horn, we'll be drowned," I yelled. The boat was beginning to angle toward shore anyway because I had stopped rowing and Maudie was on the leeward side. We beached on a sandy strip of land. To our left through the trees was the channel and the lock door. Straight ahead was the dam wall. Posted on giant buoys in the water and tacked to trees on-shore were the warning signs, but Maudie wasn't satisfied we were close enough yet. She got out of the boat and grabbed the bow rope. She began walking in the shallow water, up toward the dam.

"Now just wait a minute, Maudie," I said from my sitting position.

"We gonna go just up a little bit more. Then we be in the exact right place when they lets the extra water out of the lock and stirs up all the fish."

I sat there knowing I was helpless to do anything about it. Although we were getting closer, the spillways on this side of the dam weren't open, so our side was calm for now. She finally stopped and tied the boat rope to a tree with a warning sign on it. She motioned me to get out of the boat and bring the tea. We waded onshore to sit on the beach and sun. "And another thing," I said to her as she passed the tea. "Have you noticed that there are no fishing boats up here? How could this be a good place if nobody else is here?" She ignored me.

"See what's gonna happen is this. When the barges goes in the lock, the big lock door is closed. Then the lock is filled up with water, and when it gets high enough, they opens the other end of the lock and lets the barges out."

"I know that. My school took a field trip out

here last year. Course we weren't down here waitin' to get drowned. We were up there"—I pointed to the top of the lock—"watching the barges go through, like normal people."

She continued, like I hadn't said a thing in the world. "Now the best part is when the lockmaster blow on his horn. That means he gettin' ready to let out all that water he put in the lock to raise them barges up. Now when he do that, we gonna be ready, 'cause when that happen, all the fishes on the bottom get stirred up, and we gonna be out in our boat ready to catch us a big one." She smiled, triumphant.

"Alls we have to do is wait for the horn to blow. They say when the water starts rushin' out of the bottom of the lock, it come right over here where all the signs is at. They say they is little fishes throwed all the way up onshore. Foxes and such comes out of the woods to get 'em. Course we can't stay to see that. We got to get in our boat and be ready to throw our jugs out." She lay back on the sandy beach and put her hands behind her head. "Alls we got to do now is wait."

If this was such a good idea, why weren't other fishermen over here? I asked. She kept her eyes closed and smiled. "I guess it's 'cause they ain't smart as me."

I sat there looking out over the river. At this point, it was more than a mile wide. Other fishing boats were off in the distance in the middle of the river, far away from the spillways and nowhere near all these signs. I supposed no one had noticed us because we had stayed so close to shore as we paddled upstream. I tried to train my eyes to look only at the river, but they kept being drawn to the dam. Now that I was so close, to turn around and face it full on made me weak in the knees. Once I looked, I was mesmerized. To my left through the trees of our island I could see the top of the massive lock doors slowly opening. That whole thing was going to fill up with water once the barges were pushed inside and the door closed. I remembered from our class trip that it was the length of two football fields and when it was filled with water, it lifted boats almost one hundred feet up. After it had let its cargo out upstream, it would release all that excess water, and it was coming our way. I began to feel dizzy.

Then, splitting the air and my eardrum, the sound of a horn so loud, all I could do was hold my ears. Maudie jumped up off the sand and spun around to look in the direction of the lock.

"What in— Is it the water coming so soon?" I panicked.

"That was just the lockmaster tellin' the tow captain he can start takin' his barges in the lock now. We still got plenty of time." She smiled and sat back down. "Now when the lock is filled and them barges can leave on the other end, then that's when he blow his horn again. Then . . . then we get ready to RIDE," she shouted. She sat down on the sand and leaned back, her head in her hands, eyes closed, smiling.

I began to pace up and down. Not only did we not have a chance in the world of catching a fish with those dumb jug things but we were going to get drowned in the process. My mama was gonna kill me. "What are you lying there smiling about, Maudie?" I stood over her, hands on hips, ready to give her a punch in the stomach at the slightest provocation.

Eyes still closed, still smiling, she said, "I was thinkin' how proud the Brothers is gonna be when they walks to school the first day with they new Gene Autry lunch boxes. I'm gonna make'm the best lunch they is. Peanut butter and jelly sandwiches, a stack of Ritz crackers ten high with mayonnaise in between, and iced tea to go in they little Gene Autry thermos bottles."

"Oh brother." I let out a sigh and sat down beside her, defeated.

She opened her eyes and looked over at me, concerned. "What's the matter? Ain't that the best lunch? What could be better? Maybe I should add potato chips?"

"You could add a partridge in a pear tree and it wouldn't make any difference once that water comes. You probably won't be around to make any lunches," I said, pointing to the lock, to give it one last try. "Maudie, do you know that the water in that lock is as big as two football fields?" There was silence. She had closed her eyes again. I gave up and lay down. I might as well conserve my energy.

Five minutes passed before she said, "I done told you when we played that game, I didn't know nothin 'bout football. How big is a football field?"

I saw a ray of hope and raised up on my elbows. "Two football fields is as long as it is from the river bridge all the way up to Bainbridge House," I lied.

"Is that all?" she said, and closed her eyes again. We stayed there with the distant roar of the spillways in the background and neither one saying a word. Finally, without opening her eyes—"I guess we could compromise, me bein' such a fair-minded person and all. Compromise, now that means—"

"You told me what it means," I said, jumping up off the ground. "Good idea, good idea," I shouted. I dashed through the water to the boat and began untying the bow rope. Maudie appeared beside me and guided it out into the deep water. We both hopped on board. "Is the compromise that we paddle like crazy before the lockmaster sounds his—" Just then, it split the air. Not as long as before but it seemed to me twice as loud. "We're doomed," I sobbed, and let my paddle go slack in the water.

"Don't you let me hear you talkin' like that." She dug her paddle in. "We ain't doomed. We . . . we just a little outta sorts right now. Get busy with that paddle. I judge we still got a minute or two. Besides, we gonna put out them jugs before we get too far along. That there is the compromise."

We paddled straight out into the river, farther away from shore than we had ever been.

It began as a rumbling noise behind us that was fast catching up to our boat. I was afraid of what I might see if I turned around. I put my paddle down in the bottom of the boat and held on. The waters began to churn underneath us. The boat began to turn slowly at first, then out of control, like we were at the center of a whirlpool. Debris churned up from the river bottom banged against the side of the boat. Each time something large hit against the boat, the wooden boards would give a little to let water in. My knuckles were white from holding on as we were turned from side to side and then spun around. Any minute this boat was going to crack apart and maybe, just maybe, we could make it back to shore if we were lucky and found something to hold on to. All of a sudden my eyes fell on the jugs. They would be a perfect substitute for a life preserver. Maybe there is hope after all, I thought as I was thrown from side to side. The minute we began to break apart, I would grab a jug, one under each arm, holding on for dear life. Imagine, I thought to myself, I was able to think of such a wonderful solution on the verge of sure death.

"Maudie," I yelled as loud as I could above the

noise, "we can use the jugs as life preservers." Sure she would think I was a genius.

"Don't touch them jugs."

"What?" I knew I hadn't heard her right above the din.

"I said, don't touch them jugs. I"—just then a big wave raised us both up in the air—"am gonna catch the *big* one." As we banged back down on our wooden seat, we heard it crack under our weight.

"Are you crazy?" I screamed. "We are gonna drown here. What in the world do I care about 'the big one'?" I looked over at the jugs, afraid they might roll into each other and break before I could make good my plan. I couldn't let go with my hands, so I tried to pull one of the jugs toward me with my feet.

She saw my tricky little maneuver. "I done told you, don't touch them jugs." She began to push my feet away with her feet.

Were we not in the same boat, getting ready to drown, and I was worried about living and she was worried about the blasted jugs? We began to have a battle royal with our feet, right out there in the middle of the Tennessee River as Mr. Jake's boat creaked and leaked at the seams. No hands, just feet and mouths our only two weapons. "I am taking a jug whether you like it or not." I kicked her foot away and tried to pull the jug toward me with my feet.

"You ain't havin' one bit of no jug of mine." She kicked back.

"What did you think, Maudie?" I yelled. "Did you think you could actually catch any blessed thing with these stupid jugs?" I was kicking at random now anywhere even close to her legs.

She screamed back. "I 'spect I could if I didn't let no crackerhead like you mess everything up." She tried to stomp on my toes. It was a worthless strategy. There was so much water in the bottom of the boat that her stomping only resulted in large splashes of water soaking us both.

Presently we stopped out of sheer exhaustion and a depleted supply of insults. When we did, we noticed the boat was not turning as much. The current was still very strong. We were fairly sailing down the river, but it was in one direction and the waves were much smaller and dissipating. Maudie let go of the boat and looked around. Quickly she grabbed the jug closest to her, the one I had been fighting for. She began to unwrap the clothesline she had neatly wound around it. First the huge hook baited with water-soaked chicken, then the wire leader, followed by the lug nut weights, then the clothesline. "This is it. This is it. We gonna catch the big one," she said. She let the line down into the water and quickly began work on the next one.

"I don't know if you've noticed," I said, mustering all the sarcasm at my ten-year-old command, "but our boat is sinking."

She didn't even look up. "Well, start bailin'. You can use one of them cans with the extra chicken in it. We ain't gonna need both. Just pitch out the chicken in that one. Maybe it'll scare up more fish."

Since she was methodically throwing my life preservers overboard, there was nothing else to do. I began to bail like crazy. After a while the bailing seemed to be showing results. My tin can was scraping the bottom of the boat. Plenty of water was still left, but no more seemed to be coming in. I sat up to take a breather.

All four jugs were bobbing merrily along in the water. It was a miracle that any of them survived. The only thing missing was the iced tea jug we forgot and left on the island. Maudie was sitting there like a proud mother watching her brood. She took great care to keep the boat away from the free-floating jugs. If it started drifting ahead of the jugs, she would use her paddle to slow us down. By now we had drifted out to the middle of the river. The sun beat down on us, but there was a nice breeze. Off in the distance was the bridge into Bainbridge. We were slowly floating toward it. Maudie waved to some of the fishermen in the distance.

"Old number three," she said pointing, "was bobbin' funny a minute ago. I'm gonna have to check his bait directly. Some baby fish mighta nibbled away at him." She was sitting on the very front of the boat, her feet dangling into the water, using

215

her paddle to guide us. I was in the middle seat. "You keep count while I go over and rebait number three." She began to paddle. "Keep count. Don't take your eyes off them others." After a few more minutes, she had reached the jug. "Are you keepin' count?" she asked, not looking at me but listening as she began to pull the line attached to the jug up out of the water.

"Yes, yes. One two three, one two three," I gave a lackluster report. "One, two—" All the sudden Maudie was gone. I looked where she had been sitting and there was blue sky instead. I heard a splash and then nothing. "Maudie?" I called. "Maudieee," I screamed. I crawled to the front of the boat and looked overboard. Nothing. Panic was closing my throat and stopping my breath. For a horrible moment there was nothing but the sound of water lapping against the boat.

At the rear of the boat she burst out of the water sputtering and splashing. "We got the big one. We done got the big one." She flailed away. "Nearly 'bout took my finger off." She grabbed hold of the side of the boat. "Look round, see if you see the jug," she shouted. She began to climb back in the boat while I automatically went to the other side for balance.

"I don't see but three," I said, barely regaining my voice after being scared witless. "What do you mean, he near 'bout took your finger?" I said as I gave her a hand.

"I"—she gave a heave and came into the boat—
"I was pullin' up the string and all the sudden this
jerk done pulled me overboard. Musta struck the
bait just 'bout the time I moved it. Anyway, I had
the line round my finger and he nearly 'bout took
it off. I was down under tryin' to get shed of the
string sos he could pull on the jug instead of me
and all the time thinkin', We got the big one," she
shouted.

She stood in the boat. "He's got to be round
here someplace."

"There." I pointed to a ripple in the water. She
grabbed her paddle, still dripping-wet, and began
to row. "Get your paddle," she shouted. "This is
the most important part. We got to keep up with
him."

We began to trail after Number Three. We would
spot him as a ripple in the water and give chase. Other times the jug came to float on the surface and
make meandering paths through the water. Sometimes it would disappear altogether and we would
hold our breath until it reappeared. My arms were
on fire. Every muscle in my body ached. I thought
I could feel the water around my feet rising ever so
slightly as I tried to keep up with Maudie's paddling. If I had thought rowing upstream was hard,
it was nothing compared to this. Maudie seemed
never to tire, so caught up in the chase was she.

Finally she said, "We gonna grab the jug and tie
the clothesline to the front of the boat. If Number

Three want something to pull, we gonna give it to him. I'm plumb wore out with rowin'."

"Great. Good plan, good plan." I slumped in my seat.

"Don't stop now. This here is the most important part. We got to catch right up to him." I shoved a weary oar back in the water, mumbling, "You say every part is the most important part." We paddled on, with Maudie giving directions. "To the left, to the left. No, no, to the right, to the right. Now you can slow up. Now you got to go faster. Okay, hold her steady whiles I grab—" She put her paddle down and reached out with both hands to grab Number Three. When she did, it was as if she had caught a line attached to a rock at the bottom of the river. Number Three didn't move. We moved the boat instead.

I paddled backward and Maudie, holding the line, crawled forward to pull the jug out of the water just enough to wrap the line around the bow cleat, the only one on the boat. "Are you sure he hasn't gone under some rocks or brush? That line hasn't moved since you tied it." I peered over the side of the boat.

"Out here in the middle of the river? It must be two hundred feet right here. No, old Number Three just bidin' his time. He get to movin' soon." Sure enough, he started to move and we were pulled along with him. He had decided to head downstream with the current. Off in the distance I could see the front of a set of barges being pushed upriver. Just my luck, I thought, to be slammed into a barge, head-on, by a kamikaze fish.

There was, however, a more pressing problem. Every time Number Three inched us along, he pulled the rope attached to our old boat and that loosened the boards just enough to let in a little water. "Why ain't you bailin', Tab? It's your main job."

I began bailing again. Much more water was getting in the boat now and I had to concentrate on getting it out. "Maudie"—I was humped over bailing—"too much is getting in. I can't keep up." She was unconcerned, eyes glued to Number Three. "Maudie . . ." I pulled on her sleeve, but no answer. I bailed more and then looked up for a moment when I had gotten the water to a point just below my ankle-bone. The barge looked much closer now. It was making the slow turn to angle across the river and position itself to enter the lock channel.

"Maudie"—I pulled on her sleeve again—"we're getting closer to the channel and a barge is coming upriver."

She glanced up. "That barge ain't no bother. We be long past by the time it gets here. Past the channel and we be home free. Just under the bridge and then Miss Maydean's is right there."

"Of course," I said, stomping in the water, "we're going to sink before the barge runs over us, so why should I worry about the barge?"

"You such a baby, Tab." She grabbed the tin can out of my hand and began to bail. "It just take a little work, and you ain't willin' to do it."

"Fine"—I crossed my arms and sat back—"Miss Smartie, let's see what you can do." She began to bail, all the time keeping an eye on the line in the water. After a few minutes she appeared to be making headway and then Number Three gave a big tug. Water oozed through the cracks in the wood floorboards as they separated momentarily.

"Besides," I said, "we don't even know what's on the end of that line. It could be a big river turtle." I glanced at the barges. The tow captain had finished his turn and was halfway across the river, pushing what was, maybe, ten barges.

"Not a river turtle out this far," she said, throwing water back out over her shoulder.

"Well, maybe it's a giant carp. Nobody would pay for a carp."

"It too big for a carp." She was in a rhythm now, dipping, throwing, dipping, throwing. She wasn't making any headway. A shiver went through my body as I felt the water up to my ankles again and looked out at the two front barges that were side by side, loaded high with coal.

Her head was still down concentrating on the bailing. Dipping, throwing, dipping, throwing, she was like a crazy person.

We were drifting and being pulled right up to

the channel crossing. Maybe Maudie was right. Maybe we would be long past by the time the barge got here. It was still at a distance and we were already entering the channel.

Now we were in the middle of the channel, Maudie was still bailing, and the barge was maybe a hundred yards away. Why had I ever doubted Maudie? She knew the river. We had caught "the big one," just like she said we would. I watched her through eyes glazed over with admiration.

Then, without any warning, crazy fish decided he was tired of going downstream. Right out in the middle of the channel, with the barge coming at us, our bow began, very slowly, to turn. We were dead in the water while Number Three decided which way he wanted to go next.

I was transformed by panic. "Maudie," I screamed, "I told you people could get killed out here, didn't I? I told you about the fisherman who got drowned when he was hit by a barge, didn't I? This is all your fault," I raged.

Maudie stopped bailing to look up and see the barge bearing down on us. At the same time the tow captain, way back at the end of the line of barges, had spotted us. There was an earsplitting sounding of his horn. It was all he could do. There was no turning. There was no slowing.

Number Three casually turned and headed straight for the barge. Maudie picked up her paddle and yelled at me. "Get that paddle in the water and paddle for all you're worth." We both dug in, me headed upstream, Maudie downstream toward Miss Maydean, and Number Three to the middle of the river. "Are you crazy?" she yelled. "We goin' this way." I turned around on my seat beside her. Now two of the three of us were going in the right direction.

"We need to cut Number Three loose, Maudie. We'll never make it unless we do," I yelled. Even as I said it, I knew it was useless. We would all three make it together or none of us would make it. I could hear the sound of the lead barges cutting waves into the water.

Slowly we overpowered Number Three. Fear energized us as we pulled ourselves, the boat, and Number Three clear of the channel entrance just in time for the first barges to glide by. Again I went from panic to euphoria. I sat back and pulled my paddle in. "We did it. We did it." I turned to look back at the barges and wave to some of the deck-hands who were bow lookouts. Then I turned to Maudie. She was still paddling like her life depended on it. She looked to me with panicked eyes. "The wake," she said.

I had forgotten completely about the huge surge of waves generated by the barges. It hit us at that moment, raised us up, and sent us plunging down the river. The surge was too much for Mr. Jake's old boat. It had been our guardian for as long as its old frame would hold together, but this last insult to its integrity was fatal. We were hit from the side by a log, or the concrete pillows of the bridge that we sailed under, or some other object as we surfed along. Whatever it was, it threw Maudie and me forward. We grabbed onto the boat's front seat. The floorboards had disappeared and we held on to nothing more than the three or four boards that had made up the bow. We weren't afraid. We were too busy keeping our heads above the water and riding out the waves. Pieces of Mr. Jake's boat shot past us. Backwash from water hitting the bridge pillows threw us from side to side. We crested a wave and flew down the river.

When the churning water began to dissipate and we were finally able to look around, we found ourselves at the entrance to the fishing camp cove. I was overjoyed. We could easily swim to shore from here.

Maudie had other things on her mind. She began to feel around for the board that held the cleat that had been attached to the bow. Sure enough, it was part of what we were holding on to, and leading off the cleat straight down into the water was the clothesline, still taut with the tug of old Number Three.

She began to yell. "Miss Maydean, Miss Maydean, we done got the big one. We done got the big one."

We both began to yell and kick toward the

piers. "Miss Maydean. Miss Maydean. We done got the big one."

Presently Miss Maydean waddled out of the bait shop carrying her shotgun. She held her hand up to shade the sun and see where the noise was coming from. One of her helpers pointed in our direction.

"Lord, will you lookie here what the cat drug in." She laughed and pointed us out to the few remaining fishermen on the piers. "Ottie," she said to her helper. "Go'n out there and see what them girls is yellin' about. Dogged if they don't look like two drown rats." She took a few steps out onto the pier but not too far, mindful of its condition and her size. "I knowed you two was up to no good when the Brothers come wanderin' in here this afternoon lookin' for somethin' to drink. Go'n, Ottie. Take my boat." She pointed to a flat-bottom boat under the pier.

We wouldn't get in the boat with Ottie until he had secured our clothesline to his stern cleat. Then we allowed him to pull us on board and row to the pier.

All the fish camp watched as he began to slowly pull the clothesline in. Our eyes searched the water, waiting and hoping. Up from the murky depths, old Number Three finally appeared, a squared-off blue-gray head swaying from side to side trying to free himself of the hook he had swallowed so long ago. By this time he had run out of steam and didn't give much of a fight, but then, we knew catfish weren't fighters anyway. Sort of the sumo wrestlers of the river. All strength and no finesse. He was big, probably not as big as the one we saw at the fish camp, but in my eyes, the biggest I had ever seen. I knew he was a prize by the way Ottie reacted as he pulled Number Three out of the water and grabbed his mouth with gloved hands. "Ooh eee, you done got you a big'un here."

"Now there's one thing," Miss Maydean said as she held up the five dollars and twenty-five cents she was about to pay us for Number Three. "And this here is serious, what I'm 'bout to say." She looked straight at me. "You listenin', Tab?"

"Yes, ma'am." I couldn't suppress a grin looking at all the dollar bills she held in her hand.

"Well then, wipe that grin off your face. I done told you. This here is serious."

"Yes, ma'am." I stood up straight.

"I don't never"—she shook the dollar bills in my face to make her point—"I mean never, want to hear from nobody that you was down here today. You hear me?"

"Yes, ma'am."

"If your grandmama found out, I'd never hear the end of it. She'd be sicin' the preacher on me for lettin' you go up to the dam, even if it wasn't any of my doin', and I sure as hell don't want no preachers round here. You understand?"

"Yes, ma'am," I said, delighted she wasn't going to tell on me. I sure wasn't going to tell on myself.

She handed the money to Maudie. "And another thing. I don't know whose boat that was got tore up today. The way I look at it, if you too cheap to pay a dock fee at the best fish camp on the river, you deserve what you get." She cackled to herself. "Been tellin' old Jake for years, his boat was gonna get washed away in the current."

We let the screen door of the bait shop slam as we took off across the bottom running and jumping, dancing and shouting in the late-afternoon light. We ran on and on, the Brothers trailing behind, until we had exhausted enough of our delight to sit still. By then we had reached the top of the hill overlooking the valley. We sat down, breathless. Maudie opened her hand. We looked first at the money, then at each other, then back at the money, not believing what we were seeing, where we had been, what we had done.

Chapter 17

It was about noon, several days later, when I heard Mother having a talk with my father on the hall phone. He was at the farm and sometimes called when he came in from the fields for lunch. All the hall doors were open to let in the morning breezes, so I could hear everything she said, even if I was in my own bedroom minding my own business, which, of course, I was.

"The strangest thing happened this morning," she said. "Reverend Mengert called and asked if he could come and have a talk with you tonight. I thought it might have something to do with the historical society, so I told him you would be working late, what with getting the combines ready for harvest. I thought he would say, 'Fine, we'll make it tomorrow night,' but he said he must speak with you tonight. He just wouldn't take no for an answer, so I told him that you would be out of the fields around noon and I would try to get in touch with you. I'm glad you called. Shall I call him back and tell him you just can't make it?" She listened for a minute.

"No, he said it was a personal matter that he needed to discuss with you in private."

She listened some more. "All right, we'll have supper early. Tell him to come on around seven." She hung up the phone and walked back to the kitchen.

I sat on my bed, my mind doing flips. There were reverends and there were reverends, and this was the real thing. The one with the voice of God. The one whose Sunday service was broadcast over the radio. He and my father were friends and sometimes played chess together, but this visit was not for that. He had found me out. I could feel it in my bones. Had he already heard about our fishing near the dam, about tearing up Mr. Jake's boat? Had someone told him that I had taken John out of the basement without permission, that I played too far down the dirt road, that I almost got J.W. killed by Mr. Jake? That was it, Mr. Jake and J.W. No, wait, I'll bet it was about me and Mother making such a mess of the Ladies Help League. For the rest of the afternoon I pondered my various sins, trying to decide which one was the greater.

Of course none of it had been my fault, I would tell him. Circumstances had plotted against me. I was innocent, innocent.

Townspeople conferred with the Reverend when they had a really big problem and wouldn't trust their own preacher. He was supposed to be that wise. I knew it was because they had heard him on the radio like I had and knew he was the Real thing. He even looked the part. White collar, black suit, he was Barry Fitzgerald in *Going My Way*, only taller and not so chubby.

I had talked to him once. Maybe he would remember that and take pity on me. We had been at a meeting of the Valley Historical Society, my pop and I. Mother did not much like history and sometimes I would go along with Pop to keep him company. There was always a program about how we lost the War and then afterward there would be delicious refreshments. Most of the ladies who were in the historical society were Grandmother's age. They fixed wonderful things, brownies, tea cakes, punch, roasted salted pecans. I was usually the only kid there, so the ladies would pile up my refreshment plate.

This particular time, the time I talked to Reverend Mengert, the meeting was held at Fightin' Joe Wheeler's house. Fightin' Joe was a great hero of the War. Well, it wasn't exactly his house. He was long gone, but his daughter lived there. She was older even than Grandmother and loved to talk about the War. So anytime anybody wanted to get together and talk, she would volunteer to have the party—I mean meeting.

Anyway, somebody got up and talked about the time Fightin' Joe and his cavalry ran the Yankees off the courthouse steps in Decatur, Georgia, right before the Battle of Atlanta, but to no avail because the Yankees won anyway. Then at the end of the program all the older ladies would take their handkerchiefs out and wipe their teary eyes and then go get the refreshments—the part I came for in the first place.

The food was always served out in the side yard underneath the big oak trees. There was a grape arbor along the back of the yard with wooden benches underneath. This was where I had talked to the Reverend Mengert. I had a punch cup and a whole plate of goodies, so I needed a place to sit and eat. The Reverend said I could share his bench. "You seem to have a rather large load there, Tab," he had said in his God voice.

"Yes, sir, well, it would be impolite to take something one of the ladies brought without taking some of what all the others brought."

"I think that's very considerate of you. Can I hold your punch cup while you spread that napkin in your lap?"

"Yes, sir, thank you."

"Tell me, what did you think of Professor Wiggin's paper on cavalry tactics in the Georgia campaign?"

"On what?"

"You know, the man who talked to us before refreshments."

"Oh that! Well, yes, it seems to me like the same thing always happens. We start out good, but in the end we always lose. If it's Fightin' Joe in Atlanta or General Lee in Virginia, we always lose, but we keep on talking about it like maybe if we talk enough, we'll win, only we never do."

I leaned closer to the Reverend Mengert and whispered, "To tell you the truth, I would lot rather see a Roy Rogers movie than hear about Fightin' Joe. Roy Rogers always wins. He always wins! Nothing like—'We coulda won, but this happened,' or 'We woulda won, but that happened.' No, no, with Roy, it's simple. He finds out who the bad people are. He goes after them, he catches 'em, and then he sings a song. The end."

The Reverend took a drink of punch. He didn't have a refreshment plate. "It's certainly simpler to win than to lose."

"Would you like me to tell you about *Wells Fargo Days,* starring Roy and his dog, Bullet, and Dale and Gabby Hayes and the Sons of the Pioneers?"

The Reverend Mengert said he would like to hear about it. I proceeded to explain the whole story blow by blow. It had been on at the Majestic just the week before, and I remembered every detail.

I knew he listened, because he asked questions

that showed an enlightened comprehension of the whole matter. "Did the Sons of the Pioneers just sing or did they beat up people also?" The man was wise beyond his years. I could see that.

That night, right after we finished supper, there was a knock on the door and my pop stepped out onto the front porch so he and Reverend Mengert could sit under the fan in the big rocking chairs. The porch lights were off to keep the bugs from coming. This made it easier for me to go out the back door and sneak around into the bushes that lined the front of the house. I crouched down, fingers crossed, hoping to avoid a spanking. I raised up just enough to see the glow of Pop's Camel in the dark.

The Reverend was talking. "It came as a great shock to me, too, Charles. She seemed to be in perfect health. I think these last few years have weighed very heavily on her, what with all the work she puts in each year on the polio drive."

"But what could be so bad that she would want to give up her house? She could go to the rest home, stay awhile, and then come back here. Why sell her house?"

"Well, I think she might have other plans that would preclude her moving back into the house later on."

"Bill Mengert, if I didn't know you so well, I would swear you were trying to cover up something. This could be heaven-sent for me and my family, but it doesn't make any sense for Grace

232

Poovey to want to go to Montgomery to a rest home and at the same time want to sell her house. She's always had plenty of money, so that couldn't enter into it. When old Jesse Poovey was alive, he bought some of the best river bottomland in the county. That alone must be worth a fortune."

"That was years ago, Charles, and Grace spent a fortune sending those ne'er-do-well boys of hers off to McCallie and then W and L. It's just a shame they turned out to be so irresponsible."

He stopped talking. I saw the flare of a match in the dark, the glow from the tobacco in his pipe. Then the steady creaking of rocking chairs again. "I tried to reach her sons but no one seems to know how to find them. The last we heard, they were down in New Orleans, someplace in the Quarter. You can't find anybody in the Quarter if they don't want to be found. They probably wouldn't be of any help and might do more harm than good if they did come home.

"Her man, Ben, came to get me a few nights ago. He said Mrs. Poovey had been taken ill and wanted me to come. I went over to her house and sat with her for most of the night. We had a long talk. The upshot of the whole thing is that she is leaving for Montgomery in . . . in, uh, four or five days and she wants to sell the house before she goes."

"It's just hard to believe. She's always been a pillar of the community. Why would she want to give it all up and leave town all of a sudden?"

Reverend Mengert didn't say anything. He just rocked a few minutes, as if he was thinking. Finally he started talking. "You know, I think sometimes we expect too much of other people. In a small town like Bainbridge, we trap them in roles that they never intended to play. Only the strongest ones can break out and survive." He started rocking again.

I could feel my dad smiling in the dark. "Ever the philosopher. What in the world is that supposed to mean? After all, if anybody enjoys her role in life, it's Grace Poovey. You're getting too mysterious for me."

Reverend Mengert gave half a laugh and puffed on his pipe. "All it means is that I told her I knew of only one person in town who was in the house market and it was you."

"Now hold on, Bill," my dad said. "Mary and I have talked about moving for some time, but after this year on the farm, it's definitely out. What with the dry weather and other things that have happened lately . . ." He paused and rocked for a minute, then he said, "There's just no way I can manage this year, and certainly not a house the size of Grace Poovey's."

Reverend Mengert spoke up. "Not even for eight thousand dollars?"

My father stopped rocking. "You mean she wants half now and the rest over time?" He thought for a moment. "No, I still can't risk it. You never know with farming what the future will bring. Just last week I thought my wheat crop was a sure thing and then . . ."

"No, I mean she wants eight thousand period. That's her total asking price, provided she can get it all now."

"You can't be serious, Bill. The house is worth twice that, maybe twenty thousand. Why in the world would she take eight thousand for that house? It must have four or five bedrooms, and it's on a beautiful lot."

"It has five bedrooms, Charles. Enough for you and Mary and the children to spread out. You said yourself that you all were on top of each other in this house, it's so small. All that room would be perfect for a family of your size."

"It would be ideal, but I can't believe she wants only eight thousand dollars total. Did you tell her it was worth twice that?"

"Yes, I told her, but the circumstances are such that, well, she wants the eight thousand now. She wants to be able to leave town and not have to worry about keeping up the house."

My father took a long drag on his cigarette. Then I could hear the rocker creaking back and forth again.

"Look, Bill, you know we need a larger house in the worst kind of way, but I certainly don't intend to cheat Mrs. Poovey to get it."

"You won't be cheating Grace Poovey. You'll be doing her a favor. Believe me."

"Bill Mengert. Are you telling me everything there is to know about this situation? That's a dumb question. I know you're not telling me everything."

"I'm telling you everything you need to know. You want a house. Grace has a house to sell right away and at a very good price. I've already checked with Joe Bennett over at the bank. He said he would be glad to give you a loan on the house if you bought it. Last, but not least, I'm telling you, you would be doing Grace a great favor. Now, will you consider it or not?"

"If anybody else had come to me with this, I certainly would not, but considering the fact that it's you, of course I'll consider it. I would be a fool not to." He rocked for a moment more in the breeze of the ceiling fan. "Mary will be beside herself. Talk about manna from heaven. She's been kind of down lately, ever since—oh, never mind. She won't believe it."

The Reverend got up to leave. "Well, it's been nice to be able to deliver some good news along with all the other . . ." His voice trailed off as he walked over to the edge of the porch, about two feet from me, and tapped his pipe into the bushes. "Grace will be, uh, gone out of the house Wednesday if you and Mary want to go look at it."

"Wednesday? That's just two days from now," my dad said. "She sure is in a hurry."

"Well, you know the stores close on Wednesday

at noon, so if you like the house and want to talk to Joe over at the bank, you can look Wednesday and then talk to Joe Thursday morning and be ready to give us an answer by Thursday night or Friday morning."

"Five days? You're giving me five days to decide the whole thing?"

"You know what they say—Strike while the iron is hot. I'll call you tomorrow." Reverend Mengert stepped off the porch and down the front steps, heading to his car.

Pop just sat there. He didn't even get up to see the Reverend Mengert to his car. He took the last few drags on his cigarette and flipped it out into the front yard. Then he got out of his chair and opened the screen door to the living room. "Mary, come out here. You won't believe what I have to tell you."

Chapter 18

Mother was thrilled. Of course we took the house. The Ladies Help League was gone from our minds in the euphoria of bedrooms for all. We talked of nothing else at the supper table every night. Everybody would get their own bedroom, to be decorated, within reason, as they saw fit. Everybody except the twins, and they were too little to notice. Tina was opting for pink and white surrounded by ruffles. Charles junior was going for an Indian motif. I had listened to all ideas but felt they were too bland. I planned to surprise everyone with a nightclub theme. The idea had come to me after Maudie read me and the Brothers a story, out of *Photoplay*, about the making of *Casablanca*. I envisioned black walls with dangling beads for the door, a mirrored oval spinning in the middle of the ceiling, perhaps a record player mysteriously squeaking out sitar music. I was sure everyone would be bowled over by my concept.

There were four big bedrooms upstairs. One on each corner of the house, with a roomy hall in the middle. My room had three windows that looked out over the front yard and its own entrance off the main hall. There were built-in linen cabinets on one side of the entrance to my door. So fancy! Mother and Pop were to have a bedroom downstairs. There was a front porch as big as Grandmother's, with a hanging swing and room for rockers.

Several days passed before children were allowed a look inside. Late one afternoon, Reverend Mengert delivered the key to Mother. We pestered her until she walked us the few blocks to Mrs. Poovey's house. It was two blocks away from Grandmother's, but both were on the only fancy street in town, Ridge Road. I carried one of the twins, Tina the other. We hiked up the street like a little refugee army, Mother holding Charles junior's hand. Grandmother met us at the front door to have a look-see.

The inside was nothing like we expected. Cold and damp even on what had been a very hot day. It gave us all an eerie feeling. The furniture was gone except for a broken hand-turned Victrola. There were faded squares all over the walls where pictures had hung. On the landing in between the first and second floors was the pale outline of a cross that must have been on the wall for years. One thing was immediately obvious: The whole inside of the house would have to be repainted. When we looked closer, the curtains were dirty and rotting and would need to be thrown in the trash. And there was dust, dust in every corner and on every windowsill.

Mrs. Poovey must not have cleaned the curtains in twenty years, but it wasn't apparent, because she always had the drapes closed. On the outside, there was a fresh coat of paint. From the street, everything looked perfect.

"Well, no matter about the inside," Mother said. "I warned you not to expect too much. It's such a bargain, we can't complain. But with things like they are, we won't be moving in for some time. Cleaning and patching will take us a good part of the summer."

We began the next day, cleaning, Windexing, scrubbing. Before I knew it, three days had passed since I had been to the fort or seen John in the basement. I was beginning to think having my own bedroom might not be worth all this effort. Besides, whoever heard of a clean nightclub.

Then late one afternoon all of my hard work was rewarded. Mother sent me upstairs with a bucket of soapy water and some new shelf paper to clean out the closet shelves in my room. I cleaned for the most part of two hours, starting with the top shelf and working my way down. As I pulled the last of the old paper off the middle shelf, I noticed that someone had cut the cedarwood wall in two places on the side. Whoever did it cut at an angle so that the wood piece would fit right back in place and hardly be noticed. But I noticed. Someone had lived in this very room long before old Mrs. Poovey. Someone mysterious, like myself. This person had obviously needed a hiding place for ill-gotten loot. Positively shaking with anticipation, I pried the piece of wood out of its place. I couldn't see anything, too dark. The hole looked to be about a foot wide. Just the space between the front and back wall. I was not partial to touching spiders. I got a book of matches from the living room. The light of the match was no help. No money, no nothing. The match was about to burn my fingers when I noticed, right below the opening, a large dark green book standing flat against the wall. I had to pull it out sideways to get it free. As far as I could make out, it was just a big thin notebook. On about half of the pages there were long columns of numbers. At the top of some of the pages there were names. Disappointing, not as good or as mysterious as hard cash, but better than nothing. Maudie would be impressed. I could use the empty pages for drawing pictures. Besides, I needed a hiding place for my valuables. I put the book on the floor, replaced the piece of wood, and put down new shelf paper.

You might have guessed that as soon as the news got out, everybody in town was talking about Mrs. Poovey and why she up and left town.

Tommy was sure it was because the movies and pool had closed. "She didn't want to be in a one-horse town that couldn't even keep the Majestic and the Crystal Plunge open."

That sounded perfectly logical to me, but Grandmother said no, Mrs. Poovey didn't give a flip about the movies. She said if the truth be known, it was probably a great burden of guilt that was hanging over Grace Poovey because she was not faithful to her friends. Anybody who would just out and out go against friends she had known for years and years, friends who had been loyal to her, well, she was just bound to have a guilty conscience about it.

She was saying all this as we sat on her porch and talked in the afternoon. Me in the swing, Grandmother in her wicker rocker, as usual. She was rocking and snapping Kentucky Wonders. "You mark my words, young lady, guilt can drive a person to the depths of despair and well it should, well it should. The Bible is very clear about that."

"Are you talking about Mrs. Poovey not letting Mama into the Ladies Help League and her being a friend of yours for so many years? Is that the part she should feel guilty about?"

"I most certainly am not! Grace Poovey is free,

white, and twenty-one. She could do anything she wanted to in that situation. If she didn't like my own daughter-in-law, well, that was her business." Grandmother began rocking harder and faster. She would snap the end of each bean, then break it in two or three places. She tossed pieces into the colander so hard, they flew, some landing in the pan, some on the porch floor. "No, that was not what I meant at all, but if the shoe fits, as they say . . ."

"Well, if you weren't talking about Mama, what did you mean?"

She stopped rocking and looked straight at me. "I mean, Miss Tabitha, that what goes around comes around. You're too young to understand."

I was about to ask her to explain, but just then we both saw Mrs. Doland Myers coming up the front walk. She had her handkerchief out, wiping her wet face with one hand and carrying her garden gloves in the other.

"Afternoon, Katherine. Come on up here on the porch and sit under the fan for a while. It's just too hot this time of the day to be weeding flower beds."

She walked up the steps and took a seat in one of the spare rockers. "It just helps me to think when I go out among my little beauties and work."

These were her "new little beauties," put in after the mowing down of her "old little beauties" by Mr. Myers. Of course Grandmother and I were not so impolite as to mention it.

"I've had so much on my mind lately, what with all this business with Grace." She fanned herself with the garden gloves, oblivious to the ceiling fan cooling her.

Grandmother bent over to pick up stray beans off the floor. "Well, Katherine, if anybody has an idea why Grace just up and left us all high and dry, it would be you. I suppose you were over helping her pack before she left. How did she seem?"

Mrs. Myers didn't say anything. She just sat there, fanning and looking out in the yard, pretending not to hear Grandmother.

Grandmother raised her head from the beans just enough to look at Mrs. Myers out of the corner of her eye. "You did see her before she left town, didn't you, Katherine?"

Mrs. Myers looked to be on the verge of tears. She seemed to be studying the calla lilies planted around the birdbath in Grandmother's front yard. I knew they weren't as pretty as her calla lilies, but I thought it was nothing to cry about.

Grandmother seemed not to notice the calla lily situation. "After all, Katherine, you were her best friend. No one I've talked to has laid eyes on her. We all assumed you must have helped her pack up."

Now I was staring at Mrs. Doland Myers. Her little face was red; her mouth was starting to quiver. "I . . . I always thought we were close." She touched her eyes with the hankie. "I wouldn't presume to

245

call myself her best friend, but . . . but . . ." She stopped talking and pressed the handkerchief against her mouth.

Grandmother was getting down to business. "Now Katherine, it'll make you feel better, if you have something on your mind, just to come right out and talk about it." She reached her hand over and patted the top of Mrs. Myers's hand, which was resting on the arm of the rocker. Then she took her hand back and started snapping again. "Of course, I wouldn't want you to reveal anything that was told to you in confidence."

Now we all sat there rocking and swinging in silence while we waited for Mrs. Doland Myers to give us the inside dope, if we were lucky.

"She didn't," Mrs. Myers finally said, and then put the handkerchief back over her mouth and looked at Grandmother.

"She didn't what?" Grandmother said.

"She didn't reveal her innermost confidence or any other confidence to me. I haven't laid eyes on her since all this started."

"What are you talking about?" Grandmother was dumbfounded. "If you haven't seen her, then who has? Somebody must have helped her pack, make decisions about closing up the house, disposing of the furniture, all those things. I was over there a few days ago with Mary and the children. The place was completely empty."

"I know," Mrs. Myers said. Her chin was beginning to quiver again. "I've stayed awake nights wondering what it was that I did to insult her. I must be the reason she was angry enough to leave town without even telling me, not even wanting to see me. I called several times and her man, Ben, said she didn't want to see anyone or talk on the phone. She wasn't feeling well. A few days later I called and she . . . she was gone." Mrs. Myers looked at Grandmother. "I feel so guilty. What did I do? What could I have done to make her so, so—"

"Don't be ridiculous, Katherine," Grandmother interrupted her in midsentence. "You weren't the reason she left. Do you believe for one minute that Grace Poovey would give up her entire life here in Bainbridge, sell her home and all her belongings just because of something you did or said?"

"Well, I . . . just thought, it must be me." Up came the handkerchief to her shaky mouth again.

Grandmother stopped rocking and looked Mrs. Myers straight in the eye. "Katherine, nobody in the world would blame you. So just stop trying to make a martyr out of yourself. I won't have a bit of that nonsense. Now tell me. When was the last time you did see Grace?"

Mrs. Myers dabbed her forehead. "Well now, let's see. I think it was when we were planning the fall rummage sale, about a week before she left.

You know the one the Ladies Help League has every year in September in the empty field across the street from the fire station?"

"Yes, I know. How did she seem then? Was she tired or upset?"

"No, no. She seemed perfectly all right. We talked about the sale. It was a lovely afternoon. I always have a lovely time with Grace."

"And you never saw her after that?"

"No, I called her the next day. We were supposed to play bridge over at Nattie Foster's house. Her man, Ben, answered and said that she wouldn't be able to play, for me to get Madge McClure to substitute." Mrs. Myers stopped talking.

"And?" Grandmother said.

"And that was it. We never saw each other again. I heard that Reverend Mengert drove her down to Montgomery to the Episcopal rest home." She started dabbing her eyes. "It's . . . it's almost like she died."

"Now, Katherine. Don't be melodramatic. Maybe someday she'll come back. Have you ever thought of that?"

Mrs. Myers had never thought of that. And neither had I. "Well, I hope she never does come back. Then we might not get to keep her house," I said.

Mrs. Myers and Grandmother turned to look at me. They had forgotten I was even there. "Tab, I think it's about time for you to go home. Your mother will be looking for you for supper. Run along, dear."

I got down off the swing to go home, insulted that they didn't want my opinion.

Chapter 19

All of us were given a temporary reprieve from cleaning while Mother pondered decorating possibilities. She lived at the paint store, hauling home dozens of samples to review with Mrs. McMillan at night.

I headed straight for Maudie and the Brothers, ready to exchange the boredom of Old Dutch Cleanser for anything we might conjure up.

"Where you been, girl?" she greeted. "Miss Mama say they got you workin' like a slave over at that new house."

I smiled, put my hand on her shoulder, and waved up at the Brothers, happy at being back. By this time the Brothers would deign to move their fingers in greeting.

"Well, it wasn't all work. I did find something," I said, handing her the notebook I had found while I was cleaning the closet. I knew she would be impressed when I told her how it had been mysteriously hidden away in the wall.

"This here ain't nothin' but somebody practicin' writin' down sums." Maudie sat against a tree trunk, studying the book.

"You sure you found this here in a hidin' place? Just look like some homework somebody been doin', and they ain't very good at writin' anyway. I can't hardly make out some of them sums."

"I told you, I found it in a secret hiding place. You can believe it or not." If she wasn't impressed with my find, I knew who would be. "I'll bet John would believe me if he saw it. He would know what it is, too. He reads the *Bainbridge Times* every morning, you know." I paused and looked straight at her to see the reaction I would get when I said, "I think we should get him out of the coal cellar again to come here and look at it."

"Just hold on. Hold on. I ain't gettin' John out of no basement again. We was just dumb lucky we didn't get caught last time we got him out. What you wanta go causin' trouble again for?"

"I didn't cause trouble last time. Nobody knew. Besides, it just seems to me he should get out once in a while."

"If you wants him to look at the book, why don't

you take it and drop it down to him? Then he won't have to come out of his toy cellar."

Eager to play the game of spiriting him out of the cellar, I rambled on, making up as I went along. "Well, Maudie, if I have to explain, it's like this. If I take the book to him, somebody might see me with it and they would say, 'Tab, where did you get this book?' and then I would have to say, 'I found it in a secret compartment in my bedroom closet.' Then they would say, 'Show me where that is,' and then I would have to show them. Then everybody would know about my secret hiding place. All on account of you telling me to take John the book."

"I don't care what you say. I ain't gettin' no John out of no basement. My Miss Mama would skin me alive if ever she come to find out I had anything to do with him gettin' out of that cellar. You know that."

"Oh you're just scared, Maudie. That's all. Just chicken. Nobody will know."

"You ain't gonna pull that chicken stuff on me. I ain't doin' it and that's that." She started turning the pages of the book again, pretending she was studying the numbers.

"Okay, then, I'll do it."

Maudie looked at the Brothers and shook her head. "White peoples is crazy."

"So, John, what are you doing down there?" I was lying on my stomach, looking down at him through the open window.

"I'm reading the morning paper." John was sitting in his father's big old overstuffed armchair. On the table beside it was this cup of coffee that Miss Mama brought down to him each day. The chair was his daddy's before he died. It had been stored in the attic until this summer, when Mrs. McMillan had it brought down for John to use. If you didn't know better, you would think he was forty years old, sitting there, except that his feet didn't touch the floor.

"I can see you're reading the paper. What are you reading about?"

"Well, there is a very interesting article in here about the Ladies Help League. It says they have lots more money since Mrs. Poovey gave them all the proceeds from the sale of her house. Did you know that? Did you know Mrs. Poovey took all the money you paid her for her house and gave it to the Ladies Help League? Wasn't that generous?"

"Yeah, that was real nice, John, but don't you ever read any comics like 'Dagwood' or 'Dick Tracy'?"

"Of course I read the comics first, but Mother says it's important to keep up with what's going on in Bainbridge. Mother says my father's family has been here in Bainbridge for so long and I'm the last of the McMillans and someday I'll be a leader in the town."

He looked up at me over his glasses. "So I have to keep up with what's going on."

"You can't know what's going on if you stay down in that basement all summer."

He turned the page to start another story. "I can keep up with things. Besides, I told you before, I like it down here."

He pushed his glasses up on his nose, looked up at me, and smiled. "Would you like to see what Mother brought me yesterday? It's a new—"

"No, I'm tired of kid stuff. How would you like to see what I found in a secret compartment in old Mrs. Poovey's house?" I told him all about cleaning out the bedroom closet and the book with numbers. "The thing is, John, I couldn't make out what it was, and even Maudie didn't know what it was. I told her you would know, since you're so smart and all."

He was still looking at the paper. "Sounds to me like it's just what Maudie said, some child's homework, but give it to me and I'll look."

"Well, I can't. I left it in Fort Polio. You'll have to come out to see it."

"Why do you keep calling it Fort Polio? It's nothing but a place in the woods."

"How do you know? You never have seen it."

"You told me all about it."

"Yeah, but you haven't seen it. There's a big difference."

After another twenty minutes, I persuaded him to come see for himself.

I said I would be back when the time was right.

Chapter 20

The paper said aerosoling for our part of town would begin today at 1:00 P.M. Time to get John out of the basement for a visit to the fort. Tina was across town with her best friend, DeDe Marsh. I told Mother I was tired out from staying up late the night before. I believed I would take me a nap during spray time. Immediately she was suspicious. She felt my head for fever, then checked my throat and peered into my eyes. Satisfied, she said I could take a nap in peace and quiet because, more than likely, I wasn't catching it.

I went on to my room, pulled down the shades, turned on the floor fan, fluffed up the pillow in my bed and pulled the sheet over it. Then I climbed on out the window.

John and I ran across my backyard onto the dirt road. The cropdusting plane was beginning its run just as we reached the drainpipe.

"You know we are not supposed to be outside when the plane releases its DDT." He stood just inside the drainpipe, looking up. "We'll get stained yellow."

"I know, but we're safe in here," I said. We came out the other end of the pipe. "Well, here it is." I spread my arms wide and smiled. "So, what do you think?"

John didn't say anything. He walked up the little slope and over to the stick table Maudie had made. Then he went over to the hammock we had put up. He pushed the hammock with his hands and watched as it went back and forth. "I don't remember being in a hammock before."

"Get in and I'll swing you."

"Oh no, I might lose my balance."

"Just one swing won't hurt."

"Well . . ."

"I'll hold it and you get in."

He looked at it suspiciously but finally got in and, lying on his back, looked up at the tall pines covered in kudzu vines. I started to push him, a little higher each time.

"Now isn't this nicer than any old coal cellar?"

"Well, it is nice."

I gave him one more big push and walked over to the place in the kudzu vines where I kept the book.

"Catch." I tossed it to him on a swing toward me. He didn't catch it, of course, but it did land in the hammock, and he picked it up and started to study the pages.

"Keep swinging me." He lay back in the hammock, pretending to study the book but enjoying the ride more.

I gave him another big push and then turned when I heard Maudie and the Brothers coming through the drainpipe. Maudie took one look at John and rushed up to the hammock to pull it to a stop.

"What did you have to do that for, Maudie? He likes it."

"What's he doing here anyway? A whiskey car is coming down the road right now. I can tell by the way it's slowing down lookin' for the mailbox."

"What's she talking about, a whiskey car?"

"Shhh," Maudie said. We were all standing still except John.

"Just keep still," Maudie said.

"Why should I keep still?"

"Never mind, John," I said, "I'll tell you later. Just sit still for a few minutes and don't say a word. Then I'll swing you again!"

We saw Mr. Jake come up to his mailbox, but this time it was different. He stood there waiting for the car to come.

The car stopped alongside the mailbox. A colored man pulled up the hand brake and started to get out. He was smiling and halfway to the mail-box when Mr. Jake said, "Ain't no use comin' round here. Ain't nothin' for you in the mailbox today."

The man was still smiling. "What's the matter, Mr. Jake? You done sold all your good stuff to the white folk?"

"I ain't got no stuff for you till you put some-thin' in the mailbox. It's been three weeks since you done paid. I ain't runnin' no department store."

"You ain't never bothered to keep count on me before. Why you in such a fix to get your money now? I been comin' here for ten years and you ain't never been so smart before."

"All them years you had steady work. Now you ain't got a job no more. Besides, you drinkin' 'bout three times more than before. I remember what you told me about your boss lady. There's bound to be plenty of money. I knowed she took good care of you before she went away."

The colored man laughed uneasily. At the same time he backed up toward his car. "You ain't been listenin' to no old man out of his head with drinkin', have you? Ain't nothin' I said 'bout her true. Ain't nothin'." He backed into the fender of his car. His hands felt along its side until he reached the door handle. "I'll get you your money if you don't pay me no more mind than that." Then he got in his car and drove away.

After he left, Mr. Jake shuffled off down the road and we could move around again.

"You didn't tell me your fort was so close to Mr. Jake's house. I know about him. He's a dangerous man. Don't you know that?" John was looking at me like I was crazy. "You could get killed down here."

"Oh, we don't worry about those people," I said. "They can't see us in here. As long as we stay quiet . . ."

He took his glasses off to get the maximum impact. "You . . . you both are being very foolish." He repositioned his glasses with both hands. "Why, if my mother knew I was down here . . ." Now he was trying to get out of the hammock. "She would be so . . . so . . . disappointed."

Maudie grimaced at an attitude so insipid. "Disappointed? Disappointed? What kinda talk is that? My mama would kill me, just flat out kill me. You act like you mama don't even care about you."

"Of course she cares. She would just be greatly disappointed to know I was associating with the likes of Mr. Jake Terrance. She would be surprised that Mr. Ben was associating with him, too."

"Mr. Ben who?" I asked.

"That was the colored man Mr. Jake was talking to. He used to be Mrs. Poovey's driver and handyman before she left town. Everybody knows that. He drove her to our church every Sunday. I've seen them together many times. Don't y'all know

261

anything?" I watched as he tried to get to the edge
of the hammock.

He finally got himself out of the hammock by
putting one foot down on the pine straw and
rolling onto the ground. "Now look what a mess
I've made of my clothes." He started brushing
leaves and pine straw off of his pants and walking
to the drainpipe at the same time. "I'm not staying
here another minute."

"But wait. You were going to tell me about the
book. What is it? What do all those numbers
mean?" I walked after him.

"Oh that. I think it's just like Maudie said.
Somebody doing their homework in an old ledger
book. It's like the kind Mother uses down at the
Farmers' Co-op. Come on, Tab, let's get back.
Spraying time is over. Everybody will be coming
outside soon."

Chapter 21

It was midsummer now and polio was still on the rise. Time for the faint of heart, and those who could afford it, to leave town.

There were no plans at our house to abandon ship, but the adults were beginning to feel the pressure. Only the night before, Charles junior had started coughing at the supper table. Mother and Pop had practically run into each other getting to him to see if he had a fever. When they felt his head and decided he was all right, they sat back down and continued to eat even though Charles junior was still coughing. Finally he cleared his throat and said he almost choked to death on a piece of cornbread and didn't anybody care?

"Of course we care, dear," Mother said.

I said, "Yeah, Charles, you can choke to death all you want to, but just don't get polio. Then you'll really be sorry." Mother didn't see the humor and drummed her fingers on the table, waiting for me to stop smiling.

Several of the Scout mothers decided to send their daughters to a camp in Mentone, Alabama. It was not very far away, but up in the hills, so no polio. J.W. had gone on up north to visit his cousin in Louisville and work on his farm. Some of the other boys went to Boy Scout camp up in Nashville.

None of them was there the day it happened.

It was midmorning. I was sitting at the kitchen table eating an apple. Everybody else had left the table. Pop had gone to the farm. The little kids were playing on the front porch. Mother had put blankets over the chairs to make a large playhouse for the twins and Charles junior. Tina was sitting out on the porch reading the latest issue of *Screen Guide* and baby-sitting.

Out of my window I noticed Miss Mama. She was standing with her hand on the screen door of the McMillans' house. Just standing there. Finally she pushed the door open and started slowly down the steps. She walked on the path from her door to ours.

Mother was at the sink washing turnip greens, a job she hated.

"Hey Mama, here comes Miss Mama, and she's acting real strange," I said.

Mother sighed and turned off the sink water. "What do you mean, Tab, 'she's acting real strange'? I hate it when they act strange. I never know what to do. I wonder what she's mad about?" She glanced out the window. "Maybe a cup of coffee would help." She started toward the cabinet to get a cup, but it was too late. Miss Mama was already at our back screen door.

"Good morning, Miss, uh, Mama," Mother mumbled. She hated calling her Miss Mama. She said Miss Mama was only a few years older than she was and she felt silly saying it. Once, she had called her Mrs. Barton—that was Miss Mama's last name. The minute Mother called her that, Miss Mama started to laugh.

"Ain't nobody called me that in twenty years. Everybody calls me Miss Mama 'cause I was thirteen when my first baby come."

Mama's face got red as a beet and she never did that again.

"Won't you come in? I was just telling Tab, a nice cup of coffee would taste good right now. Maybe you would like . . ."

She stopped talking because Miss Mama had opened the screen door and we could both see these big tears running down her face.

Mother rushed over to put an arm around her shoulder. "Why Miss Mama, what in the world is the matter? Are you ill?"

"Maybe she's catching polio," I offered.

"Hush, Tab. Come over here and sit down at the table."

Miss Mama sat down slowly and picked up a dish cloth off the table. She began to fold it in her lap. She kept looking down at the dish cloth and shaking her head.

Mother tried to be solicitous. "Now Miss Mama, whatever it is, it's not the end of the world. Don't you want to tell me? Maybe I can help."

"Not the end of the world for you maybe, but for me . . . and for little John it is." She folded the dish cloth into a tiny napkin. "Ain't nothing you can do. I done called the doctor and he say he be over here directly. I told him ain't no use to hurry, 'cause I sure am sure—she stone-cold dead."

"Stone-cold dead? What on earth are you talking about? Who's stone-cold dead?"

Miss Mama took a deep breath and looked up at Mother with eyes brimming.

"I hated to tell you 'cause I know y'all is such good friends, but . . . but it's Mrs. McMillan. She— she done passed in her sleep last night."

"What?" Mama's face went white. "What are you saying? I saw her last night. We sat on the porch and talked until past dark. . . ." Her voice trailed off while she stared at Miss Mama. I was staring at her, too, with my mouth wide open and a big bite of apple in it half-chewed.

Mother began untying her apron as she turned toward the back door. I jumped out of my chair to follow her.

"No, Tab. You stay here with Miss Mama and keep her company. I'll be back in a few minutes. Maybe Edna's very ill, a stroke or something that's left her immobile."

She was out the door. I watched as she ran across the yard to the screen door. Then she slowed down and pulled it open quietly.

"She ain't had no stroke. She stone-cold dead. I knows dead when I sees it. I saw my mama when she passed. She just like that. Been dead all night, I judge."

I started chewing my apple again, mesmerized by curiosity. "Was she—were her eyes open and staring at you? Did she have a terrible look on her face, like, you know, like people in the movies when they get shot?"

"Naw, she was just lyin' there nice and peaceable, like she was restin'."

She put her elbow on the kitchen table and rested her forehead in her hand. "I come to work this mornin', and John, he was standin' in the kitchen waitin' for me. I says, 'John, how come you ain't down in the cellar yet? How am I gonna bring you your coffee if you don't go on down there? Didn't your mama tell you to go down before she left for work?' He just kinda shuffles his feet round and looks down at the floor and say, 'My mother is

267

sleepin' late this morning and you shouldn't go in to bother her.'

"I said, 'What you talkin' about? Mrs. McMillan never sleep late in her life,' and I starts toward her bedroom. Well, John, all of a sudden he come on me and starts pushin' me back into the kitchen and sayin', 'Don't look at her. Leave her alone. She's just sleepin' late. I saw her. I know if she's sleepin' late.' He pushed me plumb back to the sink and put his little hands around my waist so I could hardly move.

"I says in a real nice voice, 'Now John, you know I got to go see 'bout Mrs. McMillan. She might have took sick and need me to get her some aspirins. Now you let Miss Mama go.' I coulda just pushed him away. You know he ain't no bigger than a bean pole, but I don't wants him to feel less a man, seeing as how he the only man of the house we got. Well, all the sudden he just drop his arms from around me and turn and walk to the basement door and go on down to the cellar."

Just then I saw, through the window, Mother walking slowly back to our house. "I just can't believe it. I just can't. Miss Mama, I didn't mean to doubt your word. It's just that—I saw her only last night, and now . . ." Tears began. "We were talking on the porch. We said we would have one last cigarette before we went in for the night." She swallowed hard. "She is—she was the best friend I had here in Bainbridge—"

"So she really is dead," I said.

"Yes, Tab."

I was sure it must be something like the only death I had ever known, death on the big screen. "Is she turned all blue or something, or is there blood all over the place? Or does she—"

"Tab, this is not the time for vivid descriptions. Just take my word for it—she has passed away. It's just like she went to sleep and never woke up."

"Well, do you think she got polio in the middle of the night?"

"No, it wasn't polio. Probably a heart attack. She told me once that her mother died at a rather young age." She stood staring at the sink, like she was trying to think of what to do next.

"Did you say Dr. McAllister would be here soon, Miss Mama?"

"He say he come as quick as he can, but he have a little child mighty sick in the polio ward. He said he send the ambulance if he can't get here his-self."

"What about John, Miss Mama? I went down to the basement and tried to tell him about his mother. He just sat there in his big chair and put his hands to his ears. 'Tell Miss Mama to bring me my coffee! Tell Miss Mama to bring me my coffee.' That's all he would say. He wouldn't even look at me. I tried to put my hand on his shoulder and he screamed at me to leave him alone. He said I wasn't even supposed to be down in his basement." She choked back tears. "He said I might give him polio and then he would get sick like his mama."

Mother sat down wearily in the kitchen chair across from Miss Mama. She picked up the *Bainbridge Times* and didn't notice she was fanning herself with it. "When I tried to explain that his mother didn't have polio, he just put his hands to his ears again and started whistling to drown out my voice. Poor baby, he must have found her this morning before you did, Miss Mama."

"More'n likely," Miss Mama said. "He usually gets up every mornin' and goes and climbs in the bed with his mama, so they can have a nice talk to start the day. Mrs. McMillan used to laugh and say he know more 'bout what goin' on in the world than she do. She say, it on account of his readin' the papers all the time. Well, he mighta knowed what was goin' on in the world, but he sure don't know much about gettin' on in the world." She looked out the window at the house, blinking tears out of her eyes. They ran down her face. "He was raised a pet, you know. I done told her and told her, she holdin' that boy too close."

After Miss Mama said that, we all sat quietly for a while, letting the reality of it sink in.

Finally Mother turned to me. "Tab, you go on over and talk to John until the doctor gets here. Just talk to him through the window. Don't try to get in the basement. It might upset him."

"Well, what'll I talk about? Can I ask him if he saw his mama dead?"

"Absolutely not. Tab, for heaven's sake, child. Try to be a little more sensitive."

"I . . . I don't know what to say." Now my chin began to quiver.

"Just chat with him and keep an eye on him. Try to say kind things, sweetheart. Miss Mama and I need to go see if we can find a telephone number for the sister down in Lower Peach Tree. I think she is the closest family they have. Oh, Miss Mama, we need to call Bill Mengert—he can call her sister—and I need to see if I can get Charles at the farm." Mother went on out to the hall phone.

I walked next door, repeating to myself, "Kind things, kind things." I crawled under the red tip bush by the window and knocked. Nobody came, so I knocked again. Still nobody came. Then I slowly pushed the window open. There he sat, pretending he was reading the newspaper.

"Hey, didn't you hear me knock? Come here and hook up the window. I can't hold it all day; my hand gets tired."

"I don't want to talk right now. I'm reading the newspaper."

"Well, it must not be very interesting, 'cause it's yesterday's paper. I just saw Buddy throwing today's, not half an hour ago."

He didn't say anything, just kept turning through the pages of that old paper.

I lay there on my stomach, looking down at him. My chin was propped on top of the hand that wasn't holding the window up. I always liked lying at the window, feeling the cool air from the basement racing past my face to the outside. The grass felt damp on my stomach and the morning sun was warming the back of my legs. This was not at all like I had imagined it would be when someone died. The world hadn't stopped. All in all, it was a perfectly nice day except for John's dead mother. This was not like the movies. In the movies when people died, the sky darkened, there was sad music.

"Listen, John, I'm, uh, I'm sorry about your mother. My mama said it must have been a heart attack."

He didn't say anything. Like I hadn't even said it. Like I wasn't even there. He pretended to read the paper. In a louder voice, I said, "I'm sorry about your mother."

He kept looking at his paper. He still didn't look up, sitting there acting like he was all alone. So then I shouted at him, "I SAID, I'M SORRY ABOUT YOUR MOTHER!" I could tell he heard me that time. He jumped when I yelled.

Finally he let his hands and the paper drop slowly into his lap, but he still wouldn't look up at me. He stared straight ahead, talking to the wall. "She said nothing would ever happen to me if I minded and stayed in the basement. So I'm staying right here and I'll be okay." He pushed the paper to the floor and pulled his knees up to his chest. He locked his arms around his legs. Slowly he looked up at me, and there were these big tears in his eyes. "I'll be okay, won't I?"

I couldn't think of what to say. I just looked at him.

Then he took a deep breath, got a mean look on his face, and shouted at me so loud I jumped and almost let the window hit me in the face.

"I SAID, I'LL BE OKAY, WON'T I?"

There was a long silence while I tried to think of the right thing to say. "Well, uh, heck yeah, John. Now you can come out of the basement whenever you want to."

He didn't like that. He began to cry, staring at the paper on the floor.

Off in the distance, I heard the sound of the ambulance siren.

Chapter 22

We waited to have the funeral because Mrs. McMillan's sister lived so far down in south Alabama. She had to catch the train out of Lower Peach Tree and then change trains in Montgomery.

My father had explained to all of us that our family would act as John's family until his aunt Nelda arrived. He and the Reverend Mengert sat on the porch that night and planned the funeral. Mother and I stayed next door receiving food. Farmers from down at the Co-op came by with big bushel baskets of beans and tomatoes. They would come to the door and hand Mother the baskets. Not one word would they say. Just hand us the food out of their gardens and leave. Mother tried to get them to come in. "Won't you stay and have a glass of iced tea?" Of course they wouldn't. I could have told her that, but sweet Mama didn't know any better than to embarrass them.

For the most part, Mother was handling everything just fine until Eugene, old "Eugene, Eugene the Potato Machine" came to call. She recognized him when he got out of his pickup. He had on his Sunday suit with pants legs three inches too short. She watched from the window as Eugene fetched up his one last sack of sweet potatoes. Before he hit the front steps Mother was on the porch to greet him. He came to stand in front of her with his potatoes. "I'm Eugene Wav—"

"I know who you are," Mother said, and flung her arms around his neck, tears streaming. Poor Eugene was so taken aback, he almost dropped his potatoes.

"Well, ma'am," he stammered. "I . . . I just thought, well, she said her son, John, was partial to taters."

"Oh, yes, he certainly is. We all are." Mother sniffed, still holding Eugene in a neck lock. "You are so thoughtful to bring them by."

"Well, I thought she . . . "

"Oh, she would be so pleased, so pleased," Mother said, still holding on. Finally she let go to get out her handkerchief. "Now Mr. Waverly, I insist you stay for a glass of iced tea. Sit right down here on the porch. I'll be right back." Before he could say a word, she rushed to the kitchen to fix him tea and a refreshment plate, mumbling to herself, "He's just like you said. He's just like you said."

They sat there for a good long time, Mother doing most of the talking, Eugene, Eugene mostly shaking his head and eating his refreshments. When he got up to leave, Mother hugged him again long and hard, as if she were trying to squeeze away any sadness he might feel. She stood there watching him and crying as he cranked his battered old Ford and drove off down the block, out of sight.

Now, the town people were different. They would come and bring delicious food and then end up spending the whole afternoon or evening sitting around talking about the dearly departed Mrs. McMillan. This was not a polio death. This was a good old all-American heart attack. It was all right to come to the house and not worry about taking home germs. It was all right to visit and talk about it.

The dining table was getting piled high with things to eat. Miss Mama was in the kitchen making gallons of iced tea and lemonade. I was running back and forth to our house to get extra ice.

The Lane Sisters—they were two old maids who lived up on Ridge Road—came by and brought a homemade cake with burnt caramel icing and pecans on the top in the shape of a cross. They stayed most of the afternoon talking away to Mother about how they loved children, and "Wasn't it sad about John being all alone now?" Just as they were about to put on their gloves to leave, Miss Julia—she was the older one—called Mother aside and said they wanted to adopt John and would it be all right? Mother gave her a hug and said that was very generous but John's aunt Nelda was coming up on the train from Lower Peach Tree and she would be taking John home with her.

All this time, John was still in the basement, except at night, when he came over to our house and slept in the bedroom with me. He took Tina's bed and she slept on a pallet in the room with the twins and Charles junior.

The next morning he would get up and go back over to his basement, only there was nobody to bring him coffee. Miss Mama was too busy wrapping food and putting it in the refrigerator and making more iced tea.

All day long as the neighbors came with food, I would run halfway down the basement stairs to tell him what new goodies had arrived.

The afternoon the Lane Sisters came, I ran down to tell him about the caramel cake and how they wanted to adopt him.

He picked up a Lincoln Log and threw it at me. He missed of course. "I hate those stupid ladies. You go tell them to get out of my house right now."

"You're just a spoilsport, you know. They have

a real big house. You could put your toys all over the place."

He didn't answer.

"Okay, okay, be like that," I said. "If you want to leave, just go ahead and leave. What do I care?"

He missed me with another Lincoln Log. I stood there with hands on my hips. "You're acting just like Charles junior," I said.

He started pretending I wasn't there, playing with his Lionel engine. He was putting a pellet in the smoke stack so it would look like steam was coming out when he ran it.

"My aunt Nelda is taking me. We had a long talk when she called last night." He was fitting the engine on the tracks, talking to the engine. "Mother used to say she was very nice. She never went to college like Mother, just got old enough and started having children. She married a man named Luther, only I never met him, but I know he works in the sawmills down in Lower Peach Tree."

He had put the engine and half the cars on the track and was checking to make sure the track pieces were secure. "She has two children, you know. My cousin Butch, he's twelve and likes to play football. I'll have to share a room with him, she said." He got up and took the transformer cord to the wall to plug it in.

"I said that was quite all right, because I play football, too."

"You do?" I said.

He stopped fixing the train and looked up at me with a surprised expression. "Don't you remember when we played this summer down at Tommy's house and we won the game? I told Aunt Nelda I was the best player on the team."

"You did?"

He looked my way again, tapping his fingers on the top of the engine. Now he was getting mad at me.

"Of course I told her that. You told me I was a very good player. Remember? You said so yourself. You said I did a perfect job playing center. Remember? Remember?" He stared at me with frightened eyes, waiting for the right answer.

"Oh yeah, I forgot about that," I said quickly.

He looked at me and shook his head. I was not up to his standards, as usual. He sat back down on the floor. "Now watch when I turn the train on. It will go around the track and smoke will come out of the stack just like a real steam engine."

He turned the switch and it started around the track. It went round and round in a big circle, past the little bitty train station, over the little bitty bridge, faster and faster, only the steam part didn't work. It never did.

Chapter 23

I wore my black patents and a Sunday dress. John had his usual white Peter Pan shirt with short black pants and kneesocks. For this occasion he wore a black jacket over the shirt. John announced, the morning of the funeral, that he would sit by me because he had never attended a funeral before. I had explained to John that I was an expert on the matter, having attended the funeral of one of the colored people on the farm last summer.

We stood in the kitchen for Mother's inspection. "I think your aunt Nelda would like—"

"I am *not* sitting with Aunt Nelda, thank you. I am sitting with Tab."

Mother decided to leave well enough alone. "That'll be fine. We'll all be sitting together anyway." She poured herself another cup of coffee. It was all I had seen her eat or drink for the last week. "What does it matter anyway?" She walked over to look out the kitchen window, across the drive to John's house. "Thank heavens for the new house. I don't think I could stand to look out this window another—" She turned to look at me and John standing there waiting for instructions. "Tina will be in charge of Charles junior. I have a sitter for the twins." She stopped, tearing up, as she looked at us. "Why don't you two come over here and sit down. Would you like anything to eat before we go?" I shook my head no.

John piped up immediately, pointing to Mother's cup. "I think it would be nice if you would share."

"What?" Mother said.

"John wants some of your coffee, Mama. His mother lets—she used to let him have a cup every morning." John sat there shaking his head to confirm it.

"She did?"

"Yes, ma'am. Two sugars and lots of cream, please."

"Oh, why not." She got another cup out of the cupboard.

We stood in a small anteroom waiting for the church to fill. Most of Bainbridge was there. I waved through the window to Grandmother and all the aunts and uncles as they passed by. Then we marched in to sit down front. There was only me and John, Mother and Pop, Miss Mama and Aunt Nelda. Aunt Nelda's husband, Luther, didn't come. She said he couldn't get off work.

Tina sat up in the balcony with Charles junior in case he had to make a trip to the men's room during the services. This was Charles junior's latest trick. We could be in the middle of any activity, I mean *any* activity, and Charles junior would take great pleasure in announcing to the world that he had to go and he had to go now. Since it was a newly acquired skill and not something to be toyed with, we would rush to accommodate him immediately, even though half the time it was a false alarm.

John and I walked down the center aisle, looking everywhere but at the coffin. This was the first time I had ever been in the Reverend Mengert's church. It was smaller than the Methodist but more beautiful. The Episcopal church had been one of the first churches built in Bainbridge. It was made of old stones from the river and filled with stained-glass windows.

Immediately I realized an Episcopal funeral was nothing like my farm funeral. Where were the ladies in white dresses to bring you hankies? Where were the men in black suits to carry you out when you fainted? Where was the choir, the wonderful shouting choir?

John looked up at me trustingly. Not to worry, I said with my smile. I could handle this. I began to study the program. As far as I could tell, we would be here for at least three hours. I picked up a fan for me and one for John. We were fanning away when the music began. I grabbed the program to find my place. By the time I saw hymn 289, everyone was already singing. I whispered to John that we would skip this part and go on to the next thing. After that, it was a maze of protocol to my Methodist-trained eye. Put down the hymnbook, pick up the prayer book. Put down the prayer bench, pick up the program. Kneel to pray, stand to sing, sit to—to what, rest? I was amazed that the Episcopalians ever got anything done, they were so busy doing.

Finally, mercifully for me, the Reverend Mengert walked to the pulpit. He put a piece of paper down and began to talk about Mrs. McMillan in his God voice. He didn't sound like any preacher I had ever listened to. His voice didn't rise at the end of a sentence. It was calm, like he was telling a story we were meant to hear. I was soothed even as I listened. He said she had come to town as a stranger, that she had lost her husband to the war, that she had tried to provide a good home for her son, John, and that she treasured him above all else. We all sat there thinking about her and crying like we were supposed to. Finally he seemed to finish what he had written.

He folded the paper and the congregation moved in their seats, ready to stand. Then he cleared his throat and looked out at us. Everyone settled back down. He hadn't finished. He had something else to say.

"Edna McMillan was a wonderful mother," he said. "She tried so hard to do the right thing." He paused to look over at John, who was too busy drawing a picture of a train on the funeral program. "But sometimes things don't end up like we plan them. They never quite do," he said. "I can speak from experience. I can testify to that." He paused again as if he was searching for what to say next.

"These summers are so hard on us all. Hard because we don't know what's right or wrong. Shall we let our children drink the water, play in the pool, associate with someone who has had or might have polio?" He shook his head. "The problem is, we can't let the fear end up being worse than the polio. We can't lock ourselves away from life and living for fear of what might happen. At some point we must step out on faith."

There was silence as everyone watched him, some waiting to leave, some wanting to hear. He cleared his throat. "Do I need to tell you? Will it help to hear it once again? One of the basic concepts of our faith." He stood there with the palms of his hands open to us. "Be not afraid, for lo . . ."

He waited for us to finish it in our minds. Then he turned around and walked back to his seat.

Mother and Pop gave each other a questioning look. John finished his train picture. Aunt Nelda began to pull on her gloves.

We sang another song with a tune I had never heard before and then we went down on our knees for one last silent prayer. Mine was, "Thank you God for making me a Methodist."

Chapter 24

The next few days were taken up with everyone helping Aunt Nelda and John pack up things to ship down to Aunt Nelda's house. My father even took a half day off work at the farm to move big boxes and furniture from the cellar and attic. Mother said we should forget about our new house until all this was settled.

The more Aunt Nelda packed, the happier she seemed to get. "I can use this dining table in my house," or "Oh, won't all these kitchen things come in handy."

John was down in the basement packing all his toys in precisely the right order. He started out trying to pack them alphabetically, but when he got to ball, bicycle, and boomerang, he decided it wouldn't work. After that, he put everything in according to size.

I would go in the house and sit on the basement steps while he packed. He wouldn't let me help. He had a tape measure to measure everything and see if it was the right size to go in a certain box. If it wasn't, he would cry.

"This is dumb, John. Why don't you just put stuff in a box 'til it's full and then go to the next box?"

This did not sit well. "That's just like you, Tab. You're so messy. If you don't like the way I do it, just go home and leave me alone."

I discussed this with Mother when I went home to have a peanut butter and banana sandwich for lunch that day. "All he does is get mad at me and cry because his toys won't fit in the right box. I don't know what to do. I'm mad at him leaving here."

She was standing at the counter with her back turned to me, making more sandwiches for the twins.

"You know, Tab, your father and I were talking about John last night. If we didn't already have so many mouths to feed, we might think about . . ." She stopped to get plates to put the sandwiches on.

"Think about what? You might think about what?"

She was staring at the picture on the Blue Willow china plate in her hand, the one where the two lovers are running over the bridge to escape. "Oh, never mind. Why don't you take John some of those old shoe boxes in your closet? Maybe he can use those for his smaller toys."

The morning came for him to leave. Aunt Nelda had dressed him in ordinary clothes. She had bought him play shorts, a shirt, and some Keds as a surprise.

"Now you look like a real boy," she said.

He looked strange, completely out of his element. He was sitting on his suitcase in the front yard, waiting for my father to pack the car with all Aunt Nelda's new acquisitions. Aunt Nelda was standing with her frizzy hair piled on top of her head and her train dress and gloves on, talking to Mother about when the moving truck would come to load the furniture.

He sat there looking down at his Keds like they weren't part of the rest of him. I ran back in the house and looked under my bed. I wouldn't be needing it anymore, since I wasn't a member of The Club. I got back outside just as they were getting in the car. Mother gave him a big hug and a kiss. John didn't seem to notice much. He stepped into the car and sat there looking straight ahead. I handed it to him through the window. Of all of his toys, he didn't have a football. He gave me a glimmer of a smile and put it in his lap. Then the car backed out of the drive and drove on down Oak Street toward town. About halfway down the block, J.W.'s dog jumped out from behind some bushes and chased the car, barking it all the way out of sight.

Mother stared at where it had been. She fumbled for the handkerchief in her apron pocket and wiped away the tears hard, mad at herself for crying.

"That child is no more able to cope with the outside world than . . . than . . ." She put the handkerchief to her mouth. "Sometimes I think the fear is almost as bad as the damned polio."

She didn't apologize for cussing, just turned and walked back to our house.

All at once, I was very tired. I went around to the side of the McMillans' house and sat down by John's window that was shut fast. For the first time since Miss Mama came to tell us the news, I cried.

Chapter 25

Summer was coming to an end. The polio ward at the hospital was full of people from all over the county. I visualized what life must be like for them, sitting up in their beds with all the ice cream they could eat, donated by the local drugstore. Stacks of comic books courtesy of Woolworth's. Each day the newspaper listed new treats contributed by some local group or merchant. This day's paper had said that they would have all the free Dr Pepper they wanted. It couldn't be all that bad.

I ate breakfast each morning, trying to avoid looking out our kitchen window at the McMillans' empty house. Straight to Fort Polio, the place I felt most comfortable now. It had been so hot and dry that Maudie said we would have to take all of our things out soon. The leaves were starting to wrinkle up on us.

"Mr. Jake and all them peoples buyin' whiskey don't never need to know we was here. Next summer we can start up again." She was talking and putting empty tin cans on a shelf she had made by hanging an old swing seat from a tree branch. "Now we have us a place to put things like marbles in this can, and pencils for writin' in this can, and if we have food, we put it up here, 'cause last time the ants got to my pineapple sandwich I brought for lunch." She brushed the dirt off her hands. "All in all, this here has been a good summer, but me and the Brothers is ready for school to start. Pretty soon we gonna go shoppin' for school supplies. I been to the Woolworth's seven times, tryin' to pick out the right pencil box." She patted her pocket, filled with the money from old Number Three. It never left her side. She looked up at the Brothers playing in the tree house. "Hey Brothers, let's see how fast y'all can get down out of them trees. When I say slide, come on down that rope fast as you can." The Brothers smiled, always ready to do anything she said. "Okay, now slide!" They jumped, one at a time, onto the big barge rope and were down on the ground in no time. Maudie smiled as she watched them scramble back up into the tree house. "That's been a good lookout place if I do say so." She sat down at the stick table to mend some of the broken sticks. "Next summer we gonna have even a bigger fort. Next summer we'll build some stick chairs and some cots up in the tree house for the Brothers to rest in." She stepped over to the edge of the kudzu to get more mending vine.

We pooled our lunch that day. I had come with five baked sweet potatoes and a jar of iced tea. Maudie had stacks of Ritz crackers with mayonnaise in the middle and cornbread. We piled our food in the middle of the stick table and allowed the Brothers to come down out of their lookout to eat.

Then we settled in for the afternoon. "I guess . . . well, I guess we can be friends forever," I said. I was using the back pages of my secret notebook to draw a picture.

"What you talkin' about?" Maudie said. She was trying to braid a basket out of kudzu vines.

"I mean, I guess you won't be leaving like John, and I know I sure won't be leaving like that." I took a broken brown crayon out of the tin can holder. "It just seems to me we could be friends as long as we lived if we stayed right here and always kept our fort in the summer." I pitched the brown crayon back in the can and got out a red one. I was making the red stripes for the Brothers' shirts. I gave Maudie a sideways glance. "Well, doesn't it seem to you that way?"

She was concentrating on weaving the wet vines she had soaked in creek water. "I ain't always stayin' here," she said.

"What?" I looked up, alarmed. "You aren't leaving, too? I thought you said Miss Mama got a new job down at the foundry."

"Miss Mama is gonna be here, but me, someday I'm gonna go be a famous teacher. Remember, I done told you that."

"Oh, yeah," I said, relieved, "I know about that. But 'til then?"

"'Til then, we always be friends," she said, and smiled over to me as she reached for another piece of vine.

I shook my head yes and put the red crayon back and got out a black crayon to draw in Maudie's curly black hair.

The Brothers, back in their perch, dropped a pinecone on us. We sat there quietly, not paying much attention, as Mr. Jake walked up the path carrying a paper bag. At the same time we could hear a car coming down the road. The driver was weaving from one side to the other. When he finally came to a stop, he was on the opposite side of the road from the mailbox. I looked at Maudie and we shrugged our shoulders.

Mr. Ben got out of his car very slowly. He shut the door and held on to the side of the fender as he walked around the front. Then he came across the road to Mr. Jake. I had never seen a drunk person up close before. His eyes were red and bloodshot. He had what I thought was a silly look on his face. He was trying to smile at Mr. Jake and at the same time put his hand on the mailbox to steady himself. "I come to talk serious business, Mr. Jake." His shaky hands reached into his back pocket and brought out an empty bottle. "This here was the last of my whiskey. Can't get no more from nobody in town 'cept you."

"Well, you can't get none from me neither 'less you pay for it in cold hard cash."

"I done told you, Mr. Jake, I ain't got no cash right this minute."

"Bring me some of that money your boss lady done left you. Then you can have all the whiskey you want," said Mr. Jake.

Mr. Ben raised his hand high above his head. He threw the glass bottle on the ground. It broke into a hundred pieces. "I done told you and told you. You wrong 'bout that. She didn't have no money in the first place. She done run out of regular money two years after ol' man Poovey passed. He didn't leave her nothin' but debts and a few acres of scrub up near Scottsboro." He paused to steady himself, putting both hands back on the mailbox. "Peoples all time sayin' how rich me and Mrs. Poovey was. Wasn't a breath of truth to it."

"Now don't you go tellin' tales, Ben. Everybody in town knows Mr. Poovey was rich as sin when he died." Mr. Jake had his hands on his hips, eyeing Mr. Ben.

"Well, I'll tell you now." Mr. Ben blinked to focus. "If the truth be knowed, ol' Poovey done run hisself off the river bridge on purpose. Wasn't no accident. He done left her to face all the hard times by herself when he lost all his money. Why if it wasn't for the Ladies Help League, we woulda starved to death."

"Well, bring me what she got from them ladies, if that's where she got her money."

"I can't find it. I done looked for it all over."

Mr. Ben had tears coming in his bloodshot eyes, or maybe it was the sweat pouring off his face. I couldn't tell. He got a handkerchief out of his coat pocket and started wiping his face. "She used to keep it wrote down in a book, all we had took from the Ladies Help League. What was for our retirement and what was to spend. I figure she musta give the book to the preacher the night he come over. That was the night she got to cryin' and carryin' on 'bout what a sinner she was. I tries to tell her she just feelin' low 'cause it was the same time to the day, ten years ago, Mr. Poovey done passed. But she just keep sayin', 'I done shamed myself with so much pride. I done caused hurt and humiliation.' I told her she ain't hurt nobody. I told her she never did let them little polio childrens want for nothin'. Told her she always gets them braces, even if she did gets 'em free from the hospital in Birmingham. Didn't nobody know about it in Bainbridge."

Mr. Jake seemed to be getting very interested in what old man Ben was saying. I wished they would finish their business and leave.

"Everybody was thinkin' the Ladies Help League paid for 'em, but they didn't. That way, we can save the money from the Ladies League and use it to live on and a little left over for our retirement. She used to say it almost rightly hers anyway, seein' how she start the Ladies Help League in the first place."

Mr. Jake took a small glass bottle out of the sack he was carrying, twisted off the top, and took a drink. "Now look here, Ben. Are you standin' there tellin' me ain't nobody ever suspicioned y'all was takin' that money when it didn't belong to you? Takin' money that was supposed to be for the polio children?" He handed the bottle over to Ben to take a drink.

Mr. Ben's eyes lighted up. He took the bottle real eager and had a big swallow. Then he had another and commenced to lean against the mailbox like he was going to preach a sermon. "No sir," he said, "we had 'em all fooled. See, the way it was was this." He took another drink and licked his lips, almost smiling now. "We would send the little crippled children down to the hospital in Birmingham to get them braces. The first time Mrs. Poovey was gonna pay when they sends us the bill, only they never sends us no bill. They just mails us a letter sayin' how they fitted them braces and they was happy to be of service to the Ladies Help League. They say they foundation pay for the braces. So Mrs. Poovey done kept the money. The children done kept the braces and everybody was happy. Wasn't nobody hurt by it. After a while, Mrs. Poovey just got to where keepin' the money was natural. I knowed all about it, too, 'cause I was the driver. You see the way it was was this." Mr. Ben took another long drink. His hands had stopped shaking. He even seemed relaxed now. "Every time I was gonna drive them childrens and they mamas down to Birmingham to get braces, she say, 'Now Ben, you go on by the bank and park right in front so President Carter can see you and see who you got in the car. Take this check from the Ladies Help League and get it cashed. When you're on the trip, use only what you need for gas and give the children's mamas two dollars so they can have dinner at Brittlin's Cafeteria before y'all come home. You take enough for your dinner and bring the rest right back here to me. And not a word to anybody.' She say we need the money for our retirement. Course I knowed we needed it for buyin' food, too. Everything woulda been all right if she hadn't got to feelin' so sad of herself that night. You know"—he pointed his finger at Mr. Jake and swallowed another big gulp of whiskey— "if you don't mind me sayin' so, white peoples get theyselves so tangled up in what they suppose to do, they forget what they should do. That night she starts cryin' and carryin' on, sayin', 'Go get the preacher. I needs to confess my sins.' I say, 'You ain't no Catholic, Mrs. Poovey. You just 'Piscopal.

'Piscopals don't do no confessin'.' But nothin'
would do but she have to have the preacher. So I
goes to get the Reverend Mengert. I says to him,
'She don't know what she sayin'. She out of her
head.' He go into the living room and they starts
talkin'. Then he commences to get upset. He say
she done broke the law and she gonna have to pay
back the money.

"I'm sittin' in the kitchen listenin' to 'bout
everything they says. Then she commences to
blubberin' more and more. She say she gonna be
the laughin' stock of the town and she can't never
hold her head up again." Mr. Ben took another
big drink from the bottle he was still holding. "She
say she sure enough shamed the name of Rutherford Westmoreland. I guess that's when the
preacher took to feeling sorry for her. He say he
try to help her if he can. So now he—"

Just then one of the Brothers sneezed. Maudie
leaned her head back to put her finger to her lips.
It didn't do a bit of good. He sneezed again.

I froze, not moving a muscle. Mr. Ben was staring hard into the kudzu.

"What you got goin' on back there, Mr. Jake?"
Mr. Ben was holding on to the mailbox.

"I ain't got nothin' goin' on. Whatever back
there ain't none of my doin'."

"You got somebody back there listenin' to
everything I says?"

"That's just the liquor talkin', Ben. Nobody

cares 'bout what you say." He put his hand on Mr. Ben's shoulder to steady him.

Mr. Ben pulled away. He walked back toward his car. "We just see what we see," he said, going around to the back and opening his trunk filled with gardening tools.

"Now come on back here, Ben, and finish your story," Mr. Jake said.

Mr. Ben paid him no mind. He rummaged around among the tools until he found what he wanted. "Here it is, here it is." He lifted out a big World War II machete.

"Ain't nobody gonna go tellin' on me." He started back across the road.

"Now Ben, you workin' up a sweat for nothin'," Mr. Jake was saying. "Probably just some dogs chasin' a possum."

"You know that wasn't no dog chasin' no possum."

Mr. Jake walked over to Mr. Ben and pushed him with one hand. He collapsed on the ground. "Now sit down there before you hurt somebody. I'll have a look-see." He took the machete out of his hand and slowly walked over to our kudzu cover.

I was so scared, I couldn't move. Mr. Jake started swinging the blade in a big arc above his head. Then down into the kudzu. Leaves went flying in every direction. The big knife cut into the heavy vines like they were spaghetti.

I must have stood up and backed into the shelf

with all the cans on it, because all the sudden you could hear this big crash of cans hitting the pine-needle floor and rolling around. The cutting stopped for a minute as Mr. Jake stood still, listening. Old Mr. Ben was staggering up to his feet again and heading back to his car. He grabbed a big can out of the open trunk and staggered back on down to where Mr. Jake stood looking into the kudzu. Mr. Ben twisted off the lid and began pouring gasoline all over the kudzu. I could smell the fumes and so could Mr. Jake. He turned and grabbed Mr. Ben with one hand. With the other hand, he hit him so hard the gasoline can went flying, landing over in the kudzu, gurgling out the rest of the gas.

"You old fool," Mr. Jake yelled. "You want this whole place to go up in smoke. I got a house and the best still in the county down there. I ain't gonna have some fool nigger burnin' it up. Get on out of here," he yelled. "Now," he yelled even louder.

Mr. Ben slowly pulled himself up off the ground and staggered back toward his car door. Mr. Jake watched him go, then turned back toward the kudzu. He walked over to right the gasoline can. "Now let's just see what we got in here." Maudie's hand tightened on my shoulder. He stepped back to pick up the big jungle knife. Just as he raised the blade to swing it again, he saw, out of the corner of his eye, the book of lighted matches Mr.

Ben had thrown through the air. It landed in the gasoline and kudzu and made a big booming noise as flames raced up the vines into the trees. I couldn't believe how quick it was. Fire was all along the ground and in the trees in seconds. The green leaves were burning just as fast as the dead ones. I could already feel the heat from the flames turning my cheeks red. I looked around for Maudie. She had run over to see about the Brothers. She whispered up into the trees. "All right now, Brothers, slide down! Slide down quick! You can do it." She was half-talking, half-whispering up to them. They looked down, too scared to move. Smoke was swirling up into the pine trees. She started shaking the big rope in desperation. "I said, jump, Brothers, jump. Please jump! You can do it. I know you can do it."

I had never heard Maudie say *please* to the Brothers before. It didn't work, either. They still stood there like statues, not moving a muscle. Now the smoke had made them completely disappear from sight. I could hear the flames crackling around us.

Finally she stepped back, took a deep breath, and yelled as loud as she could. "You jump on that rope or I'm gonna blister your fanny 'til you can't sit down for a week." There was silence as we stared up into the smoke. Finally, sliding down the rope, with big smiles on their faces, came the Brothers. "You get on down to that drainpipe this minute." She grabbed their hands to pull them toward the drainpipe.

And me? All I could do was stand there holding my notebook, watching Maudie and then turning to stare out through the fire and smoke at the sun sparkling on the big jungle knife.

Maudie was yelling at me to run, yelling at the top of her voice. She didn't care who heard her now. I stood there and looked through the fire, to see Mr. Jake throw down the knife. He ran over to Ben and started hitting him. Then he turned and ran off down toward his house, leaving Mr. Ben sitting on the ground.

I could hear her from the drainpipe opening, yelling at me, "Run, Tab. What's got into you? Run! Tab, the fire is burnin' too quick to save anything! Run!"

I couldn't move. My legs were so heavy, they stuck to the ground. Smoke was in my eyes and throat. I needed to run, but I couldn't.

Flames were in the fort now, catching on all the dead wood we had pushed to one side earlier in the summer. Suddenly Maudie was there. She grabbed me by the arm and pulled me down the slope toward the drainpipe. I fell in the creek and the muddy water brought me to my senses. We all ran into the drainpipe, where we stopped to catch our breath. "We got to get out of here quick before that fire spreads all over creation. Now you gonna come this time, Tab?"

"I'm coming," I gasped.

We dashed out the other end of the pipe and up the trail. Just as we came out of the bushes onto the dirt road, he was standing there big as a tree swaying back and forth. We all stopped and looked at each other. Mr. Ben stared at me. Then, Maudie, the Brothers, and I took off running again all the way up the dirt road, past my side yard, and out to the sidewalk in front of my house. We looked around to see that nobody was following us. They weren't, but we kept running anyway. Up the sidewalk to the top of the hill, then left along Ridge Road. We probably would have run on down to town, but we noticed the Brothers were having a hard time keeping up. So we ran inside the big magnolia tree in front of Grandmother's house.

We stood there gulping in air, looking wide-eyed at each other.

I was furious with Maudie. "Why did you have to yell at me like that?" I shouted at her, between trying to breathe. "Why did you have to call out my name like that? I'm the only one in town named Tab. Now he knows for sure who it was."

"Well, what you expect I should do, Miss Smarty Pants? I coulda let you stand right there and get your whole self burned to a crisp. Don't go blamin' me just 'cause you got too scared to move a muscle. If I hadn't yelled at you, you still be standin' there."

"I would not," I lied. "I was getting ready to run.

Now Mr. Ben will go tell my mother I been playing where I wasn't supposed to. Now I'm gonna be in a bunch of trouble and all on account of you yelling my name."

"You think that's all you got to worry 'bout? What's the matter with you, girl? Didn't you hear what old man Ben say when he was talkin' to Mr. Jake?"

"Well, yeah, but—"

"But nothin'. He say he help Mrs. Poovey steal money from the Ladies Help League. Now he know you heard him say it. Now he know you can get him in trouble with the police."

"Well, he said the Reverend Mengert knew, and he didn't call the police on Mrs. Poovey."

"Mrs. Poovey a white woman. He's a colored man. Besides, the preacher don't know old Ben helped out Mrs. Poovey with the stealin'. He just think of old Ben like he was part of the house or somethin'. Now you done found out his secret. I 'spect he gonna come lookin' for you." She was breathing easier now. She sat down on the ground, between the branches, and leaned up against the tree trunk. "And another thing. If I was to guess, I 'spect that book you got there in your hand . . . I 'spect that book was Mrs. Poovey's. It probably have a lot to do with her stealin' monies from the Ladies Help League, else why would it be hid like that? That the reason Mr. Ben lookin' at you so keen back there on the dirt road."

I looked down at the book—I had forgotten I still had it in my hand—trying to decide if she was telling the truth. "You can't scare me by saying stuff like that, Maudie. What about you? He . . . he'll come after you, too," I said, desperate to find company in my misery.

"He don't care about me. I can't do him no harm."

Just then we heard the siren from the fire truck heading down to the dirt road.

"Mr. Ben won't come after me. Why should he? Besides, what did I ever do to him?"

"You so like a child sometimes, Tab. You think just 'cause you didn't do him no harm everything gonna be all right. Life don't work like that."

The Brothers came over and sat down real close to Maudie. We decided to stay hiding out in the magnolia for the rest of the afternoon.

Chapter 26

That night, trying to put Mr. Ben out of my mind, I made an extra effort to help out with supper. Mother had spent all afternoon up at the new house and was tired. It was her first time up there since the funeral.

"Poor old Grace Poovey," she said. She was standing at the sink peeling potatoes. "You can tell by her house, she never gave a thought to herself. She hadn't painted a room or changed curtains in twenty years. With all that money, it would have been so easy to have it redecorated. But no, she was too absorbed in her work with the polio children."

I bit my lip. "Yeah, well, she wasn't that great, Mama. Besides, if she hadn't gone to the rest home, we wouldn't be getting her house. So I'm glad she's gone." You would be, too, if you had heard old Mr. Ben, I thought.

"Tab, what do you have against poor old Mrs. Poovey? I know she didn't want me in her club, but she worked herself sick trying to help get braces for all the little polio victims. She couldn't be all bad."

"She didn't like you, so I don't like her."

Mother picked up a hot pad to help with taking the roast out of the oven. "Tab, you know some people here think I don't fit in, and they may be right. What I'm saying is, it may not have been all Mrs. Poovey's fault."

"You said yourself she was narrow-minded, Mama."

"Well, I thought she was, but when I go up to that house, I can see the person she must have been. No regard for herself. She truly sacrificed." She lifted the top off of the Dutch oven and steam rose up in her face, making beads of water on her forehead. "You know, maybe we should go to Knoxville for a visit after I get the house cleaned out. It would be great to see some old friends. Before we move in for good, we could go for a visit. What do you think?"

"Yeah, we could go to Knoxville and I wouldn't have to listen to old Maudie trying to scare me," I said without thinking.

"Miss Mama's child, Maudie? Now what would she scare you about?"

"Oh, nothing. We were just playing. I'll put the ice in the glasses and get the loaf bread and we'll be ready to eat, won't we?"

Mother looked up at me, surprised. "Well, yes, I guess we will. Thank you for being so helpful without my even asking."

We sat down to supper when Pop got home.

"I heard old Jake Terrance had a big fire down the dirt road today," Pop said. "They said down at the bank this afternoon that he had to call both the fire trucks to put it out." He looked up at Mother and winked. "Musta been brewing up a special batch that got out of hand."

Mother smiled back. "I could see the smoke from our backyard. I wondered what that was all about."

"Say Pop"—I hurried to change the subject—"I heard Mr. Peterson got it today. They had to take him to the hospital. He couldn't breathe and started turning blue and—"

"Never mind, Tab. We get the idea. I'm sorry to hear about Mr. Peterson."

"Yeah, well, I was thinking—that is, me and Mama were thinking. It's probably time to go to Knoxville for the rest of the summer. Things are getting too bad down here for us kids to stay."

He was startled. I knew he was thinking of how lonely he would be if we all left town. I, on the other hand, was trying to spare him the sight of his darling girl lying face-down with a machete sticking out of her back.

"Tab, you're always the last one to want to leave me. Why are you, all of a sudden, so anxious to go?"

Then Tina got into it. "Yeah, Tab, not getting to be a scaredy-cat, are you? Last summer you kicked and screamed not to go."

"Well, it's Mother's idea," I punted. "If she wants to go, then I think we should go with her."

"Mary, is that right? Do you want to take the kids and go, right in the middle of moving into the new house?"

"Well, I did mention going for a visit, but I've never known Tab to be so adamant about going."

Everyone turned to look at me. My face burned. "Nobody ever likes what I say. If I don't want to go, you don't like that. If I do want to go, you don't like that. What's the matter with y'all? Can't you make up your minds? If that's the way you feel, I'll just take my plate in the kitchen and eat by myself!"

"Well, what's got into her?" Tina said as I picked up my plate and iced tea and walked into the kitchen.

I was thinking to myself that Tina was such a baby. She probably hadn't even seen one of those big World War II jungle knives.

Chapter 27

A week went by without incident and I began to breathe easier. Mr. Ben was nowhere to be seen except in my dreams, where he appeared nightly swinging his big blade. Maudie May, the Brothers, and I were making do with a lesser hideout up the road, closer to Maudie's house. When things cooled off, we would sneak back down to our old fort and see if anything was left. Next summer we would find another place to build.

Nobody had said anything else about going to Knoxville. We were all busy cleaning up the new house. "You children have been very helpful," Mother said at supper. "Now the fun part comes. No more mops and Old Dutch Cleanser. You each get to choose the color you would like to have in your bedroom. We'll set to work tomorrow painting. Tab, we'll do your room first."

She handed me a piece of paper with paint samples on it. "Select the one you like and I'll get the paint first thing in the morning. We can start tomorrow after lunch."

"Is it gonna be just me and you painting? That'll take forever. Why can't Tina help?"

"Too many people with paintbrushes would be a mess. No, just you and me, kiddo. We'll have a good time doing it together. Then when it's Tina's turn, I'll help her with her room and you can keep an eye on the twins and Charles junior. She'll watch them while we do your room."

"They don't have the color I want on here." I scanned the color chart. "I want black, so I can make it look like a nightclub, like in the movies. Then I'll put up posters and red curtains. I'm going to have beads hanging down for the door. Did you see in *Casablanca* where the nightclub owner—"

Tina shuddered. "That's just what I need, a nightclub in the bedroom next to mine. Mother!"

"Never mind the movies and the black walls."

"But Mama—"

"You have to use one of these colors on this piece of paper." Mother reached over and poked the sample chart with her finger. "It's this or nothing."

"Okay, okay. None of these colors are any good. I choose this one."

Mother took the chart back from me and

smiled. "Sunshine Yellow! How nice! I'll get it tomorrow."

The next day, after lunch, we started painting with Sunshine Yellow. We painted straight through the afternoon. By the time we started on the window trim, it was getting near suppertime. Mother decided she better go check on Tina and the other kids. "When you finish this last front window, Tab, put the top back on the can good and tight. Wash your brush in the bathroom sink and then come straight home. It's getting cloudy out and it may rain, so hurry along. I need to start supper. Your father will be home soon. Can you do the rest by yourself?"

"Of course, Mother. What do you think I am anyway?"

"Remember to put the top on the can tight."

"I know, I know. I'm not a child."

As I painted the trim, I watched her out the front window walking down the sidewalk toward our old house. The Sunshine Yellow was not half-bad. Not as good as black, but it did cover up all the old gray paint that was there before.

When I finished the window, I went into the bathroom to wash out my brush. The electricity was still turned off in the house and the bathroom only had one window, so it was dark in there. I was feeling around for an old towel to wipe off my brush when I heard the screen door to the kitchen slam. Mother must have come back to see how my room looked. I went out in the hall and yelled down the stairs.

"Hey Mama, come see how nice it looks, all finished.

"Hey Mama!" I walked down the hall and leaned over the stair railing to see who was there. Not a sound. Maybe I hadn't heard anything after all. Maybe it was just the wind.

"Tina, is that you come to get me for supper?" I said, hoping. "If that's you, just say so. I'm coming."

I listened and strained my ears to hear her answer. But nothing. Probably it was Maudie May come to try and scare me. "Maudie?" I whispered. Still no answer.

When I heard the first footsteps sound on the kitchen floor, I knew it wasn't Maudie or Mama or Tina. The steps were too heavy for a woman. They would walk a few feet and then stop, like they were looking around for something or somebody. I leaned out over the railing, with my eyes glued to the first few steps below. There was no other way up to the bedrooms and no other way down. I waited for what seemed like an hour, hoping the footsteps would leave, but they didn't. They were looking in all the downstairs rooms. They even opened some of the kitchen cabinets. Finally I heard them come into the hall.

My eyes were hurting to see something, anything. Suddenly my heart stopped beating. The paintbrush in my hand dripped a few drops of

Sunshine Yellow down the stairwell. They fell onto the top of a gray felt hat starting up the stairs. His right hand held on to the wall to steady him as he slowly climbed to the second floor.

All I could think of was me standing on the dirt road holding that green ledger book, looking up into Mr. Ben's face.

I ran back to my room and shut the door, but there wasn't a lock on it. Damned old Mrs. Poovey was too cheap to put locks on the doors. This was all her fault anyway. I backed away from the door just enough to run smack into the can of Sunshine Yellow and spill it all over the place. Oh great, Mother was going to kill me for messing up the floor, except that I knew I would already be dead by the time it was her turn.

The footsteps had reached the top of the stairs and were coming down the hall. I heard them go into the other bedrooms and then come toward my door. Looking around for the last place to hide, I opened the closet door and stepped inside.

The footsteps opened the door and walked into my bedroom. My heart was beating so loud I couldn't hear the knob turn in the closet door, but I could see it.

He stood swaying back and forth. His eyes were circled in red. I could smell the whiskey. He was dressed in his old coat and tie, like he did when he worked for Mrs. Poovey.

"Hi, Mr. Ben." I held the brush up. "I . . . I was

just doing some painting here in the closet. Uh, how do you like the color? Sunshine Yellow, you know. I see you got a little on your feet."

He looked down at his shoes. They were spotted yellow from stepping in the spill.

"I was just getting ready to start on the closet, but it's late, so I guess I'll do it tomorrow. My mama has supper ready for me now. We're having black-eyed peas and cornbread. My favorite. I . . . I can't be late for that. I'll see you later."

He blinked like he was trying to get his eyes to focus on me. I edged past him into the bedroom and started to back toward the door. He grabbed my shirtsleeve and held it tight.

"Hold on. You ain't goin' nowhere till I say so." He was blinking his eyes like he could barely see, and every time he breathed I could smell whiskey.

"I come to get my retirement. What you done with it? I saw you with me and Mrs. Poovey's retirement book down at the fire."

"Me, Mr. Ben? Me? I don't have any retirement. I just found that book while I was cleaning. That's all I found. I didn't find anything else. Honest!"

"Don't you 'honest' me. You the one had the book me and Mrs. Poovey used to keep trace of our retirement money. Now, where it at?"

He started to shake me back and forth. It wasn't a hard shaking, though. Mr. Ben was in slow motion. "Where it at? I say." His words were slurred together.

"The book? The book? Well, it's right in there. Right where I found it." I pointed to the wall beside the middle shelf. "I put it back right where I found it, Mr. Ben, honest! See for yourself."

His bleary old eyes turned to look at the shelf. "I clean forgot about her hidin' place in the closet. I done sawed it for her myself years back," he mumbled.

Still holding my shirt, he stepped into the closet. He pulled the piece of wood out of the wall and let it drop to the floor. Then he took the notebook out but didn't even look at it. He threw it on the floor and stuck his hand back in, searching until his arm was in the wall up to his shoulder. "Here it is. Here it is," he shouted. "Maybe she done left something for old Ben after all." He pulled out an old shoe box and put it on the shelf with his free hand.

"I guess you found just what you want, Mr. Ben," I said, pretending interest. "And it sure is a dandy shoe box, too. Probably good for storing comics or . . . or, whatever it is you want to put in there." I was still trying to pull away from his hand. He held tight to me with one hand and took the top off the shoe box with the other.

I watched his face search the box, hoping he was going to be happy with what he saw.

"Ain't nothin' left but two dimes," he said, mumbling to himself, "two dimes," shaking his head.

"Well now, Mr. Ben, two dimes, you can do a lot with two dimes," I said, holding on to my sleeve and trying to twist it out of his hand. Still pulling, I stepped out of the closet and right into the yellow paint. "Two dimes can buy you two comic books or . . . or two malted milks." I gave another pull on my shirt. "You could get four Coca-Colas or four candy bars. That's good, isn't it, four candy bars?"

He looked up from the dimes he had picked up and turned toward me as I fought to get loose. "Hold on there. Now jus' you hold on there," he said, not letting go.

"I myself would buy two Baby Ruths"—I pulled hard—"and two"—I gave one last jerk—"Long Boys." With that, I slipped on the yellow paint and fell. Mr. Ben held fast to my shirtsleeve and fell on top of me. I started yelling and kicking. "Don't kill me! Don't kill me! I don't have your retirement. I'm just a kid!" I screamed.

One last pull and my shirtsleeve ripped away. I jumped up and ran out the bedroom, down the hall to the steps, taking them two at a time. At the bottom of the stairs, I looked back to see if he was following me, and ran smack into Mother coming into the house.

"Mama, Mama, thank goodness you're here," I said, breathing so hard, I could barely talk. "I, I, he, Mr. Ben—"

"Tab, what in the world is going on? Your shirt is a mess."

"It was—it was—" I was taking big gulps of air, but I couldn't get the words to come out.

"How in the world could you get that much paint on you in such a short time? You promised me you would be neat. Your grandmother stopped by the house, so I brought her over here to see how well you had done with the painting. Now look at you. You've even tracked it down the stairs."

Just then, Grandmother closed the front door behind her. She walked over to me half-smiling. "I told your mother you weren't old enough to be left alone with a bucket of paint."

"It—it wasn't like that," I gasped. "It—it wasn't my fault. It was all Mr. Ben. He tried to kill me," I shouted.

"What in heaven's name are you talking about, child?" She looked at Mother. "I believe in encouraging imagination, Mary, but this is ridiculous."

"Tab is usually very responsible for her age, Mother Rutland. I know she has a good excuse for all of this . . . this mess, don't you, Tab?"

"I do, I do. I'm trying to tell y'all. It's Mr. Ben. He made me slip in the paint! He tore my shirt! He kept saying I had his retirement, but I don't have his retirement. All I have is his green book."

"What green book? Tab, are you feeling all right?" Mama was giving me a strange look. "You're not making sense, sweetheart."

319

"If you ask me, she's light-headed from breathing paint fumes all day," Grandmother said.

Mother took a deep breath. "Let's let Tab tell us what happened, Mother Rutland."

"If she can." Grandmother sniffed. "Sit down here on the steps, child. You look all flushed."

I kept standing. "I can tell you! I can tell. I been trying to tell y'all, but you won't let me. It was Mr. Ben's fault. He saw me with the green book down by the kudzu fort the day of the fire, so I guess he thought I had his retirement. I guess he thought he could come in here and make me give it to him, only I don't have it."

Mother's eyes began to narrow. "What fort? What fire? Tab?" Her face was going white. "You . . . you didn't have anything to do with that big fire down by the dirt road the other day, did you?"

"Little girls who are allowed to run around acting like little boys have a tendency to get into things they shouldn't," Grandmother couldn't resist saying.

Mother seemed not to hear her, she was concentrating so on me. My breathing was getting back to normal now. I was beginning to get uneasy. Some fast backpedaling was in order. "No, ma'am, I had nothing whatsoever to do with that fire. I told you a million times, it was all Mr. Ben. It was all his fault. Not five minutes ago I thought I was a goner, a goner! Now you act like it was all my fault. I'll have you know I didn't do one single thing wrong."

Mother's eyes narrowed to slits. She stared at me unflinching.

I was caught. I could tell by the look. "Okay, so I took the ledger book and put it in the fort. I'll admit that."

Her hands went to her hips. One foot began to tap.

"Okay, okay, so the fort is on the road where I'm not allowed to play, but it's gone now anyway."

"Wait just one minute here, Tabitha Rutland. I've told you a hundred times never to go down to the other end of the dirt road."

"I know, Mama, but . . . upstairs. Don't you want to know how Mr. Ben—"

"No, I don't give a flip about Mr. Ben. I want to know why you went to play where I expressly told you not to. Let's hear it and let's hear it now!"

How could I have gotten myself in this mess? Now I had to tell her everything. She probably would kill me. I backed up to lean against the wall. My knees buckled and I slid down to sit on the steps. Tears were coming. Not tears of remorse, but tears of frustration at being trapped.

I began at the beginning, when we built the fort. I told all about Mr. Jake and the whiskey business. About how nobody could see us except on the day of the fire. About me and Maudie and the Brothers. Of course, I left out the part about fishing on the river and almost getting J.W. killed. I felt it was not pertinent and would only confuse her.

All this time Grandmother was saying things like "What do you expect when children go unsupervised?" and Mama was biting her tongue, she was so mad at me and Grandmother. When I got to the part about Mr. Ben and Mrs. Poovey and the Ladies Help League and stealing the money, Grandmother's ears perked up.

"Grace Poovey would never do a thing like that," she interrupted. "Why, that's unheard of. People just don't do things like that." She broke in again while I was talking. "Oh, this is ridiculous. I don't know why I'm listening to this. It couldn't be true," she said.

"You're certainly welcome to go on back to the house if you like, Mother Rutland," Mother said. "I can deal with Tab. She has a lot more explaining to do."

Grandmother didn't hear her. "This is all just idle speculation," she said. "We have not got one ounce of proof positive. If any of this was anywhere close to the truth, we would have some evidence of it."

Suddenly she looked to me. "Well, Miss Tabitha, if any of this tall tale is true, where is this green book you're supposed to have?"

"That's what I been trying to tell y'all," I fairly shouted. "It's upstairs with Mr. Ben in my bedroom, where he tried to kill me."

Grandmother gave a hard laugh. "If he is, why haven't we heard from him? Old Ben in your bedroom? Not likely. Even he has more sense than that, with or without the drinking."

I was getting frustrated. "Mama, I'm telling you for the millionth time, it's the truth."

"All right, let's just go up there and take a look," Grandmother said as she turned toward the stairs.

"No, no, he'll get you," I cried. "I don't know why he hasn't already come to get us."

"He'll get us or we'll find he wasn't there in the first place," Grandmother said, and stepped on the first stair.

"Maybe Tab is right, Mother Rutland. Maybe we should wait for Charles to come with us."

"Oh, come on, Mary. The two of us can handle a seventy-year-old man, especially since he's a figment of Tab's imagination." She marched up the stairs.

"Come on, Tab. We can't let her go by herself."

"You're gonna be sorry," I said, and waited to be the last one to start up the steps.

Grandmother slowed at the top of the stairs, out of breath, or maybe she was waiting for us to catch up with her. We all stood looking down the hall. Not one drop of noise anywhere. Maybe they were right. Maybe I just imagined the whole thing.

"All right, Tab, which is your room?" Grandmother asked. "Never mind, I can tell from the paint tracks."

"Oh, Tab," Mama groaned, "it'll take us hours to clean this up."

We turned the corner at the end of the hall and stood in front of my door. What if they opened the door and nobody was there? Then they really would think I was crazy. Somewhere in the back of my mind I was hoping Mr. Ben would be there, waiting for us with his machete. That would show them.

Chapter 28

Mother pushed the door open. He was sitting on the floor, propped up against the far wall. His jaw sagged as he breathed with the steady cadence of someone sound asleep.

I was so happy to see him, I felt like hugging him.

"See, see," I said in a whisper. "I told you he was here." I walked over to him and touched his coat to make sure he was real.

"See, what did I tell y'all? He's right here and he was gonna kill—" I stopped. Here was an old man, sound asleep and helpless.

Suddenly Mother was beside me, reaching for his coat collar with both hands.

"Why, you old reprobate. If you laid a hand on

my child, I'll—" She began to shake him as hard as she could. It was like shaking a bag of potatoes. Every time she stopped, he would go limp, eyes still closed, mumbling to himself. This made Mother even madder. "Speak to me!" She shook him. His eyes blinked open and started looking around. I was afraid Mother was going to shake his head off, so I grabbed hold of her arm.

"Wait a minute, Mama. Wait a minute. Mr. Ben didn't, uh, he didn't really try to . . . well, you know."

She turned to me. "Tab, sweetheart, where did Mr. Ben hurt you?"

"Well, he didn't actually try to hurt me that much, I guess."

Mother took a deep breath and let go of Mr. Ben's coat. "Exactly what did he do, Tab?"

"Well, he uh, he fell on me when we slipped on the yellow paint."

"Is that all?"

"He tore my shirt sleeve."

"Is that all?"

I looked down at the ground. "Well, yes ma'am."

"Are you sure?"

"Yes ma'am, but, but, he, he, mighta killed me if I'd stayed."

I looked down at Mr. Ben trying to adjust his old eyes to the light. Mother looked from me to him, ashamed she had been shaking him. She placed her hands very tenderly on his coat, smoothing it down.

"Oh, Mr. Ben, I am afraid I've done you an injustice. I let my emotions get the best of me. Please forgive me."

Mr. Ben was coming to. He put his hand down by his side to straighten up to a sitting position. "I . . . I . . ." He was half-mumbling now, so we had to listen carefully to hear him. "I done got dressed so's I could come on over here and talk to you 'bout my retirement." He coughed and cleared his throat. "Done decided to stop off on the way and have a little somethin' to drink, it bein' such a hot day." He rested his head back on the wall. "By the time I got here, wasn't nobody round but Tab." He closed his eyes and seemed to go back to sleep again.

"Mr. Ben, uh, if you don't mind, I certainly would like to know all about your retirement and what it is that you were doing up here with—" He was snoring.

She held his face with one hand and patted his cheeks gently with the other. "Mr. Ben, Mr. Ben, you need to try to wake up now."

"Oh, for heaven's sake, Mary, let me handle this." Grandmother had been standing at the door watching all this time. Now she took charge. She picked up an old straight-back we had been using for painting and dragged it over next to Mr. Ben. Mother and I backed up and leaned against the wall to watch.

She sat down and looked at him for a time before speaking. "Now Ben," she said in a loud voice. "Do you hear me? This is Mrs. Nellie, Ben. You and me been knowing each other forever. Do you hear me, Ben?" He nodded his head, but his eyes were still closed. "Fact is, Ben, you and me are some of the oldest people around here."

Ben still kept his eyes closed, but he smiled and said, "Lord if that ain't the truth, Mrs. Nellie. Feel like I'm old as dirt sometimes."

She shifted in her seat and laughed to keep him company. "Now Ben, when you been around as long as we have, you know that one of these days, probably long before these young people, we're gonna have to answer to the good Lord for all we've done."

"Yes'm, you sho right about that. You sho right," he mumbled.

"Fact is, Ben, the Good Book says that we should unburden our souls to get right with the Lord." She paused to let that sink in. Then she reached down and put a hand on his arm, working her tried-and-true formula on old Mr. Ben. "Now Ben, don't you want to tell me what it is that's burdening you?"

She let go of his arm and sat back up in her chair, not saying another word, just letting the silence fill the room. Mother and I let our backs slide down the wall to a sitting position, staring at Mr. Ben, waiting to see if he was going to do any confessing. His face didn't seem to change at first. He sat there with his eyes closed, but little by little I could see the tears start to roll down his cheeks. His head started turning back and forth slowly. I thought that this meant he wasn't going to talk, but Grandmother knew better. He wiped his closed eyes with his handkerchief and began.

"We was together all them years, me and Mrs. Poovey." He opened his eyes finally and looked up at the ceiling. "I come to work for her just before Mr. Jesse died. Nigh on to ten year ago. I done saw how she tried to raise them no-count boys. I knowed we was in trouble when Mr. Jesse died and alls we had left was this here house. I done saw how she tried to make ends meet, and her not havin' two pennies to rub together. Everybody thinkin' we had money, and we was dirt-poor. Then the Ladies Help League come along. She say, 'Ben, it sent from God, to save us.'

"We was sure enough on our last leg. We didn't even have money to buy gasoline for the car. Why, it wasn't like we was stealin'. It was either take it or we was gonna starve to death."

He took his handkerchief and blew his nose. A little smile came on his face. "Lord, me and Mrs. Poovey used to have coffee of a mornin' and plan out how we was gonna make it through. She would set at the kitchen table, with me standin' by the sink. She be lookin' over her papers with all them polio children's names on 'um.

"'Now Ben, let's see here, what souls we gonna try and save today?' And I always laugh and say, 'You mean what souls is gonna save us today, Mrs. Poovey.' Course I didn't mean no harm by it."

Now he got quiet, not saying anything. Late-afternoon clouds were building up wind outside the bedroom window. Mr. Ben got to looking at the tree-branch shadows dancing on the floor. So did I. We were back in a time when the room had furniture and Mrs. Poovey was still here. I thought I might even hear music coming from the old Victrola downstairs, but it was only the tree branches scratching the windows.

Grandmother kept watching Mr. Ben. After a while she said, very gently, "After all is said and done, I suppose going to a retirement home is the best for everyone concerned. Down in a church home in Montgomery? Is that where you said she is, Ben?"

Grandmother turned her head to look out the window and watch the wind, like it made her no mind if he answered or not. In a minute her head turned back to look down at her hands folded in her lap. She began to turn her thumbs slowly around each other, waiting, waiting. Sure enough.

"She ain't in no retirement like they say. I know better. I done seen the whole thing. It happened right in this here bedroom. It was some nights after the preacher come to let Mrs. Poovey confess her sins." He took a long breath and straightened

330

himself up, interested in what he was telling. "I found her right here lying in the bed. I come up to her room 'bout noontime 'cause I ain't heard from her all mornin'.

"I knock on the door, callin' out, 'Mrs. Poovey, Mrs. Poovey, I done finished weedin' the rose bed. Why don't you come on down and see how it look.' She was always partial to roses.

"I knowed she was feelin' poorly on account of talkin' to the preacher. She wouldn't eat nothin'. She just be there in the bed all day. I knock again and calls to her. Then I ease open the door. All the shutters was closed. It was dark and musty hot. The only sound was the fan on the floor movin' from side to side, rufflin' the covers on her four-poster bed.

"'Mrs. Poovey,' I call again to them covers lumped up in the bed. 'Time to get up.' I walks real soft over to the window by the bed and opens the shutters."

Mr. Ben shook his head and squeezed his eyes shut. "Lord, the sight I saw. There she was lyin' on them pillows, her hands out from under them covers, cut and bleedin' red all over her best crocheted bedspread.

"'Mrs. Poovey, Mrs. Poovey, what you done done here?' I say. 'This ain't no way to act.' I put my hand out and jiggle her shoulder and she commenced to moaning.

"'Now wake up here, Mrs. Poovey. What you want me to do here?'

331

"I couldn't hardly bring myself to, but I looked down at her again. The blood done run out all over the place, but the part round her wrists done dried out somewhat. She commenced to moanin' again. I say, 'What you 'spect I'm suppose to do here, Mrs. Poovey?'

"Then all the sudden, like the devil hisself done got into her, she open them eyes wide and look straight through me.

"'Jesse,' she call. 'Jesse, supper ready, sweetheart.'

"Then I say, 'No, Mrs. Poovey, this here is Ben. You remember Ben.' But she don't remember nothin'. She off in another world. It turned me cold the way she stare off in space, struggling to setup in the bed, smearin' blood everywhere, talkin' first to Mr. Jesse, then to them boys.

"I didn't know nothin' else to do but go on downstairs and call the Reverend. I didn't want to, 'cause he the one made her this way in the first place."

"You did the right thing, Ben. There was nothing else to do," Grandmother said. She sat there with one hand on her chest, where she had put it when Mr. Ben first told about Mrs. Poovey's bleeding wrists.

Mr. Ben put his hand up to rub his eyes. He looked tired, but he wasn't drunk anymore. He ran his old black hand through gray hair. "Reverend come over. Soon as he see'd her, he call Dr.

McAllister. The Doc say she didn't do no real harm cuttin' herself, but she done gone plumb off her rocker. He say it a good thing she got a lot of money, 'cause if she didn't, he would have to take her on down to Bryce and let the state take care of her.

"The Reverend say she ain't got money. Fact was, she ain't got nothin' but this here house and she rightly owed that. Then the Doc say she gonna have to go to Bryce. Wasn't nothin' else to do. The Reverend say he can't do that. That it would kill Mrs. Poovey to be took care by the public. The Doc say, 'Look at her, she's crazy as a betsy bug and she isn't 'bout to be back to herself soon, if ever.' All this time Mrs. Poovey moanin'. Once she try to get out of the bed and take her nightclothes off to get dressed right there in front of us menfolks. The Doc say, as he makin' her get back in bed, 'See here, Bill, they just ain't no way she can get along on her own.'

"Him and the Doc sat round ruminatin' on it for a hour or two and poor old Mrs. Poovey all the time moanin' and talkin' out of her head, even after the Doc give her a shot. Me, I'm tryin' to calm her the best I can.

"Finally the Doc say they got to make they minds up 'cause he got plenty of little polio childrens needs him right now at the hospital.

"Well, the end of it was they went on and called the ambulance to take her straight on down to the crazy house in Tuscaloosa, swearin' me not to tell a soul 'cause it be so hard on Mrs. Poovey. They wasn't nothin' I could do 'bout it.

"The Reverend say he feel so bad 'cause he shoulda seen it comin', say he knowed it partly his fault. Say it didn't turn out 'tall like he reckoned it would. He sit there and pray over it for the longest time. Finally he say we got to save her dignity by tellin' everybody she just wore out and got to rest up a spell down in one of them nice church retirement places in Montgomery."

Grandmother had tears in her eyes. She leaned back in her chair and sighed. "Poor Grace. Poor Grace. What a horrible predicament. No family, no one to turn to. No way to make a real living." She took off her glasses to wipe her eyes. "What was she going to do, end up clerking at the Jitney Jungle?" It was as if she were arguing with Mother, but Mother wasn't saying anything back. Mother sat there on the floor with her arms around her knees, staring at her shoes. "She had no formal education, you know," Grandmother said. She studied her glasses, then used both hands to put them back on. "Oh, what a pity. I think that was wonderful of Reverend Mengert to try to protect her. He did what any of us would under the circumstances." She looked over to Mother. "If I had been in the same situation as Grace, I would have wanted him to do the same thing for me."

"You would?" Mother said, and raised her head to look at Grandmother. "You would rather be sent to a state asylum than ask your friends to help out and—"

Grandmother interrupted her. "Of course I would. Why . . . why, she had lost every bit of who she was. Where is your sense of dignity, Mary, your pride?"

Mother said, half to herself, "Not at the state mental asylum, that's for sure."

"What?" I said.

"Never mind, Tab," Mother said.

Grandmother looked at Ben, not hearing us. "Grace Poovey did the very best she could by you, Ben. She may have made a mess of things, but she was trying her very hardest. That's all anyone can expect, you know. Why . . . why, when push came to shove, she even stole for you! Did you realize that?"

Mr. Ben didn't hesitate. "When push come to shove," he said as he began to lift himself off the floor one unsteady leg at a time, "I was the one done got shoved."

There was complete silence while Mr. Ben buttoned his coat and straightened his dirty tie as best he could. Grandmother had stiffened in her chair. I knew she didn't like Mr. Ben talking back to her like that. He leaned down to get his old driver's hat out of the paint, then stood up straight and cleared his throat. "I 'spect she mighta tried to do her best, but it wasn't good enough. Least ways it wasn't good enough for me."

Grandmother's smile was bitter. "It wasn't good enough indeed. You see, Mary? You see what I've been trying to tell you all this time? He doesn't even realize. You would think we were some redneck crackers instead of caring people trying to do the best we can with what life dumped in our laps. Do you think we wanted the responsibility?"

"What responsibility?" I whispered to Mother.

Grandmother looked back at Mr. Ben and sighed. "After all we do, and this is the thanks we get. I know she wasn't perfect. I know she broke the law to try to keep body and soul together, but don't you realize, Ben? She stole for the both of you!"

She stood and turned like a soldier doing an about-face. "Mary," she said as she headed out of the room, "I won't be taking supper with y'all tonight. I'm going home. This day has been too much."

"Yes, ma'am," Mother said, still sitting there and watching.

She paused just as she reached the door. Not looking back, she said, "Mary, do you . . . do you think for one minute Grace Poovey deserves such . . . such ingratitude from Ben?" There was silence, Grandmother standing there in the door waiting for Mother's answer. Finally she turned to look at Mother. "Well, do you?"

Mother looked up at Grandmother and saw tears welling up again. "Well, uh, no, ma'am," she said. Then she looked quickly to the floor. "I guess Mrs. Poovey did the best she could."

Grandmother took a deep breath and set her mouth in a straight line of satisfaction. "Maybe you and I are finally coming to some kind of common ground." Then she was out the door and gone.

Mother looked at Mr. Ben. She pulled herself slowly off the floor. I jumped up to give her a hand.

"I'm sorry about Mrs. Poovey, Mr. Ben. She must have been, well, I think y'all must have been good friends, well, at one time anyway."

"After all them years, it didn't go for much," he said, looking down at the paint-covered dimes. I rushed over to pick them up. I pulled out my shirt to wipe the Sunshine Yellow off.

"Mr. Ben, don't forget your money." I took his hand and put the two dimes in his white palm.

He put the money in his pocket. "Good evenin'." He tipped his hat, then walked slowly past us to make his way down the dark stairs and out the back door.

"Good evening," she called after him.

"What does 'coming to a common ground' mean, Mama? Does that mean you and Grandmama are getting along better? Does it mean you are finally getting adjusted?"

There was a look of great surprise on her face. The thought must have been jolting. "Your grandmother and me on common ground?" She stood thinking about it. "Me—and your grandmother?"

She walked over to the window and began to hit the wooden frame to break the new paint seal. She was smiling now. "No, Tab, it was just a temporary lapse on my part." The window finally gave way. She reached down to pull it open.

We could see Grandmother walking slowly down the front steps out into the yard. We could also see Mr. Delacourt, the neighbor across the street, getting out of his car and Mrs. Delacourt on the porch to greet him. That didn't stop Mother. She stuck her head out of the open window. "Mother Rutland," she called for all the world to hear, "you know Mr. Ben didn't deserve what he got, either. I think we should make sure that he gets some of the money from the sale of this house. I'll talk to the Ladies Help League." She pulled her head back inside, smiling. Then she stuck it back out again, not finished with poor Grandmother. "We'll talk to the Reverend Mengert, too. We'll set up a fund for Mr. Ben. Maybe we can call it Mr. Ben's Defense Fund." Finally she was finished and pulled her head back in, but not before she waved to the Delacourts. She was laughing as she closed the window. I looked out, to see Grandmother's shoulders sagging and her head turning from side to side as she walked on off.

I stood there with my arms crossed, tapping one foot on the ground so she would know I was disgusted with her. After all these years, just as I thought she was finally getting adjusted. She laughed when she saw what I was thinking. "I was only trying to set a good example for you." She smiled innocently.

"That was NOT a good example, Mama." I saw a little flicker of hurt in her eyes, but she would not be moved.

"Someday," she said, "someday you will know that it was."

Chapter 29

Your father won't believe this. Not in a million years." She looked down at her watch. "Oh my gosh, he's probably already home, and I left supper on the stove." She rubbed her eyes with both hands, trying to think. "Tab, pick up the ledger book and let's go home."

I looked around, seeing the yellow tracks I had made for the first time. "With Sunshine Yellow all over the floor?"

"Never mind, we'll clean that tomorrow. It's already set up anyway."

We walked down the sidewalk toward home just as the first lightning bugs were coming out.

"I guess you won't be letting me go out to play

hide-'n'-seek tonight, on account of me playing where I wasn't supposed to play."

She was walking along, looking through the ledger book I had handed her. She didn't even look up. "Hide-'n'-seek? Why, you play it every night in the summer. What should be different about tonight?" She turned pages. "Poor old Grace Poovey. All the time I thought—"

"All this time you thought she was a Goody Two-shoes, and she was nothing but a fake."

"You might say she was a fake, I suppose. She must have panicked when I mentioned helping with the books." Mother was staring off in the distance, thinking of the tea party. "She could either let me join and risk exposure or humiliate her friend and—"

She looked down at me and began to laugh. "That yellow paint all over you is a scream." She started laughing so hard, she had to stop and lean up against a tree. Finally she caught her breath. "What a day. I must be losing my mind or everybody else is losing theirs." She laughed out loud again.

She may have thought it funny, but I was on the verge of tears. In my mind I had almost been murdered and now I was soaked in yellow paint and all she could do was laugh. I glared at her. She pulled herself away from the tree trunk and put her arm around my shoulder to hug me, no matter the

Sunshine Yellow. We started down the sidewalk again.

Just then she saw my father pull into the driveway. She dashed ahead of me toward him. "Charles, we're over here."

He raised the newspaper in his hand as a greeting. She walked right into his arms and gave him a long hug. Then she started talking a mile a minute.

They turned toward the house. Not one notice of me. "Hey, y'all. Wait up. I want to tell Pop about Mr. Ben and me." They didn't hear. "Hey, does this mean we won't be leaving for Knoxville anytime soon? Hey, wait up!"

That night at supper, I was finally given center stage for my version of the day's events. Nobody seemed too interested. Mother and Pop were smiling at each other the whole time and Tina said she hoped I didn't track Sunshine Yellow in her room and it served me right in the first place. All in all, I was ignored. But I knew Maudie May would care. I knew she would be interested. So I rushed to eat and then go sit on the steps outside the kitchen door. The last of the daylight was fading when she finally came.

I could see a difference as she walked up the backyard. She was carrying a notebook and smiling. She sat down beside me on the steps and ran her hand over the front of the new notebook she had put in her lap. "Tomorrow, we gonna go buy the Gene Autry lunch boxes and me a pencil box. I be savin' the best to the last." When she opened the notebook, there were two packs of brand-new Blue Horse paper inside. She pointed to the coupons on the back of each wrapper.

"What's been keeping y'all?" I said. "I've been waiting here for hours." She was still pointing to the coupons.

"Twenty-five points each. That's fifty points. I'm gonna save up for a bicycle, too." She kept smiling as she took the pencil from behind her ear and circled the coupons on each wrapper. "I'm late 'cause I been sittin' and talkin' to Miss Mama 'bout goin' to school."

"Oh well, we still got a few more days before it starts. Maudie, now listen. You won't believe what happened to me at the new house today."

She continued as if I hadn't said anything. "I went to school today for the first time. Just for half a day. They tells you all about how it's gonna be when you starts to classes full-time, which is what we do day after tomorrow."

"Don't remind me. I gotta go in two weeks and I hate to think about it. But let me tell you about today. I—"

"I'm gonna be in the eighth grade just like you—uh—I said. Good old eighth grade. I done met with all my teachers. The best one is the new principal. His name is Mr. Abraham L. Dunwoody. He's from up in Detroit, but his mama come from around these parts. She done moved up there long time ago to find work. Anyway, he say he gonna learn us the right way to do."

She looked me straight in the eye, playing teacher again. "Now," she said, tapping the pencil on her notebook, "first off he say don't nobody ever say Negro no more or Negra or nigger. He say it always Nee-gro. He say can't no white peoples say it right and lots of colored don't, neither. He say you always say Nee-gro, Nee-gro." She said it again, this time with an even longer *nee*. "Nee-gro." She looked straight at me. "White peoples can't never say it right, Mr. Dunwoody say."

I imagined it would be easy to satisfy her and get on with my news. "Well, I can say it right," I said. "I can say it just like you said it. Nee-gro, Nee-gro. See?" I smiled. "I'm white and I said it right. Now listen, Maudie. I want to tell you all about old Mr. Ben up at the new house today. I—"

She still wasn't going to listen. I stopped what I was trying to say and waited.

She looked down at the notebook. "No you didn't. You didn't said it right." She opened the notebook and was looking at the coupons again.

"What do you mean, I didn't say it right? I said it just like you said it. I might also say, Maudie, I think you say it in a dumb way. It's Negra, not Nee-gro."

"That's cause white peoples—"

"I know, I know, 'cause white people can't say it right. But I said it just like you said it. Nee-gro, Nee-gro. How's that?" I said, knowing I had said it exactly like she had.

She looked to the Brothers, who had taken seats on the steps below us. Then she looked out into the backyard to watch the lightning bugs flashing. "No," she said slowly, "that ain't no good. You said it wrong."

It never occurred to me that if I said it a thousand times, I could not have passed her test. Not after she had discovered school and Mr. Dunwoody. But in my ignorance, I persisted. "I did not say it wrong. I said it one hundred percent like you said it." I could feel my face turning red. "You go to school one day and you think you know everything. Just because some dumb Yankee teacher comes to town. In one day you're telling me I don't know how to talk."

I jumped down off the steps and turned to face Maudie and the Brothers. "I am saying this stupid word one last time and that is positively it." I cleared my throat and wet my lips. Then I took a deep breath and slowly said the word. "Nee-gro."

There was absolute quiet except for the cicadas sawing away in the trees. We all looked at Maudie.

She thought for a minute and then began to slowly nod her head up and down. The Brothers slowly started nodding their heads up and down. I let out my breath. "Thank goodness that's over with. I told you I could say it just like you said it." I stepped back up on the stairs and sat down next to Maudie. "Now, let me tell you about Mr. Ben—"

"I wasn't noddin' my head 'cause you said it right," she said. "I was noddin' my head 'cause I was sayin' to myself that Mr. Dunwoody know his business. White peoples can't never say it right."

I jumped up and yelled, "What do you mean? Can't you hear that I said it right?" I was frustrated to the point of tears. "If you can't hear what I said, I'm not playing hide-'n'-seek with y'all." I had shouted so loud the Brothers had jumped up off the steps and were staring at me wide-eyed.

"What's got into you, Tab? You scarin' the Brothers. I don't likes it when you scares the Brothers."

"I don't care what you don't like. I tried to say your stupid word twenty times and you didn't like that, either. So tough luck. You don't know it all. I came out here to tell you all about Mr. Ben and you didn't even pay any attention," I yelled.

She was still sitting looking at her Blue Horse notepaper. She slowly closed the book and stood up to look down at me and smile. "Mr. Dunwoody give me some books to study. I'd better be gettin' on home to study'm." She stepped off the stairs into the backyard and started toward the dirt road. The Brothers were still staring, first at me and then at Maudie.

I heard a creaking noise as Pop opened the screen door to the back steps.

The Brothers took one look at him and started running toward Maudie. The three of them walked on down the dirt road into the darkness. "I'll see y'all tomorrow," I yelled after them.

I looked up at Pop. "We were going to play, but we got into some kind of argument."

"So I heard." He sat down on the step beside me and pulled out a Camel. We sat for a moment in silence before either of us said anything.

"Your mother and I could hear you all the way into the living room."

"It was about me not being able to say her word right. I said it over and over, but I didn't get it right. Least ways she said I didn't get it right."

"I heard the tail end of that," he said, and took a long drag on his cigarette. "How much older is Maudie than you, Tab?"

"She's going on eighth."

"Sounds to me like Maudie is moving on to new worlds."

"No she isn't, no she isn't. She says we'll be friends till she's a teacher, and that's a long time off." I was mad at him for even suggesting it. "You don't know what you're talking about, Pop. Me and Maudie will be best friends forever. We said so in the fort this summer."

He took one last drag and flipped his cigarette out into the backyard. Then he kissed me on the top of the head. "I hope you're right." He got up to leave. "Come in after a while. You've had a big day. You need a good night's sleep."

I leaned back, hands behind my head. The night was so clear, I could watch the stars come out. The Big Dipper, the Little Dipper, the North Star. It would always be the same.

But it was never the same. After that night, it was never the same. Like the heat lightning that darts from cloud to cloud, off at a great distance, entering our consciousness but never our reality, until finally, finally, it sends a bolt thundering home.

I had been cleaning up the Sunshine Yellow and had not seen her for the three days it had taken me. Then early one evening I was standing in my side yard, finally freed from cleaning, hoping Maudie and the Brothers would show up for a game of hide-'n'-seek. I noticed Miss Mama off in the distance walking toward me, coming home. I watched her as she came, shoulders hunched over, beat down by a long day. I walked toward her thinking to ask Maudie's whereabouts.

"Hey, Miss Mama, do you know . . . " She seemed not to see me. She came to me then walked past, without so much as a "hello." I turned to follow her. "Miss Mama, I was wondering if Maudie and the Brothers were gonna come on out and play hide-'n'-seek tonight?" I kept walking beside her, waiting for my answer. Still she said nothing. She seemed deep in thought. I noticed, as we walked, that she was not dressed in her usual work clothes, coveralls for the foundry. She had on a dress. She carried a purse. "Miss Mama. I was just wondering if you knew—"

"Hide-'n'-seek? Hide-'n'-seek? Ain't gonna be no more hide-'n'-seek round here. Ain't you heard?" She looked up at me for the first time. "No, I guess you wouldn't. It's all over town, Maudie May done come down with it last night. Truth be known she probably come down with it day before yesterday, but her being as stubborn as she is, you know Maudie. That child bound and determined to go to that school. Wouldn't tell me nothin' till three o'clock this mornin', till she already took bad sick, couldn't hardly lift her head off the pillow."

I stopped in my tracks and watched her walk on. She didn't mean "it." She couldn't mean "it." She meant something else. She never slowed in her gait, one foot in front of the other, only the thought of getting home.

I ran after her. "Miss Mama, Miss Mama. What do you mean, took sick? I didn't know it. I hadn't heard about it. Took sick with . . . with what?"

"What do you think? Polio, child. She sick with the polio."

I stood there again, watching her walk away

350

from me, my heart pounding in my head. Then I raced to catch up.

She was muttering to herself. "Done had to get Reverend Jerome out of bed at three o'clock this mornin' so he could take us to the hospital. Done been over there all day. I needs to feed the Brothers and get back." She noticed me walking along. "Lord child, I ain't got no time to talk 'bout no children's games. Get on home with you."

I stood still then, stunned, watching her disappear down the dirt road.

For days after that, I could see Maudie in my mind, sitting up there reading all the free comics from Woolworth's and drinking all the free Dr Pepper courtesy of the Dr Pepper Company. Getting fanned with the electric fans donated by Mr. Neeley's hardware store. I knew she would get well. She had to.

Then I thought about the iron lung we had seen at the movies. After that my mind would not give me a picture of what it was like for her. In the afternoons I walked past the hospital searching the windows of the children's polio clinic, hoping somehow to see her. Later I discovered that she wasn't even there. She had been taken across the river to the hospital that would accept Negro children.

I didn't tell Mother or Pop, knowing for sure I would have to go to Knoxville if they found out, but every day I watched the dirt road until finally, late one afternoon, I saw Miss Mama trudging toward home. I raced to meet her.

Not slowing down to deal with the likes of me, she said, "Them doctors say they can't do no more. They say they gonna send her on down to Tuskegee. See what they can do with her down there. Me and the Brothers gonna pack up and go with her."

"You're leaving? You're leaving Bainbridge?" I quickened my pace to keep up with her.

"I don't know if them peoples know what they doin'," she said.

"Miss Mama, did she . . . you know . . . did she ask about me or anything?"

"Sometimes I think them doctors ain't got the sense God give a cow."

"Will you tell her . . . ?" My eyes began to fill with tears. "Will you tell her . . . don't forget me?" I was struggling to get the present out of my pocket as we walked along. "Here." I handed it to her. "It's just a dumb old picture I drew of me and Maudie May and the Brothers. It's out of my secret notebook, you know."

Miss Mama seemed not to hear any of it. She opened her purse and stuck the folded picture inside. "I got a load of packin' to do," she said. "Oh, I near 'bout forgot." She snapped open her purse again. "Maudie done told me to give you this. It some gimcrack she done spent her good money on."

I slowed to a standstill holding the pencil box in my hand and watching her walk away from me down the road, her shoes making little puffs of dust in the dirt. Then my eyes were so filled with tears, I couldn't see anything.

That night, standing with my back to Mama, washing the dishes in the sink, I said to her, "Do you remember what a dandelion is like? All summer it grows into a puffy ball with millions of tiny little pieces close together making a beautiful flower. Then when you pick it and blow very hard, just one time, all the pieces float off into space separated forever." She said she remembered. I said I remembered, too. The dirty dishes blurred before my watery eyes.

That day Maudie's world had floated away from me forever.

All through the fall I thought about her every time I got a demerit and there were lots of demerits that fall. I was constantly doing something wrong, chewing gum or running in the hall or forgetting to put the date on my homework assignment.

I sat at my desk in the back of the room remembering how she taught us school at the stick table, how she pulled me out of the big fire and helped me win the football game, how we crested the waves and sailed to victory with "the big one," and how, at the very end, I never got to tell her good-bye.

Whenever memory threatened to drown me, I would pretend she wouldn't have liked school anyway. My Maudie never would have put up with the demerit system.

Epilogue

In those days, I was too afraid to ask about what happened to her, fearful of the answer. I listened in on every adult conversation that might give me some clue, but heard nothing. When I grew old enough to venture the question, so much time had passed that only rumors remained.

One said that she died on the train headed for Tuskegee.

Another said that she survived, but with braces on both legs. That rumor had it that she went on to graduate from Tuskegee Institute and then traveled up north, becoming a famous publisher of noted literary works, rubbing elbows with all the movie stars she had ever read about.

Still another rumor, passed on by barge captains coming upriver, told of a Negro woman who walked with a cane and ran a fishing camp deep in the backwaters of south Alabama. They said that she ruled the place with an iron hand, ordering about two big black men who carried out her every whim.

Of course, they were only rumors, rumors of what life might have come to.

That summer, that summer was filled with what life held in store. . . .

I am standing, hands on hips, a barefoot statue under a great stream of water that cascades off our roof. It is before gutters were built to control the flow. The water washes in huge sheets down into the roof angles, building steam as it gathers force. Then in a great arch it leaps from the roof and hits my head, spraying thousands of sun-drenched diamonds in wild profusion up into the air.

The Brothers are laughing as they dance around under my homemade fountain. Maudie May watches at a distance, wet and smiling.

It is long, long ago.

Acknowledgments

My sisters are the reason this is a book. My sister Joanne, for encouraging me to write and helping me so very much. She read everything I wrote, until, I suspect, she was sorry she had ever suggested it. My sister Sally, for, much to my amazement, being proud enough of the product to pass it on.

Thanks to Dr. Ward Pafford, and my sister-in-law, Helen Cartland Cunningham, both of whom were kind enough to read my scribbling in the first and later stages and comment. I am grateful to Nick Ventimiglia, who passed the manuscript, and me, on to Grace Ressler, who became my agent. Many thanks to Grace. How lucky I am to be associated with such a class act and such a kind heart.

My thanks also to the library at the University of North Alabama for letting me search their microfilm files.

And now the people at Warner Books. When I came to them, I reminded myself of a child carrying a few sheets of music into Maureen Mahon Egen's great concert hall.

I stood in wonder as Conductor Egen plucked the sheets from my hand and proceeded to the podium, never looking back. Up went the baton. Out came the first notes, a little legal, in the distance, like rolling thunder, to get your attention. Then the light, airy strains of the art department, followed by the staccato of editing. A wave of the baton and in came sales and marketing. The whole thing was beginning to sound fantastic. She even appointed, as concertmaster, Frances Jalet-Miller, the best editor I could possibly have hoped for. In the cacophony of thousands of words, she detects any discordant notes and, better yet, knows how to bring them to harmony. Thank you, Frances.

A grand orchestra. I began to hum along.

Hesitant, I approached the conductor's podium and tugged at her coattail. "Uh, do I need to do anything?"

She smiled. She had heard that before. "Just stand over there, kid, and hit the kettledrums when I tell you to."

"Yes ma'am."

In the end I know that if now it sings, the song is you—or y'all, as we say. Thank you, Maestro. Thank you, Warner Books.

Reading Group Guide

A Q and A with
Pat Cunningham Devoto

Q. You start and end the novel with the image of water falling on Tab. What does this image symbolize for you?

A. I think water symbolizes the uninhibited, free-flowing world of the child, "before gutters are built to control the flow."

Q. Maudie May and John are both important to Tab and they both leave her. What did you want Tab to learn from this experience?

A. With John, Tab begins to get an inkling of what death means. When John's mother dies, it's the first time Tab has come in contact with death other than what she has seen in the movies. She watches with great curiosity and absolutely no emotional involvement as the ceremonies surrounding Mrs. McMillan's death unfold, the visits from the neighbors, the food, the strange—to her—Episcopal ceremony. The emotional significance of death means nothing to her until it touches her world the day John leaves.

Only then does she begin to fathom its pain. In Maudie's case, she has already left Tab by the time she physically leaves her. Of course this leaving, by way of the argument on the back steps, is really the outside world coming to call.

Q. Tab has two strong opposing influences in her life, her mother and her grandmother. Were you trying to show that a balance of these two influences is best or did you see her eventually accepting one influence over the other?

A. Tab, like all children, wants the perfect world, and part of growing up is realizing that the world and the people she loves are not perfect. Tab would prefer that her mother be more like her socially acceptable grandmother, who abides by all of society's rules no matter how convoluted. Even after the disastrous Ladies Help League tea, Tab still tries, in her mind, to put her square-peg mother into a round hole. "See the problem here is, Mama, you have to learn to act more like Grandmother but not be like Grandmother."

But at this point, it also begins to dawn on Tab that there is a parallel between her mother being denied membership in the Ladies Help League and the fact that she is also denied membership in the boys secret club, and that maybe she is more like her mother than she would care to admit.

Q. Tab's mother could be described as a nonconformist. It is certainly harder to live this way, but do you think it is a more valuable path?

362

A. I think it depends on your reason for not conforming. One reason the mother refuses to conform to many of Bainbridge's "rules" is that she is trying to teach her children the importance of having and sticking to a set of values that will stand the test of time while living in a small town that tends to be very provincial. In the end she refuses to give in to the grandmother even though it would appear to have been the kinder thing to do. Although it would have made the grandmother and Tab happy, she knows if she does give in, her actions will be a disastrous example to the child later in life when she will understand their greater implications.

Q. What did Maudie May and Tab learn from being friends? Do you think Maudie May had a lasting influence on Tab, and if so, what was it?

A. Maudie May is the first person Tab befriends completely on her own outside the bounds of family and what is socially acceptable. The ability of the girls to make and sustain that relationship is empowering for both of them.

The first time you connect with an individual using only your judgment and it develops into something positive—marriage, business partner, friend—that can be life affirming. On the other hand, if you venture out for the first time on your own and get burned, especially at an early age, the experience can color how you perceive the world from then on. In the end, for Maudie and Tab, it was a friendship come and gone, but the memory of it will always remain as part of the basic fabric of their personalities.

Q. Did you have a central theme to your book? What was the main idea you were trying to communicate?

A. That fear, of polio, of nonconformity, of making a mistake, of revealing one's self, will not allow you to live up to your potential and, on the darker side, can even be ruinous. Certainly, in the fifties, that equated to our national fears as well and translated into a very striated society.

Q. Tab is definitely a tomboy, her sister Tina is definitely not a tomboy. Did you have any similarities to Tab growing up or were you more like Tina?

A. I was Tab, albeit not as creative and conniving, and my sister Jo was Tina, although not as frivolous and self-centered.

Q. At the end you left Maudie May's future in limbo with rumors and sightings. Why did you make her fate so uncertain?

A. As Maudie May developed, she became a character larger than life. I couldn't leave her to some ordinary fate, so I left her to the mind of the reader, a place filled with endless possibilities, as was Maudie May.

Q. Southern writing is such a strong tradition. What do you make of this tradition?

A. My mother used to say, when explaining the popularity of *Gone with the Wind*, the quintessential southern movie: "The Southerners like it because they think it makes them look *Oh, so grand,* and the Yankees like it because they get a kick out of the Southerners makin' fools out of themselves."

Q. Do you think it necessary to have this story set in the South or could it have been set in any small town in America?

A. It could have taken place in almost any small town in America in the 1950s.

Q. What will you write next?

A. You know this question is like Pandora's box. I start going back and reading old family journals and letters, and I think the poor reader is going to have to suffer through story after story. I would like to use Alabama as a setting again. Maybe I'll do follow up with stories about what happened to the characters in this book: maybe Maudie May or Tab or maybe John, and I guess every writer wants to write a Christmas story. Maybe I'll do something set in the present-day South. Now go back and look at the "maybes" in this paragraph. In any event, I don't think I'll ever write anything set outside the South.

Q. Who are your major influences? What do you like to read?

A. I'm afraid I'm a mishmash. These books are on my nightstand right now in various stages of "read": Biographies of Eleanor Roosevelt, Jimmy Carter, and

Helen Keller. Titles by Walker Percy, Lee Smith, Eudora Welty, E. Annie Proulx, B. A. Bodkin.

Q. Your description of a small town and the polio epidemic is very authentic. What kind of research went into writing this novel?

A. Hours and hours of sitting in the library and squinting at faded microfilm files of my hometown newspaper during that period and then reading very good resource material. Among the really good ones, *Patenting the Sun* by Jane S. Smith and *The Fifties* by David Halberstam. Then I reread old family letters and journals. I guess, like so many large families, I am blessed with some ancestors who liked to keep a written record before letter writing went out of style. As a child I didn't appreciate this, but now I consider myself the lucky beneficiary of all those saved times.

Discussion Questions

1. What does the title of the book imply?

2. Do you think that the fear of polio in the 1950s compares with the present-day fear of AIDS? Also, do you think that great fear of a disease can sometimes have a devastating effect that is equal that to the disease itself?

3. At what point in the story does Tab begin to have some recognition of Maudie May as a black person as opposed to her simply being a friend?

4. Do you think that Tab's grandmother wants Tab's mother to fit in because she is afraid her daughter-in-law will embarrass her or is she trying to be helpful?

5. When Tab goes down to the fish camp she realizes that "like so many things that summer, I had seen it, but I had never really seen it." What other things do you think she is referring to?

6. The Reverend Mengert makes a speech at John's mother's funeral. Why does the Reverend Mengert

choose to make the speech at that point? What effect do you think his speech has?

7. The Reverend Mengert plays several roles in the novel: friend to Tab's father, confidant, almost co-conspirator to Grace Poovey, moral conscience for the town. Do you think these roles are important for the church representative to fulfill? Which role is the most important?

8. Do you think the Reverend Mengert does the right thing covering up for Grace Poovey? What about when you take into account what happens to Ben?

9. How do you feel about the character of Ben? What does he represent?

10. There are two fires in the story. What is the significance of each fire; what results from each? Do the fires have a common purpose or result?

11. When Maudie May says her dream is to be a famous teacher, what is her motivation? Do you think that she fulfills her dream, whether or not she had polio?

12. Who in the story is afraid of being a nonconformist? Compare Tab's conformist tendencies with her nonconformist tendencies. Which do you think are stronger?

13. Tab's mother finished college, got married, moved to a small town where she didn't belong, and

had a family. Do you think she is happy at heart or do you think she is discontented? And how is this manifested in the story?

14. Some sociologists think the primary socializing factor for children in the fifties and sixties was family and today it is the media. Do you think this is true? Why or why not?

15. What do you think really happens to Maudie May?

On Writing

For me, writing is memory with hindsight—that is, events real or imagined placed in the context of my accumulated experience.

That's why I love writing now that I'm older. I have a sense of self that has taken years to evolve (read that "late bloomer"). I hate to think of what I might have written in my youth. Large amounts of gloom-and-doom drivel I'm sure. These days I'm not embarrassed to feel a disgusting amount of optimism.

Also, I think I am freer to write now because I am no longer staggered by everything I don't know. I grew up in an age when it was implied that there was a finite amount of Western European knowledge that we were all supposed to somehow wrap our brains around. And then along came the sixties and seventies—and the rest of the world. They never said anything to me about Japanese Haiku in tenth grade, at Coffee High School in Florence, Alabama, in the 1950s. Who knew?

How freeing to know it's a hopeless task, and now I can pick and choose only what I like. In this day of technological change at the speed of light, I'm satisfied that the best I can do is be open to learning—and to opening my computer.

Maybe one hundred years from now we'll just sit the new baby down in a gigantic high-tech library and say, "This is how you use the card catalogue, now go find out what it is you want to find out and when you've finished with that . . . but then, you'll never be finished with that."

The Book's Beginnings

This book grew out of a conversation I had with my mother and sisters several years ago when I was home in Alabama for a visit. We were sitting around the kitchen table drinking coffee discussing the news of the day, and the news of that day happened to be the AIDS crisis and how much fear it had spawned in our country.

I asked my mother what, if anything, in her lifetime was comparable to the fear of AIDS. She immediately said, "Oh, the polio summers in the late forties and early fifties. Every adult lived in fear, especially if you had young children."

For those of you who are not old enough to remember polio, I will tell you it was a terrible disease. It manifested itself in symptoms that were, at first, much like coming down with a cold or the flu. Then two mornings later you might wake up and not be able to move. Recovery, if you recovered, was a very painful and slow process and left many with permanent scars. No one knew who would get it next, where it came from, or what caused it. In the summer there would be outbreaks of polio in towns all over the United States. Sometimes the movies closed or the pools closed. Rumors ran rampant. If someone came down with polio, people wanted to know what they had eaten the night before, who they had played with, what they had touched.

The day after our conversation at the kitchen table and on several subsequent visits home, I went to the library of our local university and began to research that period and those summers. After many hours in the library scrolling through old microfilm of my hometown newspaper, there emerged a fascinating picture of what life was like during those summers. One day there would be an article asking for donations to the local children's polio clinic and the next day another article would report that merchants and individuals all over town had responded with everything the clinic needed. There were weekly announcements of the spraying schedule of DDT by the crop dusting plane ("don't worry," it said, "the yellow dust won't hurt you. It will only stain your clothes, so don't hang any on the line during spray time"). This coupled with lists of people who had come down with polio and helpful hints on how to avoid catching the disease: don't get in cold water, don't get tired, wash your hands constantly, and cover your food.

Yet my recollection of the time was one of childhood summers filled with grace. How interesting, I imagined, to write a book about childhood, set against such a fearful background. I hoped the setting would only exacerbate what we all come to know as adults: that our parents lived lives burdened with hopes and fears we never imagined until, of course, the mantle is passed on to us in our adult years.

After months of filling stacks of yellow legal pads with times researched and remembered, *My Last Days as Roy Rogers* came to life.

Suggested Readings

Nonfiction

Patenting the Sun by Jane S. Smith
This Fabulous Century—1950–1960, Time-Life Books
FDR's Splendid Deception by Hugh Gregory Gallager
Managing Post Polio by Lauro S. Halstead, M.D.
A Nearly Normal Life by Charles L. Mee

Fiction

To Kill a Mockingbird by Harper Lee
The Adventures of Tom Sawyer by Mark Twain
Paper Moon by Joe David Brown
Bastard Out of Carolina by Dorothy Allison
The Last of the Whitfields by Elise Sanguinetti
Cold Sassy Tree by Olive Ann Burns
Run with the Horsemen by Ferrol Sams